Mis

CW00394665

Barclay Knight

Editor

David Blackstar

Publisher

Kindle Direct Publishing

First Edition 2021

A Barclay Knight Thriller

Other work by the author: Trilogy

Blackstar – Secret Rulers
ISBN-10: 1519589433
ISBN-13: 978-1519589439

Deception – Divine Secrets
ISBN-10: 1517759781
ISBN-13: 978-1517759780

Armageddon – The Dream
ISBN-10: 1545124264
ISBN-13: 978-1545124260

&

Through Adversity To The Stars – Dexter's Journey

ISBN: 9781448663934

Missing

Barclay Knight

Acknowledgements

Barclay wishes to thank Santos Mirage for their great design layout over Shutterstock picture, where the overall effect will take your mind to what is truly Missing. Perhaps the truth.

A special thanks from Barclay to all his readers.

barclayknight@gmail.com

Missing

My world was collapsing fast. I wasn't in Majestic 12 and I certainly didn't want the President to be assassinated. However, I did know why JFK had been silenced… the world wasn't ready.

Nearly six decades later, and now Area 51 was endangering my whole existence. I wish I'd never heard of the wretched place.

Prologue

Ventura is a Californian coastal city northwest of Los Angeles and it was for this reason that Luis Kramer chose to move there. Although it was known for its beaches and long wooden pier, Kramer felt that its location with Surfer's Point could really help his new career. At thirty-eight, he was stepping back in time and returning to teach the exhilarating watersports enjoyed before attending Massachusetts Institute of Technology. But this wasn't an easy decision. There were many good reasons as to why he should be moving away from Nevada's, dry and sweltering weather conditions.

It was Tuesday late afternoon; the house move had gone well several months earlier and he was in the garage admiring his red Firewire surfboard. As the sky suddenly turned black, Kramer looked at his watch and thought about his wife, Jayne, and daughter, Libby. Like best friends, they had both gone off in the yellow Mustang to shop on Main Street. A scrub Jay darted for cover as rain began to hit the rear window, then a flash of lightning split the dark sky across Ventura Harbour; several more leaping across the Pacific Ocean. The garage lights flickered as the sound of thunder rumbled overhead. Gusting wind thrashed through the trees and rain swept in at forty-five degrees to batter his window with fury. While listening to the surprise storm, Kramer carefully polished his immaculate surfboard with pride. A garden gate slammed somewhere, then an unpredictable event; a sudden bodily jolt from behind before blacking out...

Chapter 1

Somewhere in Ventura County, California: Tuesday

Kramer lay on his back; it was pitch black, earthy and certainly not a place of his choosing. Had he known where he was, even the toughest of men would have experienced panic sweeping in. However, this innocent man lay unconscious – unconscious due to a violent abduction several hours earlier.

Through a small speaker only inches away, a man's voice now invaded his confined space.

'Kramer, are you there?' his accent, American, southern and annoyingly confident.

There was silence but for shallow breathing.

'Kramer… time is not on your side.'

The lack of response was predictable.

'Listen. We need to talk. More importantly, you need to talk.'

Still no sound, just the quietness of a sealed tomb.

'I know you're there because it's impossible to leave. See how we have considered your privacy and maximized your safety. If you have enemies, you are untouchable.'

Time had elapsed. Kramer stirred. His eyes were still closed, head muzzy and confused due to the unnatural situation he was experiencing; not that he knew anything about being drugged or his previous experience. His arms moved slowly sideways before elbows and hands collided with hard surfaces. This place was not comfortable, in fact, he ached. Kramer's eyes opened – it was pitch black and he saw nothing. He sat up immediately and hit his head, then dropped down for a double thud. A nightmare situation was unravelling rapidly as all fingers raced around to assess his confined surroundings. *Was he dreaming?* No. But reality was setting in fast. 'What the hell's going on?' he mumbled almost incoherently.

'Ah, Mr Kramer,' came the same voice; the tone annoyingly arrogant. 'We are happy that you have enjoyed your sleep…'

'What's going on?' he said struggling in his horizontal prison.

'I'm glad you asked. It seems like we are all on the same page at last.'

Kramer's hands were re-assessing the walls and surfaces as he listened. He now understood his predicament by the geometry of his tiny cell. It had to be a closed coffin, and without a lining.

The small speaker above his head ensured the conversation continued.

'What do you want from me?'

'Information. Perhaps a little task. That's all. Nothing too much for a man of your capability.'

'Who are you?'

'Who am I? With my plastic surgery, even I don't know when I look in the mirror. By the time this is all over, you may want to meet my surgeon. He is good. Very very good.'

'Let's cut to the chase…'

'All in good time,' came the smug and arrogant reply.

'Why me?' said Kramer, trying desperately to reach into his right-hand trouser pocket.

'You have information that we require, and with that vital knowledge… you are going to help us do something wonderful for the planet. It should be easy for a man of your caliber.'

'And if I say, no… what then?'

'That would not be wise. You know, and we know, that you have a nice little family. How would you like one of them to be in the same position as you… to be tortured in this way?'

Silence followed as Kramer failed to find his mobile.

An annoying laugh followed. 'Yes, just as I thought. A man who loves to comply.'

Kramer felt beaten but there was no point expressing his anger or frustration. Without warning, a light illuminated several inches from his nose. That annoying voice invaded his space once again. 'And God said, let there be light… and there was light.'

Due to the brightness, both eyes closed fast. Turning his head sideways helped, but the surface was hard and unforgiving.

'You're crazy,' said Kramer, his eyes screwed up even tighter, the heat from the lamp and his situation ensuring a light sweat.

'Oh, and if you did have a phone, there's no signal down there,' he scoffed. '21ST century technology and you can't get a signal out of a coffin. Disgraceful.'

'You've thought of everything.'

'We certainly have, Kramer.'

'So, where am I?'

'By now, you should know that you're in dead-man's land. Ironic really, but that's the way it is.'

'I meant, where have you placed this coffin?'

'You're about three feet down and covered over with soil and leaves. No one would ever find you in the middle of a wooded area.'

The cruel villain laughed before continuing. 'And if they did, it would be years from now. You'd just be a pile of bones. But I have good news for you…'

'I can't wait.'

'I know. But listen. You'll be happy when I tell you that the coffin is eco-friendly and has the cheapest of metal hinges.'

'Sadistic clown.'

'A little respect please, Mr Kramer,' his tone almost childish.

'You're deluded.'

'No, I'm not… and I can prove it.'

The light went out. Kramer opened his eyes slowly, all the time anticipating another blast. However, this time, a second one illuminated above his feet. Once again, the man spoke with arrogance. 'I have shown respect and brought you comfort. Why waste time. Let's talk like old friends.'

Still fighting light-spots in both eyes, Kramer could just about make out two photographs pinned and placed side by side on the underside of the lid. With such close proximity and poor lighting, he blinked for clarity.

'It's quiet in there,' said his tormentor. 'I guess you are just admiring pictures of your family home, plus one taken last week of your daughter, Libby, sunbathing in the garden. I love drones, don't you?'

'What do you want?'

'As I said before, we want something that you have… and if you don't have it yet, perhaps you wouldn't mind helping out.'

'With what?'

'Exposing the truth. It's time that the world knew the truth.'

'Give me a clue. I don't like guessing games.'

'Great! We are both on the same page.'

'Cut to the chase.'

'Where do you work?'

'All over the place. That's the nature of my function.'

'Where were you last week? What were you doing? And don't lie. You were being watched. You sneezed twice mid-afternoon.'

Kramer laughed. 'You seem to know everything. Tell me what you think you know, and then I can fill in the spaces.'

'You've signed the official secrets act. Correct?'

'There's no such thing.'

'But you have sworn allegiance to keep silent.'

'Thousands have done so. It's just a formality when working for government departments or agencies. You should know that.'

'What have you seen, or been privy to when in the most highly sensitive zones?'

'What zones?'

'Zones in area 51, 52 and other similar places.'

'Tell me what you know.'

'I'm calling the shots, not you. The sooner that you understand this, the better it will be for your family.'

Without warning, the conversation suddenly stopped. The foot light went out. Kramer was left listening and now the sound of water dripping slowly on his bare feet. Without a doubt, his mind was now in overdrive. What was behind this crazy game and, more importantly, how could he escape? This was torture and designed cleverly to get results. Perhaps compliance was his only chance of freedom, but in films the outcome wasn't always positive; people still died. He banged the sides of the coffin with both fists clenched. It sounded solid. *That confirms it. I must be underground,* he thought. *Damn… this is serious.*

Kramer lay still to contemplate his predicament; buried alive in a wood somewhere – totally beaten, mentally and physically. A world of silence where confinement and dripping water added to his misery… his outcome… drowning slowly. However, *there was a way out*, he reasoned. This would involve giving away sensitive information and breaching the code of practice. That probably meant a long term in prison and being discredited; his family in shame too. But there was no other choice. Besides, he couldn't endanger his family who may also end up underground and be left to die. Afterall, he was dealing with people far lower than scum. An agonizing period of approximately an hour had elapsed when the foot-light illuminated. The continual dripping stopped, but the chill of evil remained. He shivered; the water level almost reaching his ears.

'Hello Kramer. Are you still down there? I have to ask because you Area 51 boys are cunning as hell.'

Kramer decided not to play the game and remained silent.

'Oh, so that's how you want to play it?'

There was a pause.

'Trouble is, I'm the one with all the best cards. I have the aces and all the power. You have nothing. No freedom, no ability to move, no friends to chat to, no nice restaurants to have dinner in. And worst of all, no family to say goodbye to. Your position is grave.'

The villain laughed childishly. 'Sorry, but I love teasing my friends. Hey listen Kramer. I would rather be doing life than be where you are. At least I would have a window to look out of and fresh air.'

No one wanted to be in this situation, least of all, Kramer himself. He was shrewd and smart in the real world, but this was lightyears from the real world.

'Come on. All good husbands and fathers talk in the end. Why delay? Why cause your loved-ones to suffer? If they die, then you are ultimately responsible. Get wise. It would be your fault.'

No response.

'It can't be comfortable with cold water soaking through your stale clothing. I estimate that you're in two inches of water.'

No response.

'You could drown very slowly if the game goes badly. At the moment, the tap shuts off real nice. But you know what dodgy electrics are like. If the solenoid sticks, the water keeps running and you go under... and slowly, that's for sure.'

'Then you don't get what you want,' replied Kramer.

'Is this what you want your family to endure? I have two other coffins ready and more games to play. By comparison, you're in a holiday camp. It really doesn't have to be this way.'

The delay was a few seconds too long. Kramer stiffened, screamed, and sprung up hitting his head on the hard lid. Water slopped back and forth to fill his ears.

'Are you still there, Kramer? Are you ok?'

A pause. 'Listen. That was only 50 volts in the water and for a split second.'

'Ok ok. What do you want?'

'Good. Nothing like a bit of voltage to make the brain see sense. So, listen to your King. This is how it's going to work. You still need more softening-up to make sure you comply all the way to the end. That's going to be a major part of the deal. After full compliance, you go free with your family and we disappear and never bother you again. You have my full word on this matter. Let's call it a gentleman's agreement, if you wish. How does that sound?'

'When do we meet?'

'After several days.'

A satisfying laugh followed. 'You will need to lie low – keep your head down because your side will be looking for you. We have an excellent place where your safety will be guaranteed.'

'Safety from what?' questioned Kramer frowning.

'From *them*, Kramer. When *they* find out that it was you that blew the lid off the tin, you will be hunted down. And you know what they're like?'

Firtree woodland 2 miles from Ventura. Wednesday 5:35pm

Two men stood and watched as a third man used a spade to clear away leaves.

Mondor, a short stocky man with a boxer's nose, shaved head and lightning-strike tattoos above cauliflower ears spoke as he looked around in all directions. 'I love the summer, but give me yachts and pretty girls any day.'

'You're a dreamer,' said Koga with a spade and clearing. 'In the grand scheme of things, you're just like a tiny blade of grass blowing in the wind. Now if you said you had been to Kepler186F I would be impressed.'

'Koga, you're totally on another planet,' replied Mondor. 'I'm like these towering pines. Silent, but powerful. I've earned my place in this world.'

Within a few minutes, the spade hit something hard.

'He's gonna be mighty happy to see us after a day in the hell hole,' declared Mondor, looking around.

The third stooge, César, took over and cleared the last soil from the lid.

'Come on, Brazilian. Hurry up,' said Mondor peering down. 'Let's get him out of here before those crazy dog walkers see us. We should have done this after dark. Man, do I need my vacation. Hey, babes of Fort Lauderdale, I'll be coming soon like a tornado in my Corvette Stingray.'

Kneeling down on leaves, César grabbed a claw hammer and wrenched the lid open. The men peered down in silent shock, their mouths gapping.

'What the hell happened here?' said Mondor, frowning and looking spooked, the others bewildered. 'Even the damn pictures have gone. Jesus…'

'There's no point asking, Jesus,' said Koga throwing the spade down. 'I don't want to be on this planet when the shit hits the fan,' he said, eyes darting from pine to pine without blinking.

Looking redder and more infuriated by the second, Mondor shouted. 'Ok, you know the plan! Cover it up and let's go and burn the cabin. Someone's on to us and we need to be out of here, fingerprints and all.'

As the lid slammed shut, soil piled in fast. Koga trampled across the surface before leaves were kicked over, then a mad fifty-yard dash to the abandoned cabin. The rickety door flew open and nearly off its aged hinges as they burst in. Tools were thrown in the corner. Mondor grabbed a small microphone and crude communication unit from a paint-scuffed desk where a fast wrench ensured all fixed wires fractured. Loose items on the table went flying. In all the mayhem, the three men had not noticed their vehicle being invaded. As soon as it fired up, César threw his cigarette down and joined the others moving swiftly to the front door. Koga's much-loved, and highly polished Hummer was being reversed backwards at speed before a fast U-turn beneath giant pines. With the wheels spinning and gravel flying, the black vehicle took off down the rough track.

'Jeeze! That little mother's gonna pay,' shouted Koga as he watched Mondor running forward and firing his gun repeatedly.

'Hey,' continued Koga grabbing Mondor's shoulder, 'don't hit my car!'

'Don't worry about your tin box. Sakamoto's gonna kill you quick as lightning.'

'Why me? I didn't do anything wrong.'

The vehicle was bouncing and disappearing rapidly, sporadic shots still being fired as it snaked away on the winding track.

Koga looked stressed. 'Was that Kramer?'

'How the hell could it be?' ranted Mondor, pointing his gun close to Koga's nose.

'Careful. You've never experienced a Kepler186F when mad.'

'Stop giving me that kids crap!' shouted Mondor. 'I'm your boss. Fall in line and show respect,' now shooting wildly despite the Hummer being out of view.

'I hate walking,' said Koga kicking stones. 'Where I come from, we don't do it... we don't do walking. It's far too primitive.'

2 miles north of Ventura City

Mondor, Koga and their new recruit, César, arrived by taxi and through open electronic gates before finding their way to the rear garden. All three stood in bright sunshine and just yards from a grand swimming pool surrounded by a six-foot high wall built from Florida rock and all enhanced with red bougainvillea. Laid out on a sunbed by a grand pool was a mean looking man of Far Eastern appearance; dark hair, dark eyes, stubble and the aging skin of a sunbather. Despite all of this, he was toned and sporting his black boxer swim‑wear with crossed white swords on each side. He sat up on his sunbed and pointed aggressively at César. 'Hey you... yes you!' his tone, scolding. 'Move to the right. You're blocking out my sunlight. Shit man. Don't you know the sun promotes vitamin D in your body?'

The corrective move was quick by purpose. Sakamoto had a fiery temper and was highly unpredictable. 'And so, my Brazilian friend. What happened to Kramer?'

'It's a mystery,' replied César looking at the others in turn.

'I don't like mysteries. In fact, I hate them as much as I hate new recruits,' said Sakamoto, admiring a diamond encrusted ring on his small finger.

His stern and unforgiving eyes shot upwards. 'You,' he said pointing again at the Brazilian. 'Do you know how you climb to the top?'

The thinking time and silence was too long.

'Obviously not,' he said, standing up to look down on his confused victim. 'Here's your first lesson in how not to be a fool. What you should have said was this. *'Mr Sakamoto, I know where to find Kramer.'* That would have bought you time. Let's say, at least a day to fix things. The trouble is that when you mess up it makes me look stupid in front of my boss. Do you get me? Do you understand the chain of command and responsibility?'

'But...'

'There are no buts!' he glared. 'Even your two friends here know this. So, to put it in simple terms... I am in paradise, and you my friend, are in shit street. But there is good news.'

Sakamoto laughed when glancing at Mondor and Koga, then back. 'You're still my apprentice,' he said, sounding friendly. 'I was once an apprentice like you.'

César blinked, and then again.

'See this cord,' he said with a hand sweeping across an ornate drinks table at speed. 'When you catch Kramer, I want you to secure him and bring him to me personally. Is this clear?'

'Yes Mr Sakamoto.'

'Now because you messed up this time, I feel I need you to understand how the Sakamoto technique works.'

Sakamoto stood and stared at his bewildered recruit. 'Turn around and I'll show you how to secure, Kramer. He's a slippery customer. Come on, we haven't got all day, I'm a busy man.'

Standing behind, Sakamoto half smiled at Mondor and Koga as he tied his apprentice's hands together. 'There you are. Easy as that.'

The boss moved to face all. 'Ok, lesson two. Never fail the boss.'

He held his apprentice by the elbow and guided him to the pool's edge. 'Hey it's ok. I see your fear. I've been in your shoes many times, but it made me the man that I am today. You must trust your teacher… just as I once did.'

Sakamoto looked across to Mondor and Koga. 'Go and get Kramer's family and don't fail me again. There are hard lessons to learn, and who better to work on, than the weak and feeble upon this planet? I don't need weaklings in my team.'

Within a second, César felt a push. A big splash was followed by a desperate struggle. Mondor and Koga had seen it all before – another body to get rid of.

'This boy should have learned to swim in my world,' shouted Sakamoto with anger. 'Now go… and don't mess up again, unless you want to meet the devil himself!'

Mondor and Koga never turned but moved at pace.

Kramer was unconscious and laid out on top of a basic pine bed. The back of his shirt and trousers were still wet, his hair partly damp and ruffled. As a kettle boiled in the background, he stirred and slowly became aware of movement close by. Showing some beard growth, he opened his eyes and felt confused at the blurred sight of someone leaning over. Physically uncomfortable, he tried to sit up, but the effort required was overwhelming and flopped back down; both eyes shut. He spoke. 'Where am I?'

'Somewhere safe for now,' replied a man close by. 'You must have some evil friends. Perhaps you've caused an upset.'

Kramer's eyes opened slowly; a singular, low wattage bulb centrally providing sympathetic light. 'Who are you?'

'Don't worry about who I am, let's sort you out first.'

'But I need to know,' said Kramer, trying to sit up.

'I guess after your bad luck, you do deserve better treatment.'

Kramer slowly swung his legs off the hard bed and sat up with hands propping a weak body. With his head hanging down, he felt nauseous. 'What did you say your name was?'

'Fleming.'

'Ian?' said Kramer, barely looking up and trying desperately to cope with a multitude of thoughts.

'No, I'm Jack. But I like your sense of humour.'

13

'Tell me what's happening, I can't recall anything?' blinking and shaking his head.

'Drink this water, you must be dehydrated.'

Kramer put his hand out. 'How can I trust you?' he uttered through dry and parched lips.

The cup was taken.

'What were you doing in that coffin?'

Kramer frowned. Who was this man with no distinctive accent and why this light interrogation? The use of the word, coffin, had triggered his memory and glanced up for answers.

'I found you underground,' claimed Fleming taking the cup.

Kramer stared hard to gauge the man's face but the truth would be hard to assess in his weakened state.

'You were laid out and in a few inches of water which may explain why you feel damp and uncomfortable.'

Naturally, Kramer looked confused.

Fleming continued. 'I would have removed your clothing...'

'I'm glad you didn't. How long have I been here?'

'In this cabin... just an overnight stay, so about thirty hours. Luckily, I discovered you yesterday, and sometime after 4pm. Now it's nearly 10pm.'

'What day is it?'

'Thursday.'

'Thursday?' puzzled Kramer. 'I can't remember anything.'

'I must inform you. This isn't my log cabin.'

Kramer absorbed the basic surroundings. 'I'm confused. Does it belong to a friend of yours?'

'No,' said Fleming peeping past an old tatty curtain into the pitch-black night.

'You mean we're trespassing?'

'Yes. It's time to move out in the cover of darkness.'

Kramer blinked and frowned before trying to stand, but sat back down.

'You're too weak and need food.'

Kramer couldn't remember how, why or when this strange event had started. 'How did you find me?'

'I was out with my metal detector.'

'Really?' came a slow, doubtful reply. 'Where was I? The area I mean?'

'You were about three feet underground and in woodland. If I hadn't got a buzz, I certainly would never have found the coffin. I dug down and was disappointed to find electrical cable. Because it wasn't correct grade and looked new, I became suspicious and followed it. Seems obvious that you've upset someone.'

'I want to know who's behind this.'

'I'm always surprised at the evil some humans stoop to.'

'Tell me about it. I thought it only happened in films.'

'I also found lights and a small speaker on the underside of the lid... plus some waterpipe. In addition, I found these,' confessed Fleming turning away to grab something from a table. 'Pictures,' he said handing them over.

Kramer rubbed his eyes and took the photographs.

'Bring them,' said Fleming peeping out once again. 'Wanted men should never remain still.'

It would have been darker but for thick clouds now revealing the moon. Kramer sat in a Jeep Renegade and hung on tight as Fleming drove swiftly past the stolen Hummer and away from the woodland. Every puddle hit sent muddy spray shooting over the shallow grassy embankment.

'Kramer,' said Fleming handing over a small piece of paper. 'I'm going to drop you off as requested.'

'What is it?'

'Just my phone number.'

'Did you find my mobile?' said Kramer, searching all available pockets.

'A mobile? No, just wet clothing. I thought you were dead, but the very fact that you had a light pulse made me realise this was no party game, and that perhaps I shouldn't be getting involved. For a moment, I contemplated leaving you there. Lucky for you, I do have a conscience.'

'I have one request.'

'There's no harm in asking.'

'I need to phone my wife and daughter. They aren't safe.'

'What have you done to deserve this treatment?' offering his mobile.

'Sorry Jack, I'm still suffering with memory loss.'

'But you remembered that you had a phone and a family... and presumably, you remember your home number and wife's mobile?'

'What's the date?'

'Thursday, 20TH June.'

'June 20TH,' said Kramer peering out the window and thinking deeply. 'I must have been in that coffin for more than a day.'

'That's why you should eat something soon.'

Kramer had tried his home number several times, but there was no answer. 'That makes me nervous,' he sighed.

'What?'

'No answer... and the answerphone is switched off. It's never switched off.'

'You think you may have trouble at home?'

'Yes,' said Kramer trying again. 'If they've got my family, I can't bear to think what they may do. These people are ruthless.'

'Which people?'

'Those bastards who buried me alive.'

'You must have something that they want…'

'They're misguided and have the wrong person.'

It went quiet as Kramer tried to call once again.

'What line of work are you in?' quizzed Fleming, avoiding a pothole and swerving back on track.

'I fix and arrange things. Nothing too special.'

'Nothing too special? Perhaps you think it's nothing special but someone else thinks otherwise.'

'Everyone makes mistakes. Kings, Queens, Presidents. They're all human. I've made enough in my time.'

As the racing Renegade slowed down to enter a highway, so Kramer swigged water from a bottle and winced.

'Listen, Kramer. I'm an ex-cop. A crime has happened here and I'll try and help you out… not as a cop, but as a law-abiding citizen who still believes in righteousness. It's in my blood.'

'You sound more like a priest.'

'No. I'm not perfect enough for that.'

Kramer peered at Fleming in the dim light. 'Jack, I really appreciate your kindness and for saving me from certain death, but I can't let you get involved in this.'

'I've faced many dangerous situations in the past, so why not?' he said in a quick sideways glance.

'Take my advice and vanish into the night or you may end up dead. It's not worth the risk.'

'As a cop, I went to work every day knowing it could be my last. I got used to it. But now, I just want to be in charge of my own destiny so have set up as a private investigator.'

Ventura Police station had never been overrun with criminal cases, but the workload had increased in recent months. Short of staff, the station Chief had recruited a new member to the team, one by the name of Waxman. Detective, Curtis Waxman, was in his first month and keen to make a good impression. He threw a file down on to his desk. 'Not the normal stuff I'm used to,' he muttered. 'Yet another UFO story to investigate.'

A more senior colleague sat close by, a seasoned cop by the name of, Bomberger; Lieutenant Chad Bomberger. His smile was mildly sympathetic. 'Now forgive me, Curtis, but when I heard you were starting, I felt relieved and elated.'

'How's that?'

'It's policy. All the new recruits no matter what grade get the UFO shit for a while. It's just the way it is.'

Waxman pulled a smile. 'So, I get a medal for relieving you of that mundane duty, do I?'

'Well not entirely, but I'll help you out.'

Bomberger then laughed and leant over to whisper. 'Hey, I've got a PhD in rapid disposal of UFO cases.'

'That's great, Chad,' whispered Waxman as other colleagues moved around the office, some close by.

'Changing the subject, I saw a couple of women yesterday.'

'Lucky you,' an eyebrow lift.

'Yeah, I should be so lucky.'

Bomberger paused before continuing. 'It was a mother and her daughter and looking very concerned.'

'Ok.'

'Yes, the front desk referred them on to me because of special circumstances.'

'Special circumstances. I like that,' said Waxman. 'Sure beats UFOs.'

Kramer had been dropped off and was creeping around the back of his house. The lights were all off which was unusual. He glanced down at his wrist for a time check, but the villains had removed his watch for some reason. Perhaps worse was the fact that his keys were also missing from his pocket. He stopped fumbling for them and crept to the back of the garage where under a pot, he found a short wire concealed by an aged brick. The brick was cast aside and the wire pulled. From the shallow soil, a small plastic pot broke the surface. With the lid removed, two keys sat inside; one front, and one rear door. In less than a minute, Kramer was in and moving around by dim torchlight. He stood by a curtain and peeped out. The street was empty. Seconds later, he was on his way upstairs and creeping like a burglar anticipating staring down the barrel of a gun. Kramer reached the top and peered into each room. All were empty and the beds still made. In the master bedroom he grabbed a spare mobile. A dog barked, so moved to the nearest window. There was nothing to see. While searching for any clues relating to his family's absence, he was sure that a vehicle went by before slowing down. Several minutes later, he heard the backdoor creak despite having locked it.

Kramer carefully opened a window with flat-roof structure below and inched his way out. With the same window pushed closed, he crouched and moved towards the roof's edge where a grass lawn would enable a soft landing. Looking back at the house, he felt safe and leapt down. There was a thud followed by an attack. In no time at all he wrestled and fought hard with a man of equal strength, but who fought like a demon for control. Kramer had trained in self-defence, but it was a decade back. Laid horizontal on the grass and in a headlock, he did his best to elbow his attacker in the ribs. The rear garden was in semi-darkness as the struggle continued; but his fitness had suffered – maybe it was an age thing. *No*, he thought; *he had definitely been weakened through starvation, sleep deprivation and electric shock treatment.* Kramer was losing the battle and being wrenched upwards in the same deadly headlock. He began to cough and choke. Suddenly, a smashing noise and the mysterious villain let go and crumpled. Kramer was bewildered and kneeling while clutching his throat.

'Are you ok, Kramer?' a hand touching his shoulder.

The voice was familiar. It was dark but for invading street light. He turned to view.

'Fleming. What are you doing here?' he said, trying to stand.

'I thought that was obvious,' a smile in Fleming's voice. 'It's hard getting started as a private investigator. I need to make an impression.'

Standing in a slightly stooped position, hands on knees and breathing heavily, Kramer spoke. 'I never liked that clay pot anyway.'

'Yes, sorry, but it's the first thing I saw in the dim light.'

'Who is this little jerk?' said Kramer with a foot rolling the unknown villain over.

Fleming leant forward and took a picture before grabbing the villain's phone. 'I have contacts and if he has a record, we'll soon know who he is.'

'That would be useful,' said Kramer pausing. 'What are we going to do with this villain?'

'I'll reverse around and we can stick him in that coffin.'

'I'm not sure if that's a good idea,' confessed Kramer.

'It's ok,' replied Fleming. 'We'll leave it open but place a note in his pocket saying next time it'll be nailed shut.'

'I've got to find my wife and daughter,' said Kramer dusting himself down.

'I'll help you.'

'But why?'

'I told you before, I'm an ex-cop turned PI. I need clients. You could be my first. What do you say?'

Kramer peered hard at Fleming. 'Ventura cops will already be involved. My wife would have raised the alarm.'

'Don't worry, I can find that out for you. Besides, how would you explain being buried alive in a coffin? What would they say when you said a man with a metal detector found you?'

'It would be the truth, but they wouldn't take me seriously.'

'That's right. And if your wife and daughter are missing, they may think your wacky story is a coverup for their disappearance. You will very quickly become top of their, *who dun-it* list.'

'That's not great,' replied Kramer frowning and rubbing his chin.

'Listen. Grab some food and I'll bring the car around. This piece of trash needs to be taught a lesson.'

Lieutenant Bomberger brought two coffees in and placed his before offering the other. 'There you go, Waxman… black with one sugar. Unfortunately, it's becoming a mega late shift,' now glancing at his watch. 11:05pm.

'Thanks.'

'Look… if you want a break from that UFO case, let's have a chat about the ladies.'

'Sounds good,' leaning back. 'So, what's been happening?'

Bomberger seated himself. 'We don't get too many cases of missing persons, but when those who have reported a crime seem to disappear as well, then you have to sit up and say there must be something going on, right?'

Waxman nodded in agreement. 'Yes. I know it's early days, but have you tried all the avenues? Home, mobiles, workplace…'

'Yes, I've even got a lookout on their yellow Mustang.'

'That should be easy to spot.'

'It's only because I'm bored with my current cases that I've started looking at this report. People normally show up with a perfectly reasonable explanation.'

'Like he went off fishing or shooting for the weekend after an argument.'

Both laughed. Waxman continued. 'What have you got on the missing husband?'

Bomberger looked back at the new file. 'Well, Mrs Kramer said that they moved here three months back to be closer to the coast. She claimed her husband wanted to get back to teaching surfing and watersports.'

'No harm in that,' said Waxman taking a sip.

'Some day, I'd love to jack this job in and do the same. But I'm on the wrong side of fifty. Wish I was your age again.'

'The big four zero next year.'

'I celebrated that one with a hot air balloon ride.'

'Where… over Area 51?' joked Waxman, sipping again.

'I wish. Listen. Talking of Area 51, the Kramer's used to live in Nevada.'

'That's a desolate place.'

'Yes, in a town called, Rachel,' claimed Bomberger.

'Rachel? A small tight knit community with only about fifty inhabitants.'

'Are you thinking what I'm thinking?'

'It seems a bit too obvious, but if you didn't work at the base, why would you live there?'

'And listen to this. Kramer's wife said they found his shoes on the front doorstep and facing the door.'

'Odd,' said Waxman in deep thought.

'Yeah, like he had been beamed up.'

'Instant combustion?'

'It gets even more crazy by the second,' said Bomberger. 'Mrs Kramer states that his watch was placed in his right shoe.'

'Really?'

'Yep… and both socks rammed tightly down in his left.'

Waxman laughed. 'Secret Society messages perhaps?'

'There's something going on and I want to know what it is.'

'Me too.'

Ventura City: Northside 11:50pm

Sakamoto came in from his ornate stone balcony having heard a vehicle arriving at pace. He moved swiftly down the lit staircase with a firearm held firmly and approached the front door.

Mondor stepped out. Much to Sakamoto's annoyance, he was alone. 'Where is Koga!' he shouted.

'I dropped him off a couple of streets away from Kramer's place.'

'Then what?'

Mondor came closer, his shoes scrunching on the stones. 'So I left him to wait in the shadows while I went for petrol.'

'And!?'

'And…'

'Get inside,' bellowed Sakamoto, 'before I lose my temper.'

Mondor walked in, Sakamoto close behind and slamming the door shut. 'Why didn't Koga phone you if there was a problem?'

'I don't know. I tried his mobile but he didn't answer.'

Both stood in the hallway. 'Now listen to me, Mondor. You were once my best apprentice and graduated with honors. Why am I thinking that was a mistake?'

Mondor had no answer.

'How's your memory?' said Sakamoto.

Slightly confused, Mondor nodded. 'It's ok.'

'Obviously not. Have you already forgotten how and why César drowned this morning?'

'No… I have not forgotten, but…'

'Good. Send my condolences to his mother with a nice box of chocolates.'

'Don't worry, I'll make up for Koga's mistakes.'

Mondor's phone buzzed. He frowned heavily.

'Is it Koga?' demanded Sakamoto impatiently.

'Hello…' said Mondor looking at his boss.

Sakamoto's hand shot out and snatched the mobile. 'Who is this?' he growled.

Five seconds later, the call ended leaving Mondor looking puzzled. 'What was the message?'

'It's bad news for, Koga,' ranted Sakamoto marching off. He then spun round. 'Go to the coffin – Koga's in it. Shoot him and cover the grave well. He's history…. shit I hate failure!'

Sakamoto now retraced his steps with menace and shouted at close range. 'Let this be a warning to you, Mondor. If you fail me and we don't get Kramer back, you'll end up in a car crusher!'

Chapter 2

The White House: Friday

The Commander-in-Chief had called a private meeting with two of his most trusted friends. The first was Paul Penniman, Head of the Federal Reserve, and next to him, Virgil Carrozza, the second in command of all US Forces. Penniman and Carrozza were seated and talking quietly when the President walked in. Both men pushed their chairs backwards.

'Hey, don't stand up for me,' said their Commander-in-Chief looking tired, 'I'm just the President. Here today and gone to tomorrow,' his hand out to shake. 'Paul… Virgil.'

Both men acknowledged and settled back into their chairs as he took his place. 'Thanks for coming in,' he continued with his hands together and leaning on the table. 'I guess you have got new and important things to tell me too. Let's see if we can get through this meeting before the bloodhounds try to impeach me once again. It's a wretched process with far more lies than bombs fell on Vietnam.'

'You're not wrong there,' claimed Penniman.

'I second that,' added Carrozza. 'When the impeachment fails, I suggest we round up all the instigators of this dastardly act and drop them from a great height… then let the alligators do what alligators do best.'

'Yeah,' laughed Penniman. 'Clear the swamp of garbage.'

The President laughed the loudest, followed by Penniman, then Carrozza. Calm soon returned to the powerful trio. The President spoke. 'Thanks for that lighthearted moment. I value you guys immensely. You are definitely the true spirit of this great country. God bless America.'

'God bless America,' echoed his loyal visitors.

He paused and now looked deadly serious. 'Sometimes I wish I had never taken this job. Yes, I had immense challenges before, but nothing prepares you for what is thrust upon your overfilled plate. There are things I never knew about; things that I never knew existed,' he confessed, now looking at a large painting of Abraham Lincoln. 'Yes, old Abe had it good.'

'Don't feel that the whole world is upon your shoulders,' stated Penniman as the President's eyes left the great painting. 'Feel free to share your burdens with us. That's what old buddies are for.'

'Yes,' agreed Carrozza. 'I have all the best battle plans at my disposal and Paul's got all the money in the Reserve. We are bigger than the Bermuda Triangle and wiser than Russia and China put together. We can make anything happen... with your agreement of course.'

There was a moment as the Commander-in-Chief looked deep in thought. Perhaps he was changing his mind. He withdrew his eyes from another great painting. 'So, the topics I have are really for you to take away and think about. Some are way beyond top secret but will have to be brought out into the open someday. Why? Because containment will be out of our control. Yes men, even with all our might and know-how, the battles we face ahead will go down in history as the lost battles. Man's last stand. Covid–19 is just the start.'

'That sounds dire,' said Penniman looking serious.

'We know global warming is happening, and that in the grand scheme of things we can't do very much about it,' continued the President. 'American jobs need to be secure. Other countries must step up to the plate and act with responsibility. Too many criticize us without looking in their own backyard. We pay the lion's share into NATO. Other members laugh and take us for granted.'

'I agree,' said Carrozza. 'Slack members need a good kicking for not paying their full membership... some of them, the very same countries we fought to liberate from Hitler. Where is their respect?'

Penniman nodded. 'So much of our blood was lost in two World Wars to bring freedom and that's how they repay us.'

The President looked troubled before his mood changed to mild anger. 'And those same countries who deny paying their dues would cry out for our help if invaded again,' his fist hitting the table.

'Yep,' said Carrozza, 'sure as chicken shit, they'd be screaming for America to help. It's always the same. America's youth and America's blood.'

There was a pause. Carrozza continued. 'So, we continue to watch the Russians, when really our biggest threat is China right now. Every country has the right to progress, but it has to be in moderation because the planet just can't sustain such growth. Our New World Order is critical to man's survival.'

'Yes,' agreed the President. 'I was given a report by our best scientists stating that the north pole is shifting at a rate of 25 miles per year. It gave two main reasons. Firstly, the felling of millions of trees in the Amazon forests, therefore a global weight loss... and secondly, a tremendous weight gain on the opposite side of the globe as China pours billions of tons of concrete. Oh, and I nearly forgot. They've also got the massive, Three Gorges Dam, built at a cost of over thirty billion dollars. Consequently, this water storage weight adds to a world rapidly becoming out of balance.'

The President sipped from a glass of water. 'Russia should fear China sitting so close on her border. It's our policy to keep the Chinese at arms-length and to ensure we are top-dog in this world, but the day of reckoning is coming. She builds great wealth and has moved into space and with weaponry. More concerning are the seven islands that she has created, some on coral reefs as military seaports in the South China sea. The islands also have runways and fighter aircraft of all types. One island has been named, Fiery Island. What does this tell you?'

Carrozza shook his head. 'It's obvious to a child. They are gearing up for a take-over and creating strategic positions.'

The President frowned heavily as the troubles of the world bore down heavily upon his broad shoulders. 'There are so many other worrying topics to discuss, like the Chinese authorities whom have created internment camps to re-educate over one million ethic Uyghurs. These Muslims are being sterilized and brainwashed in the name of eliminating terrorism. Intelligence suggests that when the great war begins, this Northern force will be the cannon fodder to fight against us, Russia and Europe. North Korea will add another million soldiers in allegiance to China and act as the Southern buffer. Essentially, the Chinese stay safe while these other two forces fight until shredded. Then you will see China's elite forces rise up in their millions, fresh and ready to fight.'

Penniman rubbed his troubled brow. 'This type of war would punish the Federal Reserve, but we have been here before.'

'Yes,' agreed Carrozza. 'These days, the threat of atomic war is all too real. I remember the Cuban crisis like it was yesterday.'

'It's a shame because the Chinese people are good,' said the Commander-in-Chief. 'It's their political masters with their desire to takeover and control the world that is our problem.

When the time comes, even the Chinese people will be brainwashed by their own leaders and take up arms.'

'And China considers that Pakistan is their old friend,' said Carrozza. 'In the future and by design, war will break out with India over Kashmir.'

'Yes it will,' added the President. 'And China will steam through Pakistan and onwards at pace to conquer the Middle East oilfields. That's World War Three,' he sighed.

'It's such a great pity that the World's eyes are closed,' offered Penniman gloomily.

'But,' said Carrozza. 'We are the leaders of the Free World. We will resist their advances.'

'God bless America,' stated the President, the others following keenly.

Bomberger sat in the passenger seat as Waxman drove their unmarked Interceptor down a leafy avenue in Ventura.

'The best thing about this job is being able to escape the office and enjoy the sunshine,' said Bomberger, appreciating a gentle Pacific breeze. 'But the worst thing about it is finding dead bodies and never being able to bring justice.'

'Agreed,' said Waxman, stopping at traffic lights. 'The day will come when every human in the New World will be chipped with a smart device that will detect their state-of-condition through electrical pulse waves. Automatic notification will be sent to the authorities and the villain picked up for questioning.'

'I love it,' laughed Bomberger. 'Artificial Intelligence systems would be the new cops on the block.'

'Yeah. AI robots come out to pick up all the suspects before taking them away in driverless vans.'

When the lights changed, Waxman took off and continued in a lighthearted jest. 'Then once in the station, an interrogation by artificial investigators,' he laughed. 'Imagine that. An interview in a small room where your rights to a lawyer were nil and the whole process carried out by a couple of virtual robots... their eyes never blinking and able to see into the depths of your soul!'

'If it were me, I'd hate it,' admitted Bomberger.

'And these non-humans holding all the power and judging humans... the very beings that stupidly created them in the first place. Scary eh? Artificial Intelligence should be scrapped – keep manpower.'

Bomberger nodded agreeably. 'Just think, with the chipped information giving the crime scene's time, date and weather conditions, the suspect would be wrapped up in knots within half a minute. And if a case of murder, you would be out through the door marked – *Thanks for coming!* 10,000 volts... Boom, bang, puff! Next!'

'And that's it. No chance of a retrial... just smoking bones.'

Both laughed, Waxman slowing down. 'This is the place. I wonder if anyone's in this time?'

Bomberger and Waxman stepped out and strolled up the drive. The windows and garage door were shut, as was a side gate, but this didn't stop the doorbell being rung several times.

'Perhaps they're all out or hiding in the back garden.'

Waxman stood on the grass and peered in through the lounge window. 'There's no movement inside.'

'Let's go around the back,' said Bomberger, leading the way. 'It would be good to find someone and close this case.'

'Yes, I want to know more about Mr Kramer going missing and his shoes being left on the doorstep...'

'And why his watch was in one shoe and socks in the other.'

The sturdy side-gate was locked. Bomberger looked around then climbed over with minimal effort. 'Let's go, Waxman. I need cover.'

The two detectives arrived at the rear of the property. Looking around, Bomberger stooped down with a hand out. 'Look at this, a smashed garden pot.'

Waxman arrived. 'It could have fallen.'

'Not by itself.'

Bomberger was now on the lawn with fingers brushing along. 'Come over here, Curtis. There are heavy heel marks in the grass.'

Waxman looked up at the flat roof. 'Someone jumped down and landed there.'

'Perhaps?'

'There's a first-floor window that's not quite closed.'

'That's a big assumption,' said Bomberger, now trying the back door and peering in. 'Are you any good at climbing?'

'You know what they say? Send the youngest up first.'

'That's you Curtis,' smiled Bomberger. 'Don't forget, I've seen your job application. Besides, the new recruit always gets the shitty end of the stick.'

'I was about to volunteer anyway.'

The President looked troubled.

'Global temperatures are definitely rising and the polar caps are melting too fast. China and Russia are a continuous threat and now we're being visited by extraterrestrials... the whole world knows it and is supported by complex crop circles not to mention numerous sightings on land and at sea. All we need now is for gravity to start malfunctioning. Can you imagine it; people, cars, trains, planes... everything floating slowly upwards and away, people suffocating as the air becomes thinner.'

Carrozza nodded. 'I have something to add to all this doom and gloom. If the magnetic poles were to flip over or the Van Allen Belt lost its strength, then our protective shield would be eliminated exposing everyone to the sun's harmful radiation. God forbid… that would be death on a magnitude never seen before.'

'The planet Earth is mighty fragile,' admitted the President.

'That it is,' agreed Penniman. 'That it is.'

Bomberger had interlinked his fingers to form a footbridge, allowing Waxman to step up before levering himself on to the flat roof. Having gained access to the house, he let his boss in through the rear door.

'Have you seen anything?' whispered Bomberger.

'Fortunately, no bodies yet.'

'That's a good start.'

Waxman followed Bomberger into the study where both searched for clues.

'So, what have we got?' said Waxman. 'A wife and daughter who came down to the station to report a missing person before disappearing themselves. It wouldn't be the first time or the last time that a situation like this had occurred. The good news is that these things normally resolve themselves.'

'A preliminary search suggests that Kramer worked inside the Area 51 facility. I would love to know what goes on there. And how would you get a job in that place? Where do they advertise?'

Waxman picked the lock on a portable filing cabinet and flicked the lid open. 'Not sure I would want to work there,' now thumbing through folders and pulling one out. 'Just imagine they did have alien bodies there and some virus jumped to us humans. Death and a plague could follow. Who knows? Maybe bats were not the true origin of Covid-19.'

Bomberger found a solicitor's letter and was reading. Waxman spoke. 'I've got their car file and it looks like they have two vehicles. One red VW camper van and one yellow Ford Mustang. I guess we should check the garage and see if they're there.'

'Agreed.'

'What have you found?' Waxman said looking across.

'A letter from Mr Kramer's lawyer relating to the recent sale of their home in Rachel.'

'I don't think I would like to live in Lincoln County.'

'Curtis Waxman, I must agree with you once again.'

'While you carry on here, I'll check the garage for the cars. I'm an old petrol-head at heart.'

'Yes,' replied Bomberger. 'We mustn't overstay ~~over~~ our welcome. Caught without a search warrant would be a black mark for me and no chance of making senator one day.'

On his own, Sakamoto walked down a corridor before entering a staircase that led to a basement room. He unlocked the door and went in. Sat on a chair and tightly bound was a woman in her late thirties. She was slight in build, five foot six and with a fair complexion to match her brown shoulder length hair. The solid door closed. Sakamoto approached without any facial expression and could see the fear in his victim's light grey eyes. Grabbing a chair, he swung it round to straddle.

'Jayne Kramer, you have nothing to fear from me,' he said pulling a smile. 'We both want something. Perhaps we can help each other. What do you think?'

'I don't know why I'm here or where my daughter is?'

'Ah yes, your daughter. I had a daughter once, but that's a sad story. Let's not go there.'

'Where is she?'

'Dead and buried I'm afraid.'

His secured victim looked shocked. Sakamoto laughed. 'That's my daughter, not yours. Well at least, not yet anyway.'

'Is she here?'

'Don't worry about Libby, she's fine. When someone shows me respect, I show them my first-class hospitality. Your daughter is outside and sitting by the pool. If you co-operate, you may join her before my chauffeur takes you both home. How does that sound?'

'What do you want?'

Sakamoto laughed as he got up to walk around. 'What do I want? A hundred million in the bank and a peaceful life, that's what I want.'

'But we don't have any money. If you're expecting a ransom to be paid, it will never come,' she said with tears welling.

'It's your lucky day, Jayne. Today my needs are far less. I have things to do and places to go just like you... but just like you have to work, so do I.'

'Tell me what you want.'

'This is how it works. It's a trade off with no money involved. That's how reasonable I am.'

Sakamoto paused before sitting back down. He looked more serious. 'Where is your husband?'

'He should be at home. We all should be at home. Why?'

'Luis and I need to talk.'

'About what?'

The villain kept his mouth closed, shook his head and shut his eyes. They opened slowly. 'The topic isn't what you would call top secret, it's just a little private matter between the two of us.'

'I have no secrets from my husband so why can't you tell me what this is all about?' looking concerned. 'Is he in trouble?'

Sakamoto laughed. 'Not yet, not yet, Lady Jayne. Listen. All I need to do is have a half-hour chat with him and then I'll vanish into thin air and you will never see me again. That is a promise. You can trust me like I was your father. Let me ask you once again. Where is your husband? Where is Luis Kramer?'

'I swear it's the truth, I don't know.'

Although tightly bound, Jayne jumped as Sakamoto slapped his own thigh hard and bellowed. 'Stop messing around with me, stupid woman! Tell me. How well can Libby swim with concrete boots?'

'Please don't,' she cried out. 'Please please, I beg of you!' and starting to sob.

'Your husband worked at the Nellis Airforce base, sometimes on the bombing range, other times on very secretive things … and there were other places too, Mrs Kramer.'

'I don't know what you mean.'

'Remind me to tell you the story about, César. He could not swim either.'

Chad Bomberger arrived in the garage to see his colleague stood viewing an empty space beside the red camper van.

'This is where the Mustang would be if parked-up, but it's not here,' said Waxman.

'We could be jumping the gun. No one is missing… they are just all out doing separate things.'

'I think we're both on the same page. We smell a rat. That's why we're here without a search warrant.'

Bomberger nodded in agreement. 'Damn you, Waxman. I'm agreeing with you again. You'll be after my job next.'

'Offer me early retirement instead and I'll snatch it quick as grease lightning.'

'Ok then, what are you thinking?'

'Looking through the Mustang's file, I noticed that it has a tracking device…'

'And if we track the car down, we'll find them all relaxing by a lake and eating burgers,' jested Bomberger.

'That's what I'm hoping. Then we close the file down and get back on to the outstanding UFO files.'

'Little grey men with big slanting eyes! God help us Waxman,' scoffed Bomberger. 'Let's hope this is a missing persons case then we can get more villains behind bars.'

Sakamoto arrived on his sunny terrace and shouted to his second in command. 'Mondor! Where is Koga?'

Both met by the swimming pool. 'Remember when you took the call, you said he was in Kramer's coffin,' informed Mondor.

'Where is he now?'

'Still in the coffin. Why?'

Sakamoto's frowning face turned to anger as he reddened and leant forward. 'You idiot! You were supposed to use your brain. Just leave him there for a few hours as deserved punishment, that's all. Go and get him. We have additional trouble to deal with.'

'Right now?'

'Right now!'

Mondor turned to leave.

'Wait!' said Sakamoto, grabbing Mondor by the shoulder. 'What did you do with César's body?'

Mondor looked bewildered. 'I thought you dealt with it.'

'What the hell are you talking about?' he fired back.

'I said, I thought you dealt with it because when I got back, the swimming pool was clear. César's body wasn't there.'

'Oh Jesus!' shouted Sakamoto slapping his own forehead hard. 'Tell me I'm dreaming! Listen Mondor. Don't mess with me. You know what happens when I really get mad... a red film drops down over my eyes... a little voice inside my head says, *kill this pathetic creature*, and then guess what? I kill the pathetic creature stood before me.'

'But I left here with Koga. You watched César drown. When I got back there was no body.'

'Who took it, then?' shouted Sakamoto grabbing Mondor's shirt close to the neck. 'Some saint who dropped out of the sky with a band of angels!'

Mondor had no answer as his demented boss looked up to the blue sky above. 'Look up there. Do you see anything buzzing around waiting to save every unfortunate soul? No, of course not. That's why everyday people die of disease, famine and war. It's the way of the world.'

'Sorry,' said Mondor as Sakamoto pushed him away and with force.

'Keep thinking. I want answers. Now more importantly, you did well to get Kramer's wife and daughter. For this, you survive to live another day. Go get Koga out of the coffin and find Kramer. I'm under immense pressure to bring him in. Remember this. No Kramer... no Sakamoto, no Sakamoto, no Mondor,' he said nodding the stark ultimatum home with a deep penetrating stare. 'How clear is this to you?'

'Very clear.'

'Get going then... and for God's sake, don't bloody mess up again,' he said with anger, the veins in his temples, thick and prominent.

Both Bomberger and Waxman were back at the station, Waxman chasing up the missing Mustang and his boss studying another missing-person case. His phone buzzed and took the call. 'Hello, Bomberger.'

Five minutes later, and Kramer was seated in an interview room. The detective before him opened a thin file and read the few notes gathered so far. He looked up and leant back in his chair with finger tips bridged. 'So, Mr Kramer, thanks for coming in to see us. I'm glad, because what we have so far is beginning to look suspicious,' he paused. 'I gather by your expression, not all is well?'

'I would love to say the mystery has been resolved, but I'm concerned for my wife and daughter's safety.'

Bomberger's eyebrows twitched. 'Is there something that you wish to report?'

'I know it's early days, but they seemed to have disappeared without a trace. I can't get them on their mobiles.'

'Perhaps they have packed a bag and gone on a short break.'

'No. We have a close relationship. That would never happen without a discussion first. Besides, no suitcases have been used and no clothing has been taken.'

'When did you last see them?'

'On Tuesday when they went shopping in Ventura.'

'What car were they driving?'

'A yellow Mustang.'

Bomberger was now writing notes. As Kramer looked around the grey-walled room, the detective looked up. 'So, what we now have is a missing persons' report. You may not know this, but I did meet your wife and daughter last night. Normally I wouldn't have, but because the receiving officer thought the circumstances to be somewhat unusual, I thought I'd at least see them.'

'Were they ok?'

'Naturally, they were quite concerned for a number of reasons. They said you always communicated… that you had no plans to go away and that your shoes had been found on the doorstep facing the front door. Not only this, but your socks and watch had been placed deep inside your shoes. Any idea what that meant? Did you leave them there in a hurry?'

'No. And I'm sorry, but I can't explain it.'

'Could your wife or daughter have done it? You know… some sort of birthday prank?'

'If they did, it was totally out of character.'

'Where did you spend the night?'

'I don't know. I woke up on the edge of woodland.'

'And you have absolutely no idea how you got there?' quizzed Bomberger, gauging Kramer's reaction.

'No. The last forty-eight hours have been a complete blank.'

'Do you suffer from black-outs, amnesia or take recreational drugs? Otherwise, how could you explain this?'

'At this moment it's a mystery, but what I will do is inform you as soon as possible regarding anything?'

Sakamoto was pacing around the pool in his black shorts, his mobile in one hand, a large whisky in the other. He was furious. Mondor had not picked up and was now feeling pressure from someone higher in the chain… worse, a woman.

'Motosaka… where is Kramer?' her accent, Colombian.

'We are on his trail. The net is closing fast.'

'Deliver him soon or you know what will happen to you.'

Sakamoto hated being threatened or dictated to, especially by the weaker gender. If he could take over this next position, he'd be one step closer to running the whole show.

'Motosaka? Are you there?' she demanded aggressively.

Sakamoto also hated his name being abused and the slow confident delivery of every word.

She shouted. 'Motosaka!'

'Yes, I'm here.'

'Tomorrow I must have Kramer. Don't you dare let me down or Mondor will take your place. Mondor is sharp... razor sharp.'

The Colombian cut the call.

'Shit. Mondor is not sharp!' he shouted, walking back to the terrace. 'If I can't get Kramer, I will find that twisted lizard-freak and carry out an execution.'

Bomberger and Waxman sat at their desks, both eating a light snack.

'Ok,' said the boss. 'The Mustang has a tracker chip. Let's use it and solve this mystery.'

'It appears to be on the outskirts of Ventura and I've made a few enquiries regarding the homeowner. He's in Tobago for a few months and has rented out his place for $4,000 per month. Now who would have that sort of money to throw away?' said Waxman, sipping his coffee.

Bomberger laughed. 'I don't know about you, Curtis, but with that sort of money and the fact that the Mustang appears to be there makes me think villains must be involved. Drugs or car trading perhaps.'

'I agree.'

'I'm glad you agree.'

'Yeah. I just Googled it. The place has extensive grounds and a fancy swimming pool.'

'Anything else?' a sip of coffee taken.

'I did a further search on the place. It has five bedrooms, a sauna room, gym and basement... plus an integral garage.'

'Ok then,' said Bomberger urgently, and rising. 'We better get our skates on.'

Mondor had parked up near the burnt out shed with towering pines pointing toward the blue sky. Looking around confirmed that no one was about, so he made his way to the buried coffin. Two minutes later and he arrived with a short-handled spade. His mouth dropped open. The coffin was exposed and Koga had gone. Kneeling down, Mondor was looking around the woodland nervously, almost expecting Koga to leap out... or perhaps some other individual with evil intention. Feeling hot, sweaty and with eyes darting, he sprinted back to his petrol-blue, Ford-150.

Sakamoto was in the basement and interrogating his secured victim when he heard a vehicle arriving. *That doesn't sound like one of ours,* he thought. 'Sorry lady, but I'm going to have to gag you just in case you start shouting for help.'

The function was completed quickly and without much care, her mouth and cheeks distorting.

'I'll be back before you can say, *I love you.*'

As Bomberger stopped on the drive, both detectives looked around to gauge the premises. He cut the engine and spoke. 'Ok Curtis, what's your gut feeling about this place?'

'The vibe is, not overly friendly. No one has appeared at a window or come out to greet us. They must have heard the car approaching. These chippings are a dead give-away.'

'Unless of course no one's home,' added Bomberger, grabbing the door handle.

'There are a few windows open,' said Waxman. 'Either careless or just plain shy. Perhaps they're sat by the pool.'

'Ok, let's go and see who's in.'

'So, the main observation so far is that the Mustang isn't here,' confirmed Waxman. 'However, it could be behind those sturdy garage doors. Without a search warrant we won't know.'

The Interceptor's doors opened. 'Come on Curtis, let's go and chat to the butler.'

'Yeah. I'm keen to know who has $4,000 a month to pay for this place. It's got to be a crook.'

Both in plain clothes, the detectives reached the front door. Waxman rang the bell several times. A curtain twitched before the door opened. Sakamoto stood before them, unfriendly and solemn. He couldn't help it, it was embedded in his character. Too many street fights as a kid and now he had many more enemies than he cared to remember. Bomberger gauged his man – Sakamoto felt the visual scan and knew straight away this was the law sniffing around.

'Yes?'

'We are looking for Mr King, the home's owner. Is he in?' said Waxman.

'Yes he's in,' displaying the smallest smirk. 'He's in Tobago.'

Bomberger looked disappointed. 'Oh that's a shame, we were hoping to have a little chat.'

'About what?'

'Let's just say that it's a private matter,' informed Bomberger staring.

'I can't help you then,' said Sakamoto, starting to close the door.

'Just before you go... when will Mr King be coming back?' enquired Bomberger, his foot fast to block.

'I don't know. That's not my business.'

'I guess you're right,' added Waxman. 'But it should be your concern if residing in a house with a stolen car in the garage.'

'No. There are no stolen cars here.'

'If you get the garage key,' said Bomberger, 'we can clear this up very quickly, can't we?'

'Are you the law?'

'We could be,' added Waxman slowly.

'Let's see your ID. There's a lot of fraud going on and that's not a police car.'

Both Bomberger and Waxman produced their ID.

'Lieutenant Bomberger and this is Detective Waxman.'

'I do feel privileged,' came the sarcastic reply.

'Good, you make us feel welcome,' said Waxman. 'So, can we have a look in the garage. We have just received information to say that Mr King heads a ring of thieves in Ventura who steal cars for export. These cars are laid up until the heat dies down before shipping. We think there may be a couple in his double garage. It's certainly big enough.'

'Sorry to disappoint you boys,' laughed Sakamoto, 'but there is no key. What I'm prepared to do for you is contact the agent and ask if they forgot to give me a set.'

'Would you do that for us?' said Bomberger.

'Sure,' replied Sakamoto with a pulled smile. 'Why not? I'm always happy to help the law.'

As they drove out of the gate, the boss spoke. 'It looks like we may have to pay this place a visit after dark.'

'That's a shame, I was going out tonight.'

'Oh yeah? Doing what? Cookery classes?'

'Salsa actually.'

'At your age?' smiled Bomberger. 'I suppose you are single.'

Kramer was back at his house and standing in the lounge looking at a framed picture of his wife and daughter. He peered at his watch and then back to the recently taken picture before glancing out into the street. A young family arrived opposite. They had two kids and all looked happy as they stepped out. If only that was his position. Guilt swept in as he considered that somehow this disastrous affair was all his own fault. Afterall, the life that he'd been leading for the last decade was certainly his decision. Looking back, he thought, *if only* – if only he had stayed teaching watersports. Yes, the money may not have been so good, but at least he would be in a far more open and happier environment. However, this was reality. Kramer snapped out of his trance as a car pulled up outside. He checked his watch; 8:27pm... his visitor was three minutes early.

'Come in, Jack,' he said, peering out quickly before closing the door.

'I'm a bit early.'

'It's good of you to come,' now turning to walk.

'I want to help. If there's one thing I hate, it's villains.'

Kramer led the way with Fleming just a few steps behind. Arriving in the lounge, Kramer flicked a switch; silent motors closed the curtains.'

'Have a seat,' he said pointing to several. 'Coffee?'

'No, I'm fine... but thanks.'

Kramer sat down opposite. 'I know it's early days, but did you have any luck with your contacts?'

'I've had limited success so far. At the moment I can only use trusted friends based in LA.'

'Yes, I remember. You said that you used to work in the LAPD until recently…'

'That's right. Traffic cop first and then quickly progressed to investigations.'

'I admire you for giving up a steady income to go it alone.'

'Some would say foolish, others may say, gutsy. To me, it's a new dawn.'

Kramer was busy listening when it fell quiet for a moment. Fleming continued. 'Any news about your wife and daughter?'

'I've met two of the investigating officers on the case…'

'What were they like?'

'They seemed to ask all the right questions but, so far, they have no new leads to follow up.'

'If they're any good, they'll be making progress.'

'What about you? Any thoughts on where to start?'

'I've made a few enquiries,' he winked, 'with an old trusted colleague still plodding away in the force.'

'It's good to have contacts.'

'Ok,' said Fleming looking serious. 'This is what I have so far. A yellow Mustang is registered to your wife – town Rachel, in the Lincoln State.'

'Correct.'

'The car has a tracking device and I have an address,' informed Fleming.

'I'm impressed.'

'I say let's get over there as soon as it gets dark and we'll steal it back.'

'Shouldn't we just break into the property and find my wife and daughter?'

'Just because the car's there doesn't mean to say they're there too.'

'I agree,' sighed Kramer.

'Ok. We get the car and take it, but if there is a chance to spy and get more information, let's do it,' suggested Fleming.

Later that evening, Bomberger and Waxman parked in a side street before using an alleyway leading to a small field. It was dark enough not to be seen, but light enough to see their subject, a house just fifty yards up ahead. Not far away a dog barked, and when it stopped, another started. Both detectives stooped as they approached a high brick wall that fortunately didn't contain any further obstructions on its top face. Bomberger was first to scale the wall using an old discarded crate; a fly-tipper's rubbish was his gift. Both were soon creeping through well-watered gardens, most of which contained up-lighters beneath trees, some on the actual building. Several rooms were lit; window blinds down and shielding against prying eyes. The dogs had stopped barking. Bomberger knelt down just ten yards back and under a tree. He beckoned to Waxman who approached. 'It seems very quiet inside,' he whispered. 'No music, no movement...'

'They may be out. It's only 10:40. They can't have gone to bed.'

'Perhaps the villains are quietly planning the next job,' offered Waxman.

'Come on. Let's go around the side and check out the garage. That Mustang has got to be there.'

Bomberger stood at the double garage door with his treasured tumbler keys. The lock clicked open. Although Waxman was on lookout duty, he noted a satisfying smile arrive on his boss's face.

'I've never been beaten yet,' admitted Bomberger with pride.

He pulled gently on the door before reluctantly applying more force, but it remained firmly fixed.

'Shit,' he whispered. 'I definitely heard it tumble,' now trying once more to pull the sturdy doors open.

Waxman moved forward. Bomberger wasn't a man to admit defeat but nodded as he stepped aside. Seconds later, the senior officer grimaced. 'I knew it wasn't going to open.'

'I think it's bolted on the inside,' puffed Waxman still trying.

'I'm inclined to agree with you, Curtis. You know what that means, don't you?'

'It means two things. Firstly, we call it a day and go home, or secondly, we gain access some other way.'

'I agree with that analogy,' said Bomberger. 'Tell me. How was the salsa class this evening?'

'Great. I have a cute teacher.'

'Is she single?'

'Hold on a minute. I thought we were on a mission?'

'We are Waxman. Come on, let's go and peep through a few windows.'

'I must remind you Chad, we still don't have a search warrant for this place.'

'I know. But you know what? I thought to myself, Waxman's a clever guy, he'll figure something out when the FBI show up.'

The following day, Bomberger and Waxman were in work by 8am and sat at their respective desks. The senior detective looked over at Waxman, who in turn looked back as if a telepathic call had been received. Something was definitely coming. Bomberger rolled across on his computer chair and leant in. 'What the hell happened at Sakamoto's place last night?'

'I suggest two rival gangs came together and had a fight over something...'

'Surely not the Mustang?'

'Well, it wasn't there,' admitted Waxman looking perplexed.

'If it wasn't there, why would you bolt the garage doors on the inside? You would only do that if there was something else of value in there... and we had a good look around. There was nothing to see.'

'I agree.'

'I'm glad you agree. But it doesn't solve anything.'

'Yes but,' said Waxman looking a little more hopeful, 'we did find Sakamoto and some other individual laid out on the floor.'

'It's good that we got their mug shots.'

'So where has the Mustang gone?' demanded Waxman looking puzzled. 'The search data said it was at that location.'

Bomberger had rolled back to his workstation. 'Perhaps it was never locked away at all,' he said, 'but driven off the drive during the day... you know... before we got there.'

'That's the only logical explanation. So where does this leave us in the hunt for Mrs Kramer and her daughter? You know what's going to happen next? Kramer himself is going to come back to us very soon asking if we've found them.'

'I hate to admit it, Waxman, but I'm afraid that you're right again.'

'Why don't we do another search on the Mustang? With that chip, we'll find it... and this time, let's move straight away.'

Kramer had got up early and took off down the road in his lightweight tracksuit. Heading for the park, he enjoyed the fresh air but was deep in thought about the events unfolding the night before. Certainly, Fleming had proved to be a formidable private investigator and had led them straight to the Mustang. A car drew up alongside and stopped abruptly before he stepped in. Kramer slammed the door as they took off sharply.

'Morning Jack... good to see you. How's Jayne?'

'She's a little shaken up but I left her to sleep off her ordeal.'

'I wanted to phone her...'

'I know, but it's not safe. Phone taps and bugging devices are everywhere... your house included.'

'What about, Libby? She still hasn't come home. Any news?'

'That's a little trickier. Sakamoto is a shrewd villain and knew that someone would come calling, so he wisely separated them. But we have Jayne. Something tells me he'll be one mad dog right now – that's the man he is.'

'When you stormed in, how did you deal with Sakamoto?' quizzed Kramer.

Fleming laughed lightly. 'Secrets of the trade.'

'How can we find, Libby?'

'While you helped untie Jayne in the basement, I put bugs in Sakamoto's house phone, bathroom, kitchen and bedroom. If he's on his mobile or walking around, we may get lucky.'

'Ok, what now?'

'I'll take you back to my place. Hopefully, Jayne is up. I left her a note to say I was picking you up.'

'Jack, I can't thank you enough. I owe you big time.'

'Thanks for the opportunity.'

Bomberger and Waxman were back in the Interceptor after gaining further information on the Mustang. Driving down Freeway 101, both had many unanswered questions to resolve.

'So where are we heading? Mexico?' laughed Waxman in the passenger seat.

'Hopefully not that far. No, the latest is that the tracking service puts the car down at Joe's Café on York Street. Then we can catch the villains red-handed.'

'What's the chance it's the wife and daughter out for brunch?' said Waxman.

'If it is, I have a pile of questions requiring concise answers.'

Turning into the Café, the two detectives soon observed the near empty car park. Bomberger looked disappointed. 'Bloody technology these days is crap. The Mustang isn't here. Shit!'

'Wait,' said Waxman using a hand-held device. 'Let's see if this thing is working,' tapping in and staring at the screen.

'Where did you get that thing from, eBay or Orion's belt?'

'Very humorous. No. I forgot to hand it in when I left my last job.'

'A dishonest cop, eh,' said Bomberger frowning.

His hand shot forward to shake. 'Join the club.'

Both laughed, Bomberger stepping out first.

'Damn. The battery's low,' grumbled Waxman, 'but there is a signal.'

'Great. Let's find this elusive motor. It could be around the back.'

The bleeping got louder then died back as Waxman changed direction. Bomberger was right on Waxman's shoulder as the signal increased. Both arrived at a bin.

'Jesus!' exclaimed Bomberger looking and sounding frustrated. 'It's damn obvious that the tracker's been removed and chucked in there. If there's anything I hate, it's smart villains giving us a wild goose chase.'

Waxman looked deflated. 'Do you want to hold this?'

'Why? Is it radioactive?'

'I didn't think you wanted to put your hand in the bin and search for the tracker.'

Bomberger looked in. His nose twitched. 'You're right, Curtis,' his hand out. 'I'll hold the tracking device while you have a good deep rummage. God bless America.'

Sakamoto had been laid out on the floor and was groaning as he came to. A vase lay smashed close by. Still on his side, he felt the worst headache that he'd ever experienced in his life. His vision was blurry and the slightest movement caused waves of pain. The groans grew louder as he managed to crawl up on to a chair where he sat and tried to make sense of it all. The place was a mess. He noticed blood on his hands and touched his head; the stabbing pains ensuring he looked more miserable than normal. Feeling fragile, he called out. 'Mondor.'

With no reply, he staggered off to search the house.

Reality suddenly hit home when Jayne came to mind. He now moved at double-snail pace until reaching the stairwell where he trod carefully till reaching the basement. Pushing the door open, he saw Mondor tied to the chair. Sakamoto closed his eyes for a second and shook his head. 'What the hell happened here?' he half shouted, then being punished with more self-inflicted pain.

He approached Mondor who sat with his head flopped down. 'Hey wake up, dopey clown,' he grumbled, pulling Mondor's head up by his chin. 'You were supposed to be on guard duty last night. What the hell happened? You goofed up!'

Mondor was released and given a few slaps until regaining consciousness. The boss was just about to shout at close range when he heard the front door being knocked.

'Oh shit,' he grizzled. 'It's the law... I can smell their stale clothing a mile off.'

Bomberger and Waxman stood on the doorstep and waiting patiently.

'Beautiful day,' said Waxman, looking over towards the pool.

'Yeah.'

'Who trashed this place last night?'

'Some bad ass,' admitted Bomberger. 'Sakamoto is a brute. Legs like tree trunks, arms thick as telegraph poles. Who in God's name put him down so easily? We need to recruit them on to our side.'

'And a blow to the back of the head with a thick-walled vase meant a stealth move.'

'Ex-commando maybe?'

'What would an ex-commando be doing here?' said Waxman.

'You tell me. Seems like you're the clever detective.'

'I wish... but thanks, Chad.'

Fleming pulled off the road and parked in front of his garage. Kramer stepped out and eagerly caught up at the front door. Fleming looked around and placed the key before entering the bungalow. It was quiet and the living room was empty.

'Luis, go and see if Jayne's awake. I will make us some coffee.'

Jayne was still fast asleep; must have been her recent ordeal. Kramer crept back out of the room and joined Fleming in the kitchen.

'Silly question,' he said, 'but I suppose the Mustang is still in your garage?'

'Yes. But don't worry about people around here thinking anything is suspicious. I've only been renting for a few weeks. They don't know me and I don't know them. That's the way I like it,' he said, stirring the coffee as a cup filled.

Kramer nodded. 'I'm much the same. I enjoy distancing myself from some folk, but welcome the interaction with others.'

'For example,' said Fleming carrying the cups through.

'I don't care for nosey neighbours, but I like working with young people, especially if I'm teaching them something they're passionate about. For instance,' he said sitting down, 'teaching them watersports and having lighthearted conversations... you know... non-intrusive.'

Fleming placed the cups down. He looked bright. 'Hey Curtis, I love watersports myself.'

'That's great.'

'Yeah, I love speed boats, kayaking...'

'Do you like surfboarding or windsurfing?'

'I wish, but I just don't have the balance for that,' laughed Fleming, seating himself. 'That's a young man's game.'

'Listen. When all this has blown over, I'll teach you. They have some great surf here.'

'I know, I've been down to the beach and watched the Pacific rollers breaking.'

Sakamoto was on his mobile and looking out over the pool where a light breeze caused gentle ripples to fan out.

'Motosaka, have you got, Kramer?' demanded Salamander.

'No,' replied Sakamoto, sounding frustrated. 'It's just not that simple...'

'I don't care about simplicity or complexity. I don't want to hear excuses. I demand you get him for me and I'll do the rest.'

'Ok. Just give me until the end of the day...'

Salamander laughed. 'The same old Motosaka. That's all I hear from you... just give me until the end of the day!'

'This is complicated.'

'But why, why?' came an angry response.

'Something's going on...'

'Like what?' she shrieked. 'Come on, convince me.'

'We buried Kramer alive in dense woodland and miles from anywhere. He was in a coffin and three feet down. How could he escape without help?'

'You are the great, Motosaka. Are you telling me that someone has out-smarted you?'

There was a slight pause; the interrogation continued. 'You know what happens to non-performers, don't you? I know you do. It's simple. We kill off anyone who threatens the organization through stupidity and lack of co-operation. This is not some trashy little outfit. Look around you. A nice residence all paid for, plus money in the bank every month... for you and your stupid stooges. Motosaka, are you completely brainless?'

'Listen...'

'No!' she shouted. 'You listen to me. I'm your boss. We have never met before, but I can see that I will have to pay you a visit.'

'Don't waste your time…'

'Shut up! Think before you open that ugly mouth of yours.'

Sakamoto cut the call. Looking angry and humiliated, he turned to Mondor, seated under a parasol. 'I hate that ranting woman, and I'm not going to take that shit from her anymore. This is a man's world.'

'But Salamander and the upper chain will come for us.'

'No, I don't think so… not that gutless bitch. What she will do is send an execution squad. We either stay and fight like men, or vanish like rats until the heat dies down.'

Mondor looked worried. 'I would rather vanish.'

'No. I say stay and fight, or you will forever be looking over your trembling shoulder.'

Bomberger played back the bugged recording. Waxman had moved in close to listen. He spoke. 'So, the picture gets more complicated by the day. Sakamoto is in the chain and obviously under instruction to capture Kramer for certain information. It must be hellishly important to someone if they're prepared to go to this length and expense.'

The senior detective nodded. 'And the fact that Sakamoto cut the call means he isn't going to comply anymore. What is it that Kramer knows that these criminals want?'

'Yes, who is at the top of the chain and paying for all of this?'

'Obviously Kramer is the key,' added Bomberger, sipping his diet coke. 'If he was living in Rachel, he must have been working in Area 51. So, this has to be the most likely reason as to why he's a magnet for these criminals.'

'Area 51 is just a secret base for trialing new aircraft, weapons and wacky control mechanisms, that's all,' said Waxman.

Bomberger laughed. 'Why all the secrecy, high fences, guards watching from afar and their own Boeing 737-600's with long red stripes along the fuselage?'

'Military stuff always has been a covert game thanks to the Russians and now the Chinese. With spy satellites cruising over sensitive areas, obviously things have to be kept undercover,' explained Waxman.

'I'll tell you something for nothing, Curtis. You and I could get a job in there if we wanted to.'

Waxman frowned. 'Would we want to do that? All that secrecy and nothing but sweltering in the desert. It's not for me. I like trees, parks and the ocean view with a nice breeze. No, let's leave that for people like, Kramer.'

'What do you think makes him tick?' asked Bomberger looking at his screen and sipping from his can.

'What makes him tick?'

Waxman paused and then continued. 'I think he's just an ordinary guy... obviously he has got certain talents and expertise. But at the end of the day, Kramer is just a family man...'

'Ok then, let's look at Sakamoto. I've got his mug shot and have requested his file. I know you shouldn't judge a book by its cover, but looking the way he does demonstrates a life of crime. That's my hunch.'

'I've just had a good idea,' said Waxman, looking bright.

'I'm all ears,' looking across and finishing his diet coke.

'We could recruit, Sakamoto.'

'What?' said Bomberger looking horrified, leaning back while crushing his can noisily in one hand.

'Sakamoto now finds himself in a tricky situation with his life on the line. Why not at least consider him? He helps us and we whistle him away to some remote Caribbean Island afterwards.'

'Yeah,' laughed Bomberger. 'Then we send a hitman over.'

Both detectives had been quiet for half an hour, Bomberger looking at another case and Waxman on a UFO report. He looked puzzled as he read the details, then looked up to stare out of a window with picturesque clouds. The episode of the Phoenix lights came to mind, then the Bermuda Triangle and so many unexplained events reaching back seven decades or more. Whilst in a deep trance, Bomberger seemed to be speaking. He looked across. 'Sorry Chad. What was that?'

'I just got some new info.'

Waxman shuffled across on his computer chair to arrive next to Bomberger who was still engrossed in his own screen message.

'It's a short but useful mobile conversation between Sakamoto and Mondor. Sakamoto asks where Mondor is. Mondor said he's on his way to Wacky Mac's supermarket. Sakamoto instructs Mondor to go and pick the girl up about 11pm and bring her to the house. Unfortunately, he doesn't say which house… and there are at least two Wacky Mac's stores in Ventura.'

'This has to be Libby, unless they're implicated in something else,' offered Waxman.

'Come on,' said Bomberger, standing up urgently and moving for the door. 'If we get to the supermarket before Mondor leaves, we can put a tracking device on his vehicle.'

'Then follow at a distance tonight…'

'Yes,' agreed the boss, 'but if we get to the wrong Wacky Mac's store, then we'll miss this golden opportunity,' he said moving swiftly down a stairwell. 'I should have traced Mondor's vehicle details.'

'It's ok, I had a break from UFOs and traced them myself.'

'You are good, Waxman,' said Bomberger looking bright.

'Yeah, I know.'

Jayne now sat with her relieved husband; the small group discussing the recent events.

'Curtis, we must leave now and go down to the police station,' she said, looking pensive.

Strangely, he didn't jump at the chance.

'Curtis,' she said standing, 'come on, we must find, Libby.'

'Sorry, my mind was somewhere else,' he replied, now by her side. 'You're right.'

He looked over to Fleming. 'Jack, I really want to thank you for all your help so far. It's right that Jayne and I go down to the police station and update them as soon as possible.'

'Yes, get going, but not in the Mustang. Its disappearance and whereabouts would be an added complication to explain. We will think of something. Use my car this time.'

'If you drop us off at our place, I can use my camper van.'

'The red VW combi?'

'Correct,' said Kramer looking mystified. 'How did you know we have one?'

'I've been to your house with you. Remember?'

'Yes of course. There's so much going on, I can't keep up.'

Bomberger and Waxman cruised down the 101 Freeway before turning off towards Wacky Mac's largest store. A quick drive around the car park brought frustration.

'Damn,' said Bomberger behind the wheel. 'Mondor's either been and gone... not arrived yet, or at the other store. We don't need this complication.'

Swinging out of the car park with urgency, their unmarked Interceptor nearly hit a truck coming the other way.

'Shit, that was a close one,' said Waxman hanging on. 'I would put a call out to all cars in the area to locate Mondor, but we don't want to spook him. We need to get Libby back alive.'

'It's just a thought,' offered Bomberger, 'but it may not be the daughter. It could be Kramer's wife, Jayne. We don't know yet.'

'Ah yes, but don't forget... Sakamoto said, *pick up the girl*. It has to be, Libby.'

'Curtis, you do have a good point,' pulling a face and nodding.

Bomberger soon arrived in the other Wacky Mac's car park. 'Remind me what we're looking for? What make? What model?'

'Ford F-150 pickup. Velocity Blue.'

'Any scratches,' smirked Bomberger, getting smart.

'Just five at the last count.'

Fleming had dropped the Kramer's off at their new home, a home that they'd hardly lived in and got to know.

'Why don't we phone the police station for an update?' said Jayne stripping in the bedroom.

'We could do that,' replied Luis, grabbing clean clothing.

Although the shower started, she called out. 'Luis, come in here and tell me again what happened to you. Exactly how did you escape from the coffin?'

Luis arrived at the sink and looked in the mirror. 'God, I look awful.'

'How did you escape…'

'Miraculously, Fleming was out with his metal detector and searching through the woods for any Indian artifacts. That's what he said and I believe him,' picking up his shaver. 'He's an ex-cop and now a private investigator…'

'I'm desperate to find, Libby – ' she said, grabbing the soap.

'So am I… and just like you, I love her like crazy.'

Tearful and soaping quickly, Jayne spoke. 'What's happening to us, Luis? This whole affair is frightening me to death.'

'I'm as baffled as you are…it's got to be mistaken identity.'

'I can't bear to think what may have happened to our, Libby.'

'Remind me again how you were kidnapped. You said from the Ventura Mall car park.'

'Yes, at gunpoint,' and still rinsing. 'At first, I thought it was a prank. We were petrified,' stepping out and rapid towel drying.

'You read about these things but it always happens to someone else,' he said, looking in the mirror.

'I'm not sure about your friend, Fleming,' said Jayne, grabbing her underwear.

'Why? What do you mean?' flicking a comb through.

'I don't know,' pulling on her jeans. 'But it seems odd that of all the miles of pine woodland, he happens to be right there with his metal detector.'

'It was a fluke. Just like someone winning the lottery.'

'But he may be a plant to gain your confidence,' her hairdryer starting.

'I don't see it like that,' he said, frowning and thinking.

Bomberger and Waxman arrived back in the office. The boss grabbed another diet coke from the vending machine. The can fizzed before he enjoyed a prolonged gulping session. 'That was thirsty work,' he admitted.

'I don't know how you can drink that stuff,' said Waxman standing at the vending machine.

'Don't get me wrong,' said Bomberger plonking himself down. 'I really like coffee, but for me, this is the lesser of the two evils.'

The phone started ringing. Bomberger looked at Waxman. 'I do believe it's your turn. I'll get on with the coffin case and you deal with this one before getting back to your UFO junk files!'

'Thanks,' said Waxman, walking back with his coffee.

'No problem,' said Bomberger booting up his computer, a satisfying smile arriving.

'Waxman here,' he answered hurriedly.

'External call for Lieutenant Bomberger,' said the redirecting control room.

'It's for you,' the handset thrust forward.

Bomberger rolled his eyes, a hand over the mouthpiece. 'It's the commissioner giving me early retirement for outstanding service. 'Bomberger.'

'Lieutenant, I have Mr Kramer on the line. Can you take the call?'

'Yes, put him through.'

A pause. The line connected.

'Lieutenant Bomberger speaking.'

'Hello lieutenant, it's Luis Kramer. I'm just ringing to see if you have any updates regarding my wife and daughter?'

'Thanks for calling in. My colleague and I were going to drop in to your place later on... hopefully with some good news.'

'Oh. Can you elaborate?'

'I'd rather not say anything over the phone about this. Will you be in later on today?'

'Would you prefer that I come in and see you?'

'I would have said, yes, but I have quite a few commitments so that won't be possible.'

'Ok. I'll wait to hear from you.'

'Thank you for your understanding, Mr Kramer.'

'That's fine, Lieutenant.'

'Bye.'

Bomberger hung up. 'We need to make some progress today on this one.'

'We?'

Bomberger looked across. 'Yes... we. While it is true to say that you are on UFO cases, I need your mind to hover, as it were, and still be active on this case. What we don't want is a backlog of cases piling up when holiday season arrives.'

'Has anything new come through on Sakamoto's phone tap?'

'No, but perhaps we should pay him a visit. If he has messed up and his ruthless masters have turned, then perhaps we can persuade him to help us. That way, we get information... and he will get minimal protection from us.'

'Minimal?' quizzed Waxman. 'We don't have the authority.'

'The odds are he'll get wasted and end up six foot under. That's my assessment.'

After the phone call to Lieutenant Bomberger had ended, an argument followed. Jayne was reluctantly packing her case.

'Luis,' her tone one of frustration. 'I just don't get it. We're in dire straits and wanting our daughter back and the only person able to help is Bomberger. Why did you blatantly lie to him on the phone just now!'

'It was something that I had discussed with Fleming...'

'Fleming?' she said, raising her voice further. 'Since when was he leading the case?'

'I have great respect for him. He's an ex-cop...'

'Stop telling me he's an ex-cop,' she said throwing more items into her case. 'Tell me something new like, he's found Libby.'

'Fleming thinks that with two missing people, Bomberger's team will work harder to solve the case.'

'Huh. Since when was a small-time investigator like Fleming more knowledgeable than a Lieutenant in the police force with all the search facilities at his disposal?'

'But I must remind you that it was Fleming who found me and not Bomberger. Without him, I'd still be in the woods and three feet down... probably dead by now.'

'Fleming hadn't been assigned to your case. He wasn't looking for you. It was just a fluke. You said it yourself.'

'I did, but please remember... I'm only standing here because Fleming found me. And you're only standing there because he helped find you. So... in conclusion, don't you think he's the best person to find, Libby?'

Chapter 4

The Pentagon

The President walked down a long wide corridor and deep in conversation.

'It was this section that got hit by the hijacked airliner in 2001,' said Carrozza, second in command of all US Forces. 'That was a bad day for America.'

'I agree. Who would have thought that we could receive such a devasting blow from our enemies,' replied the President barely acknowledging staff coming their way.

'The terrorists really hit us hard. I shall never forget the Twin Towers coming down,' said Carrozza stopping at a door and engaging the handle.

'We paid a very heavy price that day. It must never happen again.'

'I'm afraid it's just a matter of time.'

A quick knock and in they went.

'Hi Paul,' said the President with his outstretched hand.

The Head of the Federal Reserve, Penniman, had been writing but stood as his two colleagues entered the spacious office. Once seated, the President took control of the conversation. 'How are the families,' he said, gauging each in turn.

'Fine,' said Carrozza, 'except my eldest wants to join the CIA and deal with all the guys who upset him at high school.'

The group's response was one of mutual amusement.

'As you know, both of mine graduated from Stanford long ago,' added Penniman, sitting back. 'Peter wants my job and Joe wants to be an actor,' he said with an eye roll. 'He's still hung up on the Blues Brothers – he's watched that film a thousand times.'

'Great,' said the President. 'If only our lives were as simple as that.'

Both Penniman and Carrozza nodded solemnly.

'So where are we with the great exposure case. Any news Virgil?'

'Every day we get a little more information. Sometimes we still have to send the Men in Black out to ensure secrecy.'

He then laughed lightly. 'It's the old story. Keep it quiet, down play everything and spin your way out.'

'It's quite a burden to carry,' admitted the President, shuffling on his seat. 'Kennedy wanted to tell the world what was really happening, but it was never going to happen. There would be a time in the future… but that time had not come. In the fifties and sixties, the people of the world were still getting used to peace after the Second World War.'

Penniman looked deep in thought. 'What could Kennedy have gained by breaking the news, except for having the glory and going down in history? Honesty is very commendable.'

Carrozza cleared his throat. 'What he hadn't thought through was the reaction of the people. If the timing was wrong then the response could have been disastrous for humanity. So, despite the cold war and Cuban crisis, to announce that we had made contact with other civilizations would have spooked the world. People could cope with warring neighbours, but not advanced beings from outer space.'

The President looked serious. 'And that's the great deception. They're not all from outer space… some have been living here amongst us for generations.'

Penniman scratched his head as he engaged the Commander-in-Chief. 'Hal, you don't really believe this stuff, do you?'

The President's smile was small and closed; his look almost expressionless. 'You are my closest friends and I trust you totally, for both of you also hold many secrets that you'll take to the grave too. What I'm about to tell you is probably widely known anyway... just not confirmed by myself or the government.'

A hush followed. 'Every new President taking office is briefed by the CIA on the extra-terrestrial subject. I always sat on the fence with this matter. Sure, it made sense. There could be life out there. Equally, we have now gathered so much evidence... evidence pointing to the fact that some of these beings never left planet Earth in the first place. And so, why shouldn't there be life forms more advanced than ours. Remember, that in a short space of time, man has reached the moon. America made world history, for the first man on the moon was more than just a visitor. Neil Armstrong was in actual fact now an alien to that planet.'

The President paused. 'That was one small step for man, one giant leap for mankind.'

Penniman took his opportunity as the President looked his way. 'This is fascinating. But are you really admitting that aliens are here?'

'Yes. And while we always thought that they were visiting, the general consensus is that they are still here. Many never left. And while we live on solid ground breathing oxygen, some species are amphibious and hide in the deep oceans.'

'Some species!' laughed Penniman nervously.

'Yes,' replied the Commander-in-Chief. 'Just as nations went out and colonized Africa, and the Americas etcetera, so they have done the same in other solar systems... maybe other Galaxies. And like the English, French, Dutch and Spanish fought long ago to maintain their colonies, these visitors are doing the same... but!' he said, raising a finger, 'they do it all covertly.'

Penniman looked to Carrozza and back. 'Really, Hal?' he said with some doubt. 'It can't be possible.'

The President continued. 'The Russian Navy have seen them under water. In fact, many sightings include craft flying in and out of lakes and oceans. What sort of technology lets them enter water at speed and cause no splash. I'm sad to say, there isn't much that we can do about it. They have the upper hand, especially with their advanced materials and flying technology.'

Carrozza had been quiet and listening. 'Yes Paul, this is all true. I might be second in command of all US Forces, but I'm sure that if it came to a war with them, these beings would win hands down. How can I be so sure? We track them on radar... we've scrambled jets to intercept them, but they've out maneuvered us every time. In some instances, they've vanished at an exceedingly high speed. On other occasions, their craft had done ninety degree turns at two Mach which defy our laws of physics. A further worry is that these beings can just switch our power off... yes, black out our communications and kill all electrical systems. Our whole world runs on electrical systems. Surrender would almost be on day one... should their secretive agenda change.'

Penniman looked both mystified and horrified. 'I have never really taken this subject that seriously.'

The President laughed respectfully. 'Paul, think about the pyramids. We couldn't build one today with all our know-how. Therefore, the Egyptians could never have done it three thousand years back. Impossible. So, it confirms that while our ancestors may have witnessed the event, the Rendlesham binary code holds the key. We are definitely not alone in the Universe.'

'What happens now?' added Carrozza.

'It's as simple as it is complicated,' said the President. 'We are doing our utmost to keep it under wraps, but there are people out there who want us... me... to tell the truth once and for all. I just don't know that the world could take such a message.'

Frowning all the time, Penniman took his opportunity. 'What about the Christianity thing?'

'For sure, the church definitely won't like it,' said the troubled President. 'Historically, they hated scientists and any theory dispelling one true God. But if you remember, the three wise men followed a star. Consider now that this was not a star at all, but a spaceship. Look how the International Space Station shines so brightly as it passes over the Earth. Now you see how complex the reveal would be. The whole world-system could fall into a never-ending abyss.'

Ventura police station: Sunday morning

Bomberger was at his desk when Waxman dashed in to miss a short heavy downpour.

'If I'd known, I wouldn't have showered.'

'I just missed it,' said Bomberger staring out. 'I'm still hacked off that we didn't manage to find Mondor's car yesterday. The Sakamoto call definitely said he was going to Wacky Mac's store.'

'Have any other leads come up?'

'No,' paused the boss. 'I say we pay Sakamoto a visit and see if he would like to jump ship.'

'Are you taking your firearm?' asked Waxman.

'I wasn't going to. It's Sunday.'

'What will save your life? A gun or a prayer?'

'Going home... that will save my life.'

'Yeah, more fun watching the Boston Red Sox. Back to reality. My experience is that anyone with lightning strikes tattooed all over his back, a few long scars and built like a treehouse should be regarded as highly suspicious... may even be dangerous.'

'I hate to say it, Waxman, but you're right again. I'll bring my firearm.'

Both were soon out on the road and heading for Sakamoto's residence.

Fleming peered out of his front window. Convinced that no one was spying on his place, he grabbed his mobile. The call connected. 'Is that you, Luis?'

'Jack?'

'Yes... it's Jack.'

'Where are you?'

'At my place. I have some good news.'

'You found, Libby!'

'Not quite, but I've had a tip off. It is a long shot from someone I know.'

'... in the LAPD?'

'Sorry, I can't say on the phone.'

'Yes, I get that. What's the next move?'

'Come around this evening about 10pm. I would do it on my own but, if Libby is there, I want you to be there too.'

'That's great, Jack. Anything else?'

'No. I now have some urgent work and must go.'

'Thanks again. Should I call you?'

'No. I'll call you.'

Once the call finished, Fleming went into the spare room at the back of his rented home. 'Ok Mondor, you can't fool me. I'm not who you think I am. Your world is not my world.'

Mondor was sat with his hands tied behind his back, where marine rope also secured his legs to the chair. A gag would have kept him quiet, but it wasn't necessary. The unfortunate villain was dazed.

'I know where you've hidden, Libby... César told me?'

In his trance like state, Mondor's mouth moved, but no sound came out.

'Yes... you are shocked at what you have heard and seen.'

Fleming paused. 'Oh, and if you should see Koga, tell him I enjoyed driving his Hummer... and don't worry, this will soon be all over... you won't remember me.'

Kramer had arrived at a small motel just on the northside of town. He checked in alone and grabbed the keys from an old man who looked like he didn't want to be there. Back in the car park, he met Jayne and carried their two cases up to Room 102 on the first floor. The door closed.

'Tell me again what Fleming said,' came a desperate plea.

Kramer sat down on the bed. 'It's a hard mattress.'

'Luis!'

'Jayne, you need to keep this quiet, remember?'

'Stop treating me like I'm stupid.'

'It's very sensitive...'

'Come on then.'

'Jack has had a tip off from someone in the LAPD regarding Libby's whereabouts...'

'How would the LAPD know?'

'I didn't ask.'

'Perhaps you should have,' her voice raised again.

'Don't forget, he's a Private Investigator. Fleming doesn't have to give all of his contacts away. Besides, he isn't charging for this work.'

'That's odd. What about, Libby?'

'Jack will pick me up tonight and we'll go and get her.'

'Where from?'

'I don't know.'

Bomberger drove the Interceptor through the open gates and approached Sakamoto's residence.

'There are no cars on the drive,' stated Waxman.

'It was a fifty, fifty chance that he would be in.'

The unmarked car drew up in front of the expensive rental. Waxman's hand was already on his door handle. 'We could always call in on Kramer and see what he's doing. Hopefully, clearance for a background search has come through.'

Bomberger stepped out and placed his sunglasses. 'Somehow, I don't think we'll get anything worth looking at. People working on the Area 51 site and similar places will be protected by the CIA and various non-disclosure docs.'

Both doors slammed. Waxman spoke with amusement. 'That should have made Sakamoto sit up in bed,' placing his shades.

'Unless he's riddled with bullets and in a shallow grave.'

The front door was knocked. With no answer, they walked around the property. Five minutes later, and Bomberger had his lock-picking device out.

'What if he's home?' said Waxman looking around. 'He may put a complaint in – intrusive police behaviour without a warrant never looks good in the newspapers, or on the Chief's desk.'

'It's easy. We heard someone scream inside,' said the boss as he fiddled with the lock.

Bomberger smiled to himself as the door opened, now leading the way. 'Hello, anyone at home?'

As expected, there was no answer. Entering the front room ensured their inquisitive nature kicked in. Bomberger reached over to a small table and picked up a scribbled note.

Waxman craned over as his boss read out the message. 'Koga & Mondor; deliver Kramer by midnight or Sakamoto dies. Take the mobile. I will call.'

'Looks like someone means business,' stated Waxman pulling a face and picking up the mobile with a tissue. 'We may get finger prints or DNA,' the phone dropping into a plastic bag.

'We know who Mondor is, but not Koga,' added Bomberger. 'Shit this case is getting more involved by the minute. And we still haven't got Kramer's wife or daughter back. I'll tell you something for nothing. The Chief won't be too impressed with our clear-up rate.'

Waxman took the note, flipped it over and back again. 'What happened to our weekend off?'

'Nothing unusual there,' said Bomberger, mooching around. 'Looks like we need to go and tell Kramer he's wanted tonight.'

'He's a civilian and not on our payroll. We can't implicate him any further in this mess.'

'Have you got a better idea?' said the boss with his hand out for the phone and note.

'Unfortunately, not… much to my annoyance.'

'Ok, so we go back to the office via Kramer's place. We lay it on the line that Sakamoto is key to getting his wife and daughter back. He will cooperate, I know it.'

'Chad, I like your confidence,' said Waxman, peering out of a window.

'It's my gut feeling, that's all.'

'I'll go with that.'

'Come on. If we are coming back here tonight, we may need an easy way in.'

'Through the garage door?' offered Waxman following.

'No need.'

'No need?'

'No need,' said the boss. 'You are going to stay here…'

'Why?' frowned Waxman heavily.

'When I come into the house with Kramer, I'll do the swap with Sakamoto. If it looks like it's going to go wrong, you come in all guns blazing.'

'I know I'm good, but this isn't a movie with cameras, mics and a BAFTA hungry producer. I'm flesh and blood. I feel pain.'

Bomberger walked out of the front door. 'It's nearly midday. Go and have a swim… but if I were you, I'd plan where I was going to hide.'

'You better give me your firearm too. I don't want to run out of ammo.'

Waxman took the gun.

'Now don't worry, Curtis. This will look good on your CV.'

'A CV isn't much good if you're no longer breathing.'

'Many good books were written about Jessie James after his demise. You could still be useful and entertain the world. Think about it… your gallant actions making great stories.'

'Thanks. I appreciate this opportunity immensely.'

Bomberger looked back as he walked away. 'I'm counting on you, Waxman.'

'Thank you, Chad. I've got it covered… A-Z.'

'Could be worse,' he replied with a smile in his voice. 'You could be back in the office working on UFO reports.'

As soon as Bomberger got back to the station, he headed for a new section; a small forensics department.

'I know there have been cutbacks, but I've got an urgent case here and I need results within the next two hours. Get me finger prints, DNA and anything else going. Most importantly, if the mobile rings, under no circumstances do you answer it. Let me know the second anything happens. I can't emphasize enough just how urgent this is.'

Back in the empty office, the busy Lieutenant switched on his computer, popped a diet coke open and took a quick drink. He grabbed his mobile, moved swiftly out into the cark park before tapping in a number.

'Waxman, it's Chad. Anything happening over there?'

Waxman was sat by the pool in the shade of a parasol, his feet up and contemplating life. 'It's the quiet before the storm.'

'The mobile's in forensics. A lead may put us on to Sakamoto's kidnappers. Let's see what turns up?'

'Did you contact, Kramer?'

'Not yet. That's my next job.'

'Without him, there's no trade tonight…'

'I know,' said Bomberger sounding frustrated. 'I'll call him and lay it on the line. It's going to be a risky moment. Anything could happen.'

Bomberger decided not to go back into his office, but rather, he drove to Kramer's house. Once parked up, he knocked the door. In less than a minute he was rewarded. 'Mr Kramer, may I come in? It won't be for long and it is vitally important.'

Both stood in the hallway. Bomberger held his sunglasses and cut to the chase. 'Regarding, Libby.'

'You've found her?' said Kramer looking hopeful.

'We are close, but I need your help.'

'Yes of course.'

'You can say no,' said Bomberger looking serious, 'but right now, it's our only chance.'

'Let's go for it.'

'Ok, but you must understand... there are risks and there are no guarantees.'

'I accept...'

'Listen carefully to what I'm about to say. Tonight, those holding Libby are willing to trade her for you.'

'For me?' replied Kramer in slight shock. 'It's normally for money, a ransom.'

'I know. But for reasons that are unclear to me, they want you, not money.'

'No problem. I'll do it.'

'Tonight, I will pick you up. Wear black or dark clothing. I'm taking you to Sakamoto's place.'

'What happens at the exchange?'

'You get traded for Libby, but I will have put a tracer on you. Once she's safe, we'll come for you in the early hours.'

'Ok.'

'But it is dangerous. Anything could go wrong.'

'I can't see any other way. I just want Libby back.'

'Before I go, there are just a couple of questions.'

'Fire away.'

'I know that it's a sensitive subject, but did you work inside Area 51?'

'Yes, but I think you already knew the answer.'

'I did.'

'And have you any idea what this is all about?'

'That's the million-dollar question. I wish I knew.'

'So… you don't know?'

'Until the kidnappers tie me to a chair and start asking me questions, I remain completely in the dark… like yourself.'

'And lastly, have you any idea where your wife might be?'

'Unfortunately, it's a mystery.'

As soon as Bomberger got into his vehicle, Kramer was on his mobile. 'Jack. It's Kramer.'

'Is everything ok?'

'Yes and no.'

'What is it?'

'I've just had a chat with Bomberger, and he claims that Libby is going to be traded for me tonight…'

'What else?'

'After the trade, I'll be taken somewhere for reasons unknown. Then his team will trace me via a bugging device and get me back in the early hours of the morning.'

The response was unexpected silence.

'Jack… are you still there?'

'Yes, I'm here.'

'I thought the line had gone…'

'No.'

'So, what do we do?'

'To avoid complicating Bomberger's plan, I say we suspend ours by twenty-four hours. Let's see what happens tonight. Perhaps he knows something that I don't.'

'Ok, sorry to put a spanner in the works.'

'If it means getting Libby back, it's for the best.'

'You're right,' said Kramer.

'Where is the swap taking place?'

'At Sakamoto's house. That's all Bomberger has told me.'

'That's the place where I rescued Jayne from the basement,' said Fleming, his voice almost hypnotic and calming.

'I don't know how you did it all by yourself. All I did was sit in the car.'

'I just got lucky.'

Lieutenant Bomberger had received a call from forensics, so made a quick dash down to the busy department. He grabbed the brief report containing fingerprints and the frustrating message that the mobile had buzzed several times. Back in the office, he sat down to continue his investigation. Ten minutes later and the mobile became active. *Here we go,* he thought. *So, who's calling Mondor or Koga?*

'Hello,' said Bomberger, disguising his voice.

'Mondor?' the accent, South American, perhaps Brazilian.

'No, it's Koga.'

'Where's Mondor? It doesn't sound like you, Koga...'

'I've had some shit flu bug.'

'What's the arrangement?' quizzed the caller.

'Are we still meeting tonight?' throat clearing.

'Meeting where?'

'Don't be so suspicious,' said Bomberger, coughing. 'Have you got Sakamoto?'

'And if I did, who would you have?'

'Kramer. I would have Kramer. Have you got a problem?'

'Ok,' said the caller still sounding doubtful. 'No tricks or you are dead.'

'All we want is Sakamoto. All you want is Kramer. Let's cut the crap. What time?'

'Make it 10pm at Sakamoto's place.'

Kramer parked in the motel's car park and casually made his way to room 102. He knocked. The door opened.

'Hi Jayne, how are you?' stepping in and looking sympathetic.

'I'm in a miserable place at the moment,' she said, moving aside and looking fed-up and anxious. 'It's early evening and I've not seen or heard much from you all day.'

'Yes, I'm sorry. It's been hectic.'

'Lucky you,' she said, sitting back down on the double bed. 'So what's happening? Any news about Libby, I'm worried sick.'

'I know. I feel the same as you,' joining her.

He paused. She knew him well… something awkward was coming.

'What is it?'

'Please bear with me,' he said, shuffling.

'Come on Luis, tell me.'

'Things have changed…'

'What things?'

'The plan was that I join Fleming to go and find Libby after the LAPD tip off.'

'And?'

'And that's off now?'

'But why?'

'Fleming indicated that the intelligence had changed and we delay by a day.'

'I knew we couldn't rely on him.'

'That's unfair. But listen. Lieutenant Bomberger also has a plan to get Libby back…'

'When?'

'Tonight.'

'But how?'

'It's an undercover operation with risks...'

'I don't want Libby's life put at risk.'

'I agree. Listen, I'm going with the police tonight but purely in a supportive role for Libby.'

'Is it safe?'

'Just remember this. I'm in good hands and Bomberger knows what he's doing.'

Waxman was now indoors as the evening approached. It had been overcast, and the low cloud ensured darkness fell sooner on Ventura. All curtains and blinds were closed, all internal doors shut. However, the front door could not be secured as Bomberger had picked Sakamoto's lock, and unfortunately, internal bolting devices were non-existent. He checked his gun, then the time; 8:45pm. The downstairs lights were on, but he was upstairs in a dark bedroom with minimal moonlight coming in. His window view allowed sight of the gated-entrance and adjoining road. Waxman's mobile was on silent mode but vibrated.

'Hello,' he said quietly, knowing the caller.

'Are you all set, Waxman?'

'Yes, I'm in position and watching the drive from upstairs. Any updates?'

'No. It's still on for 10pm, but don't hold your breath. You know what villains are like. Unreliable, untrustworthy and best behind bars.'

'Agreed.'

'And don't forget, Waxman. I'm counting on you.'

'No problem. I take it that Kramer is still coming.'

'Yes. But he thinks the trade is for his daughter, Libby. As you know, he's being traded for Sakamoto.'

'He won't be happy about that?'

'We will say the kidnappers double-crossed us. Once we get Sakamoto, he'll lead us to Libby… I'm sure of it.'

'Ok. So tonight, Kramer is traded?'

'It is a risky strategy, but there's no other way.'

At 9:20pm, Bomberger parked outside Kramer's home. The lights were off and it looked like no one was in. Just as the detective considered cutting the engine, there was a knock on his passenger window. Bomberger swung round… it was Kramer now gaining access.

'I didn't see you,' he confessed. 'The dark clothing worked well.'

A short time later and they were parked at Sakamoto's rented house. It was dark but for a light on in the living room.

'How are you feeling, Kramer?'

'A little nervous. To be truthful… a lot nervous.'

'That's to be expected when dealing with villains. Come on, let's go inside.'

Both walked in through the unlocked front door, Bomberger first. 'We can sit and wait for them. Not long to go now,' he said looking at his watch.

The detective withdrew something from his pocket. 'Here. Roll up your trouser leg and clip this on. It's your tracking device.'

Kramer took it and, while halfway through the operation, the mobile that Bomberger had acquired, buzzed. Looking at Kramer, he took the call. 'Hello.'

'Koga. Bring Kramer outside… we are waiting.'

Bomberger frowned. 'You're early.'

'Just bring Kramer outside.'

'I don't think you're there.'

'Why not?'

'I didn't hear your car arrive.'

'Who said I came by car?'

'You walked?'

'No…stupid. I parachuted,' shouted the villain. 'One minute and I'm gone from here. Hurry up. Bring Kramer out, and no funny business.'

The call cut.

'Shit,' said Bomberger. 'That's not in my plan.'

'Have you got back-up just in case?' quizzed Kramer.

'Let's get this over and done with,' replied the senior detective checking his gun holster under bomber jacket.

Both moved to the door.

'It's dark out there,' said Kramer. 'Anything might happen.'

'I know. Unfortunately, they hold all the cards.'

Once outside, only Bomberger's Interceptor could be seen as some light escaped from the house.

'This is eerie,' whispered Kramer, hardly moving his lips – eyes darting.

The mobile buzzed.

'Yes?'

'Koga. Drive out the gate, turn right and then at the crossroad, make a left. A car will be waiting there.'

'That was not the plan,' said Bomberger sternly.

'You don't call the shots, Koga. I do,' shouted the caller. 'That's how the chain works, remember? Now hurry up.'

The call was cut. Bomberger looked frustrated. 'Sorry Kramer, the goal posts have shifted,' he said, moving toward the car.

Within a few minutes, they made a left at the crossroad and sure enough, a car was up ahead with sidelights on; rear view facing and engine running. Bomberger slowed down to stop some fifteen yards back. He decided to have greater illumination and left his dipped beam on. 'Ok Kramer, let's see how this pans out. It's all about getting Libby back safely. Just go with the flow.'

'There's no other choice,' he replied with a sigh.

Their doors opened almost in unison.

'This is it,' mumbled Kramer to himself. 'It's for you, Libby.'

Three doors opened on the car up front; each with a man stepping out. Bomberger was sure that he recognized Sakamoto's profile despite the distance and poor light conditions.

'I don't see, Libby,' said Kramer squinting.

'She maybe in the car,' added Bomberger, his face dark with the lights behind.

The villains had stopped at the rear of their vehicle and looked menacing. One stepped forward and then shouted. 'Come here, Kramer.'

'Follow their request,' said Bomberger calmly.

'Ok. I really hope this works. If it doesn't, tell Jayne and Libby that I love them and that I'm sorry for the way things turned out.'

'Sure, but it'll be fine. Trust me.'

'Come on, Kramer!' demanded the lead villain.

Bomberger shouted, 'Where's Libby?'

Kramer was now walking towards the gang.

'Libby who?' came a scoffing reply.

'That was the deal,' shouted Bomberger knowing his deceptive plan.

'No, Koga. You asked for Sakamoto.'

'You're double-crossing me.'

'No I'm not! You're a liar. And I don't believe you are Koga.'

'We never met, stupid!' fired Bomberger, sailing close to the wind.

Kramer was grabbed and hauled away at gunpoint while the two remaining villains shot several rounds over Bomberger's head. The gutsy detective hit the ground fast. 'Mad bastards!' he grunted under his breath.

The gunmen were laughing as they shoved both Kramer and Sakamoto into the rear of their car. The wheels spun, spitting small stones up in the lawman's direction, some bouncing and stinging as they hit. 'Damn, that didn't go to plan at all well.'

There was no point giving chase with so many hostile gunmen, so made his way back to Sakamoto's place. Once parked, he went in.

'It's ok Waxman, it's only me... your blundering boss.'

There was no answer, so he went in search of his second-in-command. This was mystifying as the hunt revealed no sign of his trusted friend. Fearing the worst, he walked outside and looked over toward the partly lit pool. He grimaced. 'God, will I have some explaining to do. Surely those bastards never came here first and found Waxman?'

'You are right,' said Waxman, stepping out of the shadows.

Bomberger had flinched. 'Jeeze! You made my heart stop.'

'What happened?'

'They now have Kramer.'

'Where's Sakamoto?'

'I had to ask for Libby... that's what Kramer was expecting.'

'And?'

'And when I tried to make it look like they'd double-crossed us, they decided I wasn't even going to get the trade at all. Those bastards took Sakamoto and Kramer.'

'This is not a good day at the office,' stated Waxman.

'Please don't remind me. My ego is as flat as a pancake.'

'Essentially, the whole Kramer family have been kidnapped.'

'That sums it up well,' said Bomberger heading for the car. 'We have now only got one last chance to redeem ourselves.'

'What's the plan?' said Waxman catching up.

'Fortunately, when my useless little brain was working, I gave Kramer a tracking device which he secured to the inside of his trouser leg.'

'Now that was good thinking, Chad.'

Both stepped into the car. 'It's not ideal, but we need to get Kramer back just after midnight when the villains have gone to bed. At the same time, we also grab Sakamoto. I still think he knows where Libby might be.'

Sakamoto and Kramer had been pushed at gunpoint into a shabby building that had taken about thirty minutes to reach. Once inside, the leader opened a door and waved his gun. 'Get in there and make yourselves comfortable. Tomorrow you will be transferred again. Sakamoto? You have upset someone so much that even I would not want to be in your shoes. As for you, Kramer, I don't know what you have done, but someone wants to talk with you. It maybe the devil himself.'

'Do you know where my daughter is?'

'If I did, I could have some fun.'

The closing door was locked and bolted from the outside. There were no facilities, windows or furnishing; not even beds. As Kramer was just about to speak, the light was extinguished via an outside switch.

'I don't think much of this hotel,' said Kramer finding a wall and crouching down to sit on the floor.

'Yes, I won't be paying my bill.'

There was silence. Kramer spoke. 'Tell me Sakamoto, why are you in here? Afterall, you originally kidnapped me?'

'I was only doing my job.'

'Do you know why I was chosen?'

'Chosen?' frowned Sakamoto.

'To be kidnapped.'

'Mine is not to ask, but to do. That is the chain.'

'You just take orders?'

'Take them from above and pass them on down the line.'

'I have to ask you about my daughter, Libby. Do you know where she is?'

'You were split up for obvious reasons... someone would be coming to rescue both of you.'

'Ok. So you don't know where she is?' quizzed Kramer.

'No.'

Kramer didn't like the silence that followed or the answer.

'What now?' he said, feeling for the small tracking device.

'You ask a lot of questions.'

'I don't feel like sleeping,' he replied. 'It's hardly luxury.'

Somewhere in the building a radio came on playing South American music; rhythmic dance.

Kramer was aware as Sakamoto cursed and stood up. Next, the door was being pulled and rattled aggressively. 'Shit! These scumbags will pay for this,' he said aggressively.

'Do you know them?'

'No, but I know who they work for. Trust me, we will not be leaving here alive... unless gods in chariots arrive.'

'Or we overpower them,' stated Kramer.

'Tell me about you,' said Sakamoto. 'Why are certain people so interested in you?'

'If I was to be honest, I'd say it's a case of mistaken identity. It happens all the time.'

'I was asked to frighten you first...'

'It worked. You did. When I woke up in that coffin, I thought I was going to die. Then when the electric shock treatment started, I prayed to die quickly. Have you any idea what that was like?'

'Let me tell you something Kramer, these people are much worse. You didn't talk for me, but you will talk for them.'

Jayne lay in bed reading after trying her husband's phone numerous times. Naturally, she was very worried and finding it hard to concentrate. A quick glance at the clock; 11:59pm. She flinched as her door was knocked. *It must be Luis,* she thought, throwing back the bedcover. In her pajamas, she made her way to the door and called out. 'Who is it?' her heart starting to race.

'Fleming.'

'Fleming? What are you doing here so late?'

'Can we talk? It is important.'

Jayne bit her lip nervously and was silent.

'It won't take long,' he continued.

'Where is Luis?'

'That's what I want to talk to you about.'

Reluctantly, she unlocked the door but kept the securing chain in place. The door opened slightly and she looked through the gap. Fleming's small smile was encouraging although she had her suspicions; *why was he being so helpful?*

'Jayne. I would have called, but I don't have your mobile number.'

'What's happened?'

'Intelligence suggests Luis is in trouble.'

'What sort of trouble?' sounding alarmed.

'I believe he was meeting up with, Bomberger.'

'Yes, he was.'

'And he's not back here?'

'No,' she said, pausing. 'You said Luis is in trouble?'

'I fear so,' offered Fleming looking over his shoulder. 'Listen Jayne. Stay low and don't answer the door to anyone. I'm going to see if I can track him down...'

'Now?' said Jayne in slight shock.

'Yes. My work is intelligence led. If my contacts are worth their salt and things go to plan, there is a small chance I can find him.'

Fleming put his hand out and offered his card. 'Call me if you ever feel threatened...'

She looked down and read the details:

Fleming

Private Investigator:

'Thank you,' she said looking up.

Her face was one of surprise. Fleming had vanished.

Music was still playing somewhere down a corridor.

'This place doesn't smell good,' said Kramer still in the dark and seated on the floor.

'It smells like a wretched toilet,' added Sakamoto.

'I'm inclined to agree with you. No light, no bed, no sink, no toilet... this place is the pits.'

'I had something crawl on me just now,' confessed Sakamoto.

'A cockroach?'

'A small lizard or gecko,'

'How do you know?'

'Its tail came off when I trapped it.'

Kramer laughed lightly. 'I don't believe you.'

'It's a survival mechanism with some species.'

'That's a good story to pass the time,' added Kramer feeling itchy.

'Put your hand out…'

'Put my hand out?'

'Is there a parrot in here?'

Within a few seconds, their hands touched.

'Open your hand, palm up.'

As Kramer did so, he felt something wriggling.

'Damn,' he cursed, as the squirming tail slipped off quickly.

Sakamoto laughed. 'It was thrashing around to the Latin beat.'

'You learn something every day.'

'And while the predator is distracted by the lively tail, the lizard escapes and a new one grows back…'

'That's amazing.'

Both flinched as a gun battle started close by. Although the music still played in the background, the sound of ricocheting shots could never reveal who the attackers were. In between the urgent cacophony of battle, the two had leant in to be closer, and although they could not see each other, both covered their ears.

Kramer shouted. 'I hope they're on our side!'

'A rival gang looking to profit,' returned Sakamoto. 'It might be best to take a stray bullet.'

'You can have mine.'

'When these shits are torturing you, you'll wish you hadn't been so damn generous.'

Chapter 5

The White House – The Oval Office: Monday

The Commander-in-Chief stood looking out of his window at the view so many great Presidents had been privileged to enjoy. As he waited, he spoke to himself. 'It makes me proud to think that I follow in the steps of that great man, George Washington. And Ted Roosevelt, yet another wonderful leader of our nation. Hey, you guys, I sure could do with your great wisdom today.'

He turned from the tall window surrounded by thick yellow curtains and looked at the great wooden table. 'Imagine I had all the great Presidents sitting here in the Oval Office. Wow, I could benefit from the awesome wisdom of such wonderful men.'

The door was knocked.

'Come in,' he called out, looking at his watch.

'Ah, Virgil,' he said, walking over to shake hands. 'You bring sanity to my world.'

Virgil's smile had begun closed but now widened to show his teeth.

'Nice job, Virg. Remind me who your dentist is?'

'Was.'

'Was?'

'He's now retired and living it up in the Bahamas.'

'Lucky man, but a bit too close to the Bermuda Triangle for my liking,' now pointing. 'Have a seat.'

'Is Penniman not coming over today?'

'No. I excused Paul this time,' seating himself. 'He has some special family get-together later on. There's no point rushing around like there's no tomorrow.'

Carrozza nodded. 'I agree with that.'

The Commander-in-Chief spoke. 'I wonder what the planet would be like today if Kennedy had got his way and told the world we are not alone. Would there have been shock on a massive scale, or a gradual acceptance? All I would ask of *them* is that we be respected as the human race... and not taken over.'

'It's a great burden to cover up what is blatantly obvious. Orbs whizz around in famous places... they get filmed and put on the internet... and yet, the majority ignore them... considering all to be nothing but a hoax.'

'Yes but,' said the President, 'there are a growing number of people who have become wiser with time. Did you see the bright orb that came down vertically over Jerusalem in 2011?'

'I did,' acknowledged Carrozza. 'It came down directly over the Dome on the Rock. The thing almost kissed the spire before shooting back up vertically at an estimated speed of 4,000mph.'

'Cameras caught it from many angles on that clear night,' said the President, his folding arms arriving on the historic table. 'I suggest we call a meeting and discuss the extraterrestrial subject and the much-dreaded timetable... the timetable to change our delicate world forever. Time is not on our side... others seek to expose the truth before us. What a dilemma.'

'I guess Hauk will be involved as usual?'

'Hauk is everywhere. The CIA are the absolute foundations of America's security.'

Bomberger was back in the office although not as early as usual. *A day off would be nice,* he thought, *but that's never gonna happen!* He grabbed a can of diet coke and wrenched the ring-pull fast. It fizzed and overflowed. 'Damn!' he said doing a leg dance. Five minutes later, he was reading information on his screen when Waxman strolled in. The boss looked up to acknowledge. 'Another tired looking face,' he said, back to reading and typing.

'Yes, I'm getting too old for this game. I got into bed at 4:20 and then back up three hours later to shower. Thankfully it doesn't happen every day, or I'd be ready for the scrapheap.'

'Have ten minutes, then we'll go down and get Sakamoto out of his homely cell. Let's see if we can win him over.'

'That shouldn't be difficult,' said Waxman rubbing his eyes and booting up his computer. 'We saved his butt.'

Fifteen minutes later and the two detectives were down in the interview room. Waxman stood in the corner of a windowless room, while Bomberger sat opposite Sakamoto.

'Ok, I guess you know why you're here?'

'Yes,' replied the prisoner. 'You brought me here.'

'It is for your own safety,' claimed Bomberger.

'Do I look like a man who needs protection?'

Bomberger looked up and over to Waxman whose position was slightly behind Sakamoto. The boss smiled. He re-engaged.

'At the moment, perhaps not, but at 1:30am, I'd say you were pretty vulnerable. Therefore, to answer your question... yes, you do look like a man needing protection. Our protection.'

Sakamoto stared at Bomberger without blinking, Bomberger returning the same treatment. Silence followed. Sakamoto spoke. 'I want my lawyer.'

'I didn't know you had one.'

'I do, but he's in Brazil.'

'On holiday?'

'No. That's where I live.'

'Well that's no good to you, is it?'

'I don't have to say anything...'

'That's up to you, Mr Sakamoto...'

'You're right. I have nothing to say without representation.'

'Have you got money to hire a lawyer in Ventura?'

'What do you think? You're the smart cop... I'm the dumb villain. Right?'

'If I was the smart cop, this would all be over and I could be watching the Boston Red Sox and eating popcorn.'

Waxman stepped forward. 'Mr Sakamoto, we know you have money because the house you're renting costs $4000 a month. What is your line of work? FI racing driver?'

'Very funny. Who said I work? Did it not cross your mind that I'm a retired entrepreneur?'

Bomberger continued. 'I love entrepreneurs. This is what made America great,' he said, nodding and glancing at Waxman doing the same. 'So, what is the business, or should I say, what have you invented?'

'Listen Bomberger...'

'I'm listening with open ears.'

'You know what's going on...'

'Do I?'

'Yes. That's why you tracked us down. It wasn't to save me. No. This was all about, Kramer. Am I right?'

'You might be,' admitted Bomberger poker-faced.

Sakamoto relaxed and leant back in his chair to smile. He turned and glanced at Waxman. 'Hey, I'm not just a pretty face,' then laughed.

Waxman immediately looked at Sakamoto's tattoos, especially those lightning strikes on both forearms. This villain certainly looked tough, but perhaps he wasn't too stupid after all.

'Ok,' said Bomberger. 'We can keep you in here for further interrogation or let you go...'

'It would be wise to let me go.'

'Hold on a minute. It's not that easy. I think you owe us a big favour.'

'Why?' frowning.

'I think you have a very short memory.'

'I don't think so...'

'You were a prisoner last night...'

'I'm still a prisoner now.'

Waxman move forward. 'But in much better circumstances. No one's going to put a bullet in your head or torture you to death.'

'Who were those people last night?' said Bomberger.

'I don't know exactly, but vermin in the chain...'

'The chain?' quizzed the lead detective frowning.

'Look here... why am I talking to you? Let me go.'

'Because, we want you to jump ship and join us.'

Sakamoto burst out laughing. 'What?! Jump ship and join you cops? Give me a break.'

'It would make your life so much easier. You work undercover for us and we keep you out of prison... but be warned, if you double-cross us and start shooting cops, you'll never see the light of day.'

'Working for cops would be like having poison in my blood. It would be impossible... and if the other side found out, I would quite literally be crucified.'

Bomberger leant forward in his chair. 'Listen Sakamoto, you are not really in a good position to call the shots. We think you would be wise to sleep on it.'

'You mean, I'm not being released today?'

'That's correct,' said Waxman. 'It's for your own good.'

'I've already thought about it. I would rather be on the outside looking over my shoulder than working for you cops.'

'Look, do I have to spell it out for you? Act dumb and you'll soon be behind bars on death row. Work with us and you could get an amnesty for anything done so far.'

'Huh. I'm not falling for that garbage.'

'Help us find Kramer's wife and daughter.'

'It's your turn to listen to me.'

Sakamoto paused and now looked doubtful. 'I told you, I'm in the chain. In the chain you know those below you, but not those above. I got my instructions to kidnap the Kramer family. That's all.'

'That's all?' said Waxman. 'Then what? Just hand them over?'

'No. I was to interrogate Kramer and find out what he knew about Area 51 and other stations he worked on.'

'But why?'

'I don't know fully, just to say that if stories about alien contact or real evidence existed of captured UFOs…. then *they*, whoever *they* were, wanted to know.'

'Hold on a minute. Are you saying that this is all about UFOs and extraterrestrials?' quizzed Waxman.

'Seems that way,' confessed Sakamoto. 'Sounds like bullshit.'

'What did you find out?' said Bomberger frowning.

'Not much…'

'Not much?' said Waxman looking disappointed.

'No. Once we had kidnapped the family, we split them up. 'I had Mrs Kramer at the house. Kramer himself was buried under ground.'

'Sorry,' said Waxman in slight shock, his mouth open. 'You buried Kramer underground?'

'Yes. It's a torture method that works really well.'

'I bet it does,' admitted Bomberger, looking across at Waxman.

Waxman spoke. 'See how good we cops are to you. Imagine if we employed those methods?'

'Maybe you should,' said Sakamoto. 'Who knows, perhaps you do this, but no one has ever lived to tell the story.'

'We'll be in the last days if that becomes the norm,' confessed Bomberger.

There was a pause.

'Alright,' continued the boss looking at his watch. 'Sakamoto, you have been helpful and cleared up a few loose ends. I know that you are suspicious of us cops, but it's worth remembering that without law and order, the world would be in a total mess. We would be back in the dark ages.'

Sakamoto nodded in agreement. 'I know that I'm not perfect, but I do agree with what you say. Since a teenager, I have always sailed close to the wind.'

'And now you've capsized your boat,' stated Bomberger. 'The sharks are circling. But we are your lifeguards. Accept our help and work with us. We need to find the Kramer family and then put the chain members behind bars.'

'I make no promises.'

'At least we have a starting point,' said Waxman, hopefully.

'Yes,' added Bomberger. 'Sakamoto? The chain will be looking for you now. Stay in here for a few days and keep a low profile. In the meantime, we can find you a safe house.'

Waxman spoke. 'You can't return to your rented place now, that will be too dangerous.'

Directly after the daring rescue, Kramer had /bedded down _ed_ on Waxman's sofa for a few hours before being dropped off at the motel. Both husband and wife then checkout before 10am and got a cab back to their house in Ventura. After a quick sort-out, and packing a change of clothing, the desperate couple took off in their red camper van making for the coastal road, northside of Ventura City. It was sunny. For disguise, Luis was driving with Ray-Ban aviator shades while Jayne had chosen Wayfarers, plus a baseball cap – her hair trapped underneath.

'Where are we going, Luis?' she said, looking unhappy.

'Just heading north to join the 101 Freeway. Let's go and sit on Faria beach for a while. I need to think… we both need to think.'

'What about Libby? Every day that passes makes me fear the worst.'

'I know. We just have to put our faith in Jack and Bomberger.'

'Can't we do anything. Every hour Libby isn't with us, makes me feel so guilty. There must be something I can do… we can do.'

'I've thought about this a lot…'

'Thought about what?'

'Perhaps I just have to hand myself over to this organization that wants me to confess all…'

'All of what, Luis?'

'It's obvious that this is about my work on the base.'

'I never wanted you to work there.'

'I never intended staying more than a year. I thought it would lead on to bigger and better things... less secretive things.'

'For instance?'

'I wish I knew. The trouble is that one year becomes two, two becomes three, and then before you know it, a decade has gone by. Besides, Libby was settled with friends and schooling. It's such a tough call.... moving on, I mean.'

'Well, there's one thing for sure...'

'What's that?'

'We can't turn the clock back. Not now.'

'You're right. That time has gone.'

Jayne looked over. 'Luis, if Bomberger set you free last night, didn't you ask him about, Libby?'

'Yes, I did. He said they're doing all they can to find her. If you remember, when originally kidnapped, Sakamoto held you at his place.'

'I remember, but I can't recall precisely how we got out of there. I seem to have memory loss.'

'It was Fleming who found us. He is very good at his job.'

'Is he looking for, Libby?'

'He is.'

There was a pause. Luis continued. 'I feel that it was a mistake not to tell Bomberger that you have been found. If he finds out that you have miraculously appeared, but Libby remains missing, then the spotlight will be back on us as prime suspects.'

Jayne was close to tears. 'Just a week back and I was feeling so happy to have left Lincoln County. Rachael was too quiet with nothing really going on. Ventura seemed the ideal move. When you suggested it, I was over the moon. Now look at us... this is such a mess, Luis. I can't cope.'

'I agree, it's a nightmare situation. All I wanted to do was give both you and Libby a better life. A new career in watersports... and Ventura City seemed to hold so much promise for us.'

'Why don't you contact Fleming and see if he's got any news?'

'I'll do that as soon as we get off the Freeway. It won't take long to find the beach.'

Lieutenant Bomberger sat opposite Sakamoto, while Waxman stood close by. The interview room door was closed.

'How was your night?'

'Not as good as yours,' claimed Sakamoto.

'At least you were safe. No one in the chain knows that you are here, and if they did, they'd expect us to charge you for previous crimes... then lock you up and throw away the key.'

Sakamoto laughed. 'You really think so?'

'Why not?' quizzed Waxman.

'They have friends in prison all over the US. Someone would get me eventually.'

'You can't be certain,' stated Bomberger.

'I can. You forget that I too, was in the chain. I passed on information and people behind bars got hit. It was the norm.'

'Good,' said Bomberger.

Sakamoto frowned.

'I say good, because you won't be trapped on the inside with no protection. If you want to work with us, then you will be on the outside. It's a much bigger world with many places to hide.'

'The big question is,' said Waxman. 'Do you want to work for us and redeem yourself, or do you want to have a record and spend years behind bars? You're not exactly a young man. Life is short. Surely it's an easy decision?'

'Ok,' said Sakamoto. 'If I help you by working undercover, when do I get paid?'

Bomberger laughed. 'Your big reward is your freedom. I'm afraid you'll have to live off your previous earnings.'

'Where am I going to stay?'

Waxman stepped in. 'The best place is your old place.'

'The chain will kill me. I didn't deliver the information on time. There's no turning back. Plus, you two came in all guns blazing and killed two of their men. The one who calls herself, Salamander, will be seeking revenge...'

'Salamander?' quizzed Waxman. 'That's a strange name.'

'She's a strange person and fast going insane by all accounts,' informed Sakamoto. 'Yes. Salamander will be looking to drain your blood.'

'Unless,' said Bomberger, looking smug, 'you make contact with the chain and tell them you escaped police custody. We can put out a fake story in the papers to cover it. Fake news. Hey what's new,' he smiled, looking over at Waxman.

'It's the best way out of this for you,' stated Waxman. 'But if you reject the offer, you'll be put away for kidnap, and anything else we can pin on you. I bet there's felony as long as my arm to secure a significant prison sentence.'

'Ok,' said Sakamoto. 'I'll do it, but just for two weeks once I leave the cell.'

Bomberger laughed. 'Listen carefully. I'm your unofficial boss now. It's me who decides when and how you breathe. Mess up and we'll be back on to you like a ton of bricks.'

Medium sized rollers crashed on to the beach and soon turned to white surf leaving patterns in the sand. It was nearing midday when the VW camper arrived and parked to face the vast ocean. Only one other car sat there, although without occupants. Kramer cut the engine. 'This place brings back memories,' he said, still holding the wheel and looking out.

'Luis, give Fleming a call now,' said Jayne looking pensive.

'Yes,' he replied, reaching for his mobile.

'I pray he has news. I can't take much more of this.'

'Me too,' he said, tapping in a number. 'Jayne, I thought you had his number as well?'

'I have, but he never answers.'

The dialing tone continued. Jayne looked away from the blue ocean. 'Come on, Fleming,' she moaned. 'Pick up!'

Luis looked strained as he listened and waited; the scenic view not compensating for his disappointment. 'I don't understand it,' he said, now staring out at a ship on the horizon.

Fleming hadn't answered, so they walked southward along the sandy beach.

'I know I shouldn't ask, Luis, but things have changed so much in the last few days... I have a right to know what's going on. You must know something?'

'Jayne, I'm just like you,' he said picking up a seashell. 'I know it's something to do with me because of my previous work.'

'Can't you tell me what you did at the base?'

'I know you have seen the TV programmes relating to ancient aliens and the extraterrestrial theorists, etcetera. Did you ever believe any of it?'

'I didn't because you said that you didn't. It was always so far-fetched,' she said, her hair moving in the breeze.

'It was, I agree. That's how most of the world perceives the idea that we have been visited.'

'Have we?'

'Been visited?'

'Yes.'

'If I said no, would you be pleased or disappointed.'

'Pleased of course.'

She paused and stopped to face her husband. 'Luis, please phone Lieutenant Bomberger now. He may have news for us.'

'I'm sure that if he did, he would keep us informed.'

'He should, but you never know,' sounding hopeful.

After a forty-minute walk, they were returning along the beach and a hundred yards from the car park. Luis looked up and could see that the other car had gone. However, there was a black 4x4 parked several spaces away from their camper van. Jayne had not noticed and was talking. He squinted to enhance his view. Two men in dark clothing with sunglasses stood looking their way, a third using binoculars. *More trouble on the horizon*, he thought.

'So, when you transferred to Area 52 hanger 4, what was there that you witnessed?'

'In that important role, I was mainly involved in advanced weapons which we tested on a range nearby.'

'What sort of weapons?'

'Direct laser that could be used from space. These were very special and reverse engineered.'

'What does that mean?'

'Put simply, you observe a more advanced technology and make it your own.'

Jayne stopped. 'Are you saying, alien technology?'

'Yes. From crashed space craft initially...'

'But that's all a hoax... Roswell 1947 was a fabrication.'

'Yes. That's what the world must believe.'

'Why?' she said, looking concerned.

Luis turned to face full on. He took her hands. 'Jayne, you might as well know the truth. We are not alone in the universe. Some are visiting, others never left. I'm afraid it's true… they are here.'

Sakamoto was seated in the back of the Interceptor, Waxman driving and Bomberger in the passenger seat. Twisting round, he spoke. 'Ok, so we drop you off at your place. You will lie low and get your own contacts. Your priority is to find Libby and Jayne Kramer.'

'What about you? Are you still looking?'

'Yes of course. The County has a missing person list as long as your arm.'

'What about, Salamander?' said Sakamoto.

'Remind me what Salamander wanted you to do.'

'I already told you at the station.'

'I know, but tell me again… you may reveal something new that you forgot.'

'I don't think so.'

Bomberger looked cross. 'Listen Sakamoto. I need you to be fully compliant and on our side. Two weeks isn't long for you to redeem yourself.'

'I may have to fly to Rio. Who's going to pay for that?'

'You are…'

'Why me? I'm working for you.'

'Yes, you are working for us and there is a great prize for you. I may not have the full authority to get you a standard, State amnesty, but what you get is a, Bomberger amnesty. What does that mean? Simple, I get off your back, you disappear and I close the file. Your name vanishes from our records.'

'How can I trust you? You're a cop?'

'How can I trust you? You're a criminal.'

'Time will tell,' smirked Sakamoto looking out of his window.

'And one last thing… make sure you communicate with us. No communication is a bad sign.'

'I was born under a bad sign.'

'Use your mobile only. And remember, I'm not Bomberger. I'm the chief. Just call me chief.'

'Chief?'

Early evening had arrived. As Fleming prepared to leave his house, his mobile sounded. He looked at his watch then took the call. 'Hello.'

'Jack. Good to speak to you.'

'And to you, Luis.'

'I've been trying to get you today…'

'Yes, sorry. I saw the missed calls but I've been out on urgent business.'

'Any news about, Libby? We are desperate,' said Kramer.

'I feel we are getting closer…'

'Can I help?'

'No. This is something that I have to do alone.'

'Ok. I trust your opinion on this. We'll wait to hear from you.'

'Yes. As soon as I have something, I'll let you know.'

'May I ask about your lead?'

'I have to go now but will soon make contact.'

Once Sakamoto arrived back at his house, he soon made his way to the basement. He grabbed a handgun, a few grenades and a small semi-automatic from a lockable steel cabinet. Moving around as if on a mission, he filled his camouflage jacket with ammunition and snatched a knife and small torch. Sakamoto knew his destination and hurried into the study where he found the Land Cruiser keys. Snatching a small bottle of water, he locked up and made for the garage.

After breaking all speed limits and jumping traffic lights, he drove east until reaching an old derelict windmill. There were two buildings some two hundred yards away, one uninhabited, the other, a drugs relay station.

Sakamoto had seen the lights in the house extinguish despite arriving on side lights. *A horse ~~would~~ with rubber shoes would have been better*, he thought, now on the desert landscape.

He stopped and gently pushed the driver's door closed. Only armed with a knife and handgun, he crept to the rear of the vehicle. The windmill was whirring overhead with a repetitive squeak; his eyes slowly becoming accustomed to the darkness. Stooping down, he moved towards the derelict house where he wanted cover and the ability to spy. On arrival, a shot pinged nearby.

'Shit. The bastards must have night vision,' he grumbled.

Now another shot; bits of wooden walling flying and hitting his neck. 'Very friendly,' he whispered aggressively to himself; eyes searching.

Two seconds later and he was pounced on from behind. Sakamoto had no choice but to step-up his game, and rapidly. A strangle hold was starting to choke him fast. It was an easy choice to aim at the ground just behind. Two quick shots and the strangler let go with a cry of pain. Sakamoto didn't care what he had hit... he was suddenly free. He spun quickly to pin the assailant to the ground using his superior weight; now the gun pushed hard into the attacker's neck. 'Who's in the house?'

'Who are you?' came a moan.

'Your executioner if you don't talk. How many are there?'

'Go find out yourself,' came a pained and disrespectful reply.

'That's my intention… goodbye.'

Just a dull thud followed as Sakamoto pulled the trigger on his silenced gun.

The man slumped as the stealth visitor let go. Moving off around the building, he felt certain that other villains would be nearby and ready to take him out. Peering around the far corner, he could see the other wooden bungalow and still in darkness. Suddenly a spotlight from the rear of that building came on and whizzed around until landing directly at his position. A burst of shots came flying over and too close for comfort. Reluctantly, he dived back for cover.

Sakamoto was just taking stock of the situation when torch lights flicked on, and more alarmingly, closer that the spotlight. He immediately turned and started running back to his vehicle. Turning for a split second, he fired two random rounds. Shots were fired back. Now his direction changed; he was cutting out wide with the idea of circling back around. After a mad five-minute dash, he guessed they would be cautiously looking around by his Land Cruiser. *But what did that matter – it was stolen and with false plates.* However, his semi-automatic lay in the boot with other kick-ass equipment. Once in between the enemy and the derelict bungalow, he threw a handful of stones that landed sporadically. Someone fired and gave their position away. He crawled slowly to close the gap… then saw a stooped figure moving. Sakamoto fired. A torch from another direction flicked on and pointed his way, but over his head. He fired close to it. The torch dropped followed by a painful groan. Sakamoto's hand searched sideways, grabbed a large stone before throwing it at the Land Cruiser. With the metallic sound reverberating into the darkness, and no further shots fired, he assumed all villains to be incapacitated, so set off running at pace for the bungalow. Suddenly, shots were being fired aggressively, some whizzing by, others ricocheting off the stony desert floor. Reaching the target bungalow, many things were running through Sakamoto's head. Most importantly, *could Libby be held captive there?*

Luis and Jayne were fearful of returning home despite the fact that lightning rarely ever struck in the same place twice... *so the saying went.* The camper van was now parked up in woodland.

'I don't like it here, Luis,' said Jayne, seated at the table.

Kramer pulled the curtains more tightly to ensure all gaps were closed. 'I have to agree with you, it's not my favorite place either... pine woodland can be eerie when the wind is howling.'

'It's so dark, I'll never sleep tonight,' confessed his wife.

'You have me and I have a gun.'

'I hate them...'

'You know me, I'm no gun-lover myself, but if I have to use it, I will,' admitted Kramer sitting down. 'It's legitimate and fully licensed.'

A sound came from outside, not loud and not exactly quiet. It had happened so quickly that it was hard to identify.'

'God, what was that?' whispered Jayne, her eyes full of fear.

Luis had felt the hair on the back of his neck stand up in a split second. He slowly and carefully reached for his gun.

'Luis,' she said quietly and grabbing his arm tightly. 'Please can we go home?'

'It's probably only a black bear or cougar,' he said, switching the light off.

'What are you going to do?'

'We wait and listen.'

'Please don't go outside, will you?' she squeezed harder.

'No. Not unless someone knocks on the door for help.'

Sakamoto had been nicked on his lower right calf muscle by a ricocheting bullet where blood now seeped. However, he had gained entry to the dark bungalow and encountered yet another gang member. Fighting hand to hand in the dark and crashing to the floor after tripping over furniture, the two rolled and threw punches at any opportune moment. The invader was now in trouble as the center light came on. Two men had barged their way in during the fight, both dropping down fast to secure and lean heavily on Sakamoto. The villain that Sakamoto had been fighting broke free and delivered his revenge with a few wild kicks to the ribs.

'What are you doing here, Minimoto?' he shouted, 'the one who failed the chain?'

Sakamoto grimaced and groaned, a small trickle of blood in the corner of his mouth. 'What am I doing here?' he said leaning on one elbow. 'I came to talk...'

Another kick in the ribs. He groaned.

'Huh. You came to talk,' a foot arriving on his chest to push back down. 'That's a funny way to come here for a talk. Arriving in the dark unannounced... sneaking about and firing a gun.'

Sakamoto's face twisted in pain as a boot heel arrived fast on his bloodied shin. 'What did you want to talk about? Sunday school?'

'I have Kramer and that's what Salamander wanted. I got the information that she was so desperate for.'

'Why didn't you pass it up the chain?'

'It's complex and involves binary code...'

'That is shit man!' blasted one.

'No. This is like classified information. That's why I need to take it directly to Salamander.'

'Tell us what it is,' came an aggressive shout and now a gun held against Sakamoto's head. 'I'm going to start counting...'

'I told you that it's complex. Get it wrong... send Salamander the wrong message and those responsible in the chain will be smoked. And that's you, Mr Big Time.'

The gun's barrel was pushed even harder into its target. The owner laughed. 'Ok, stupid. Give me the message and let me be the judge of its complexity.'

'Ever heard of Chinese whispers?' said Sakamoto, looking at the three in turn.

Silence.

Yeah you dumb asses, of course you haven't, he thought. *It looks like I'm ahead of the game.*

'Listen to me. I learnt about it in second grade,' informed Sakamoto. 'Chinese whispers is when you pass on a message secretly and by the time it has reaches the end of the chain, the original message has changed. Why? Because the majority of people ain't too bloody sharp at listening...'

'Bullshit!'

'Don't be fooled by my looks... my tattoos or my accent. I went to Harvard.'

'Window cleaning, maybe. I'm not stupid.'

'Ok,' said Sakamoto. 'Are you listening?'

'Stop messing with me!'

'Sure…'

'Jesus! Did you get a degree in annoyance?'

'Yeah. First class,' smiled Sakamoto.

For this cheek, another hard kick was delivered.

'Ok ok! But listen closely…'

'Tell me now or die!'

Sakamoto cleared his throat. '1001101000101110…'

'Shut up!' cried the gunman.

'I will deliver it personally to Salamander,' declared Sakamoto. 'You will take me to her.'

'Salamander does not deal with people like you…'

'People like me? What kind of shit is that?'

'Protection from those who have big ideas, like you… stupid.'

'I'm just working in the chain and I have what she wants. Wait until she finds out that you caused the delay.'

'And what happened to Mondor, Koga and César?'

'You're so clever, you tell me.'

The Kramer's arrived back at their home just after midnight. With caution, they locked up the camper van and went in. Most people had gone to bed and their homes were now in darkness. Jayne stood in the unlit hallway while Luis systematically went slowly through every room in turn, a torch in one hand, a gun in the other. All windows and doors had been checked.

'It seems ok,' he called down.

She hurried up the staircase while her tired husband went back out to the camper van. He opened the vehicle and pulled out their two cases. Placing them down, he locked the sliding door as quietly as possible. Seconds later, and he was creeping back up to the doorstep. With cases held, he nudged the door open using a knee and walked in. Once dropped, he returned and peered out. A quick glance before closing... but something caught his eye. A small brown envelope on his windscreen and trapped under the wiper blade. *Shit, that wasn't there a few seconds ago.* Back inside, he closed the door and withdrew the typed note. *We saw you today on the beach. Do not give in to them.*

Chapter 6

Swan Lake Golf Course, Manorville NY: Tuesday

The President stood on the fairway and selected his driver. 'Hey Virgil, I just love it here.'

'Yes,' said Carozza, looking skyward, 'a few fluffy clouds and the best fresh air. You can't beat it.'

'When the extraterrestrials arrive,' said the Commander-in-Chief, 'do you think they would want a round of golf first or a McDonalds burger with ketchup?'

'Good question,' said Carrozza pausing before continuing. 'With all our technical advances, life's still a mystery. I remember the first time I investigated Flight 19 and the five Avengers that disappeared over the Bermuda Triangle.'

'1944?'

'December 1945,' smiled Carrozza with satisfying confidence. 'The practice bombing and navigation raid started off well, but for some reason they never made it back. Some say, unusual and fluctuating magnetic fields upset their compasses so they went off in the wrong direction, ran out of fuel and crashed in the sea.'

'I heard engine fumes leaked into the cockpit.'

'Surely not on all five aircraft,' said Carrozza. 'That would be too much of a coincidence.'

'If you want this President's view, I say that they were brought down by extraterrestrials.'

The Commander-in-Chief struck his ball.

'Great strike!' said Carrozza. 'You could have taken down a UFO with that one.'

'And that would start a war,' replied the President, picking up his tee.

'Hey, let's not go there, Hal. They would win hands down,' confessed Carrozza, placing his ball. 'But if I was a betting man, I'd say they've been on this planet as long as us... maybe longer.'

'So why are they so secretive? Why not just come clean and reveal themselves to us?'

'In my opinion, they are. They know we have seen them in their fast-flying machines. They know we have picked up their crashed craft. Revealing themselves is all about timing.'

Carrozza struck his ball.

'Hey, good shot Virgil,' clapped the Commander-in-Chief. 'That's why you're second in command of all US Forces.'

'It was a good shot, Hal,' he smiled. 'But not as good as yours.'

'You're too kind,' said the President, enjoying his status and playing ability.

Carrozza bent down for his tee. 'Look at that ant. Now here is a prime example of our situation. That creature is programmed for survival and, clever as it is, it has no idea about our world, our monetary system, planes, boats, trains, holidays etcetera. We are superior and, by comparison, we are the kings upon this planet. However, suddenly we learn that this is no longer true. Mankind is now playing second fiddle to them.'

'Are they really living here amongst us?' said the President.

'How could you tell? There's no proof,' offered Carrozza. 'But I think the CIA has more knowledge in this area.'

'Let's get Hauk over for a chat.'

'Maybe we should pay a visit to area 52. I hear that they have something new going on.'

'Yeah, let's do that. Come on Virgil,' a pat on the shoulder. 'Let's enjoy this beautiful sunshine... while it belongs to us.'

Bomberger was seated as he checked through his, to-do list. 'How's it going, detective Waxman?'

'I still can't get Sakamoto to pick-up. Do you think he's done a runner?'

'It's possible,' admitted Bomberger with his pencil tapping on the table. 'If he has, then that would be foolish after what we offered him.'

'If it were me, I'd have taken the amnesty route, but then I'm thinking like a cop and not like a criminal.'

'Yeah,' replied the boss, swapping his drum beat for a sip of coke. 'We could swing by his place this afternoon.'

'Smart thinking, Chad. And while we're out, why not cruise by Kramer's house and see what's happening. It's annoying not to have any new leads.'

Bomberger looked puzzled. 'Do you think there's something Kramer has failed to tell us?'

'Previous case studies demonstrate that people do hang back with information. Sometimes they don't exactly lie, but more so, set out to deceive... or divert attention.'

'So why would our friend, Kramer, be holding back or even diverting from the truth when his wife and daughter are missing? Surely you would give every scrap of information available.'

'These are all good questions,' admitted Waxman, opening a new report.

'Not another UFO sighting?' moaned Bomberger peering over.

'Yeah, it looks like it.'

'I've been here a couple of decades and the sightings have definitely increased lately. I always used to close the files quickly because they wasted so much police time. You could never prove anything. Resolution of real crime is what the taxpayer wants.'

'I agree,' said Waxman.

'That's absolute music to my ears,' confessed Bomberger with a satisfying smile. 'I love it when people agree with me.'

Sakamoto sat in the back of a car being driven at speed. Not only was he hooded but his hands were tied behind his back making the journey far less comfortable.

'Hey, Minimoto?' laughed the driver looking at his victim in the central mirror. 'You're in trouble. Why? Because Salamander is severely pissed off for messing her around with this binary code shit.'

'I'm just doing my job.'

'Salamander is female and bad shit.'

'I'm giving her a hi-tech code only meant for intelligent people. That's why you, with your withering brain will never understand its meaning...'

'Listen Minimoto, any more insults and I will stop the car and take you to the edge of your worthless life.'

Sakamoto laughed. 'Be warned. If you damaged the goods and Salamander can't get the message, I wouldn't want to be in your pink ballerina shoes. In fact, when I can't remember the binary sequence, I'll say that it's because you just kicked the hell out of me for fun.'

'Salamander won't fall for that crap,' he sneered.

'You're like a parrot, and one day I'm going to pluck you good... scruffy bastard.'

Sometime later, they arrived at their destination. Still hooded, Sakamoto was grabbed and hauled out where he landed on the hard-stone drive. He groaned as his shoulder took the full force. 'Hey, you are going to pay for this. I know who you are!'

Another kick to the ribs arrived before being pulled up by the shirt collar.

'Come on, you dog. It's time to meet your maker.'

Half stooped, Sakamoto was pulled along without respect. He tripped, tumbled forward and hit his head.

His two guides laughed foolishly, the driver the most. 'Sorry Minimoto. Did I forget to tell you there are steps to this grand slum?'

Sakamoto did not move. Another kick in the ribs. The door to the residence opened. Two beefy looking henchmen appeared, possibly Mexican.

'Hey you!' scowled the first with threatening body language. 'What the hell is happening here?' still approaching. 'Have you forgotten the chain protocol?'

'We have brought Minimoto to see Salamander…'

'You stupid fools,' shouted the first arriving and giving a hard-backhand face slap. 'You know you should never bring anyone here without permission.'

'But that's what we were told.'

'By who?'

'By the next one up in the chain.'

'Well they told you wrong. Ugly heads will roll starting with yours!'

'I get the message. You want us to go now?' said the driver turning his stinging face toward the vehicle.

'Not until you carry Sakamoto up these steps.'

'But he's like a bull elephant,' laughed the blundering driver. 'Throw some water over him... he can walk himself.'

The house guard moved forward and grabbed the driver by the shirt collar; cotton tearing – buttons popping. 'Hey you dopey shit. Don't you tell me what to do,' he shouted. 'Carry Sakamoto into the hallway and then get the hell out of here before I use you as live shark bait.'

Late afternoon, Waxman drove out towards Sakamoto's rental, Bomberger in the passenger seat. 'Let's hope he's there,' said the boss checking his gun. 'We need progress and we want results before any more work lands in our laps. The last thing we need is a black mark on our record sheet.'

'I agree...'

'I just love it when you agree,' confessed Bomberger feeling stressed. 'It makes life so much easier.'

Turning into the drive through black gates, both noticed a vehicle parked up.

'Hmm,' frowned Bomberger. 'Sakamoto has visitors.'

'The meter reader?' said Waxman slowing to park adjacent. His door swung open. 'Let's go and see his new girlfriend.'

'Or his criminal network,' said the boss closing his door and looking up at the building.

Both arrived at the front door. It was ajar. Bomberger looked at Waxman. 'I'm not sure if this is a good omen,' ringing the bell.

While Bomberger peeped in and pushed the door gently, Waxman looked the opposite way and towards the pool area. Although it wasn't fully in view, he frowned. 'I'm not sure if I just saw something move,' he declared without blinking and scanning the same spot, now craning. 'It could have been a bird or cat, I guess. Even the light breeze moves things.'

Bomberger had been listening. 'This place has either been turned over, or Sakamoto's had a leaving party,' he said in a loud whisper and going for his gun.

Waxman took his eyes off the pool area to see for himself. However, Bomberger was already moving in with his gun pointing forward, both hands securing the weapon. Pointing in different directions, he was now alone. Waxman had gone off to investigate the rear garden and pool area. Mauve bougainvillea provided the residents with privacy, but equally, somewhere for villains to hide. Waxman was very alert and also had his gun out. Suddenly, a shot from inside the house made the hair on the back of his neck stand up so fast that he spun round and made off to support Bomberger. Now several more echoed around in the building. Stooping for cover, he arrived at the front door, and looking in all directions. *Perhaps Bomberger had gone down*, he thought. Waxman's tactic was to go in low no matter how risky. Passing through the hallway, now a creak from the wooden staircase that wound upward and round a corner. He heard the front door behind click, but he hadn't closed the gap himself. *Not Good! Potentially one in front and one behind*, ran through his mind. With a fast-beating heart, the new recruit glanced front and back, his eyes wide and nostrils flaring. Even more confusing, the car outside started. Waxman wanted to jump up and look out of the window, but it was far too dangerous; one false move and he could be dead. Another creak on the staircase. He spun round and aimed, his finger squeezing down on the trigger. Bomberger suddenly appeared. Both looked relieved and dashed for the window.

'Damn, they're escaping,' claimed Waxman.

'Not all of them. One's upstairs.'

'Dead or alive?'

'If Jesus arrives, he'll be ok. I didn't mean to kill him, but in a split second it was me or him. It was an easy decision... I've paid too much into my pension fund and I'm sticking around to get it.'

Waxman turned for the staircase, Bomberger following. 'Hey Curtis, did you get that number plate?'

'Yes. It's probably false but I've got it locked in.'

'Damn. Now I have another report to fill out. That's the second one in a few days. The chief is going to think I'm trigger happy.'

Waxman arrived in the upper hallway. 'I say this. If you want to continue breathing, you can't be trigger shy.'

They approached the dead man. 'Do you know him?' asked Waxman. 'He looks like a man from south of the border.'

Bomberger bent down and started going through the dead man's pockets. 'We need something to go on.'

Waxman peered in more closely. 'Chad, our friend has a tattoo on his wrist.'

'Yes, a chain,' added the lieutenant, pulling out a few items.

'What have you got?'

'A petrol receipt and some dollars. He can have the dollars back. They may help with his funeral expenses,' said Bomberger. 'And we have the car registration plate to help trace the driver.'

'I don't wish to sound negative, but it could be stolen,' said Waxman looking out of a window.

'Yes, it could be,' replied Bomberger standing up with a sigh.

'I'll ring the recovery squad and arrange for forensics.'

Sakamoto had been moved once again and had no idea where he was... except that the temperature was comfortable.

Surely, he thought, *this was still Nevada.* The burly prisoner was once a strong man and very much in control, but now was being pushed around by criminals in the chain. His hands had been untied; however, he was outnumbered by Salamander's cruel protection squad – four armed men looking mean and aggressive. Sakamoto stood inside a cool building with whitewashed walls and wooden shuttered windows. Like something out of a film, he was staring at the back of a wide, high-backed leather chair. Someone was sat there, but he couldn't determine who. *Why the mystery?* he thought. *But it's a game… a game that even he had played.*

'Ok Sakamoto, you have messed up,' said one of the four men. 'But by the grace of God, you have been allowed to come here and redeem yourself. What have you got to say?'

'I have done my best and brought the information that was requested.'

'And what was requested?' quizzed the same man with scars to frighten the timid.

'It's only for the one called, Salamander.'

'My name should not be on your lips,' came a woman's voice, slow, high-pitched and almost theatrical. She spun round to face Sakamoto. 'I am Salamander. It was I who put the instruction out. I wanted Kramer captured and tortured for information. Where is he?'

'I had him,' claimed Sakamoto. 'The chain had him…'

'So where is he now?' she said with venom and eyes of fire.

'It was bizarre. He escaped from an impossible place…'

'What place on earth is impossible?' she shouted, looking him up and down as if he were worthless.

'My men buried him in woodland…'

'The chain buried him?' leaning forward, her teeth clenched.

'Yes, in a grave three feet deep. He was in a coffin and no one could have known that he was there.'

'So how did he escape?' she fired, jumping up from her seat.

'I really don't know, but someone must have found him. It's impossible to dig your own way out.'

Salamander scowled, her fists clenched and white. 'Ok idiot. So you have come here saying that you have information. What is it and where did you get it from?'

'From Kramer himself...'

'But you said he escaped! You're lying through your back teeth to me.'

'Before he escaped, he revealed the code during torture.'

'So?' said Salamander looking very impatient. 'Tell me what Kramer said! Tell me, tell me.'

'I must warn you, it is technical...'

'Stop delaying!' she shouted. 'Do I look like I have all day?'

'Ok, but it's in binary code.'

'What!?' she almost screamed, leaning forward, hands on her scrawny hips.

Sakamoto spoke precisely, all the time staring at her enraged face. '10011010001...'

'Stop!' she shouted, 'What is this? Some kind of delinquent joke,' her greying, blond hair with extensions shaking wildly during her tantrum.

'It's computer language – designed not to be understood easily in the wrong hands.'

'Rubbish! You are trying to fool me. No one on this earth fools me.'

'I have the full code at my house... it's hidden.'

'Where?' she demanded aggressively, her arms folding.

'In my swimming pool pumphouse.'

'Take him back there!' she said angrily. 'If he's lying, drown him slow as a rat and bring me the picture evidence.'

Her heavily sleeved arms displaying dragons and serpents were waving around. 'When you have the code, get it translated immediately within the chain and then returned to me before midday tomorrow, or else.'

Two henchmen grabbed Sakamoto by the wrists and pulled him toward the exit door, the other two behind and with guns, one prodding, jabbing and pushing.

'Shift!' said the leader from behind.

The group soon arrived outside. 'Come on, Sakamoto. And don't try anything smart unless you want us to feed you to the dogs... one leg at a time. Best part... you can watch their sheer enjoyment as they eat you with pleasure.'

The Kramer's were at home and busy packing their cases. The front door was knocked. A quick peep out from behind a curtain confirmed the worst; unwanted visitors. Dressed casually, Luis moved downstairs and opened the door. 'Hello. Are you passing, or would you like to come in?'

'Do you have a minute?' said Lieutenant Bomberger, Waxman to one side.

'Yes, of course. Come in.'

All arrived in the sitting room, the very room directly under the master bedroom.

'Have a seat,' offered Kramer pointing.

'Thank you,' said Waxman, 'but this is just a flying visit.'

'How can I help?'

'I guess you have no news for us,' said Bomberger.

'Unfortunately not.'

'As far as we're concerned, there are a few leads to chase.'

Waxman spoke. 'How's your Private Investigator doing?'

'The same as you really. He's trying all avenues.'

'What was his name?' quizzed Waxman, looking at a family photograph.

'Fleming. Jack Fleming. He's an ex-cop and used to work for the LAPD.'

'Yes,' said Bomberger. 'It's often a natural progression,' he smiled. 'I might even take that route myself one day.'

'How are you coping?' added Waxman. 'It must be quite tough dealing with this on your own?'

'It is. I miss my wife and daughter immensely.'

A moment of silence. Bomberger was looking around the floor then engaged Kramer. 'Have you any idea what's going on, or what may have caused this situation? I would have said kidnap, but even this is unclear at the moment.'

'No, it's a mystery,' he paused slowly.

Both detectives waited.

'Unless it's work related…' offered Kramer.

'Area 51, you mean?' said Waxman hopefully.

'Yes. While I can't talk about what I did and what I saw, there are others perhaps who are prepared to go to any length and blackmail me.'

'Any letters or other communication yet?' said Bomberger.

'No. I'm just waiting.'

Back at the police station, Bomberger plonked himself down, his finger hovering over the computer's power button, an eye glancing at his wristwatch; 6:55pm.

'Here's your coke,' said Waxman.

However, the boss had a Eureka moment. 'I'm a clown.'

'What?' said Waxman, looking bewildered.

'I'm a complete fool. I've overlooked vital evidence,' he said releasing the ring-pull slowly.

'Oh yeah?' said Waxman, seating himself and booting up his machine.

'I'm surprised that you forgot too.'

Waxman frowned. *Bomberger's got coke saturation syndrome,* he thought.

'Listen. We had Sakamoto's place heavily bugged. Therefore, those who raided it recently will hopefully be taped. It may also give us a clue as to where Sakamoto is... right?'

'Right,' agreed Waxman, nodding. 'Now I see how you made Lieutenant.'

Once dark, the Kramers left their home heading for a campsite just forty-five minutes away. Fortunately, the couple had been there before and knew what to expect; a small privately owned piece of land ideal for those who wanted a quiet and scenic break. Kramer parked their red camper van away from the keeper's cabin and went straight down to sidelights. 'That's perfect,' he said, 'and only two other vehicles for company.'

'What's happened to Fleming?' she quizzed while looking around outside and not seeing much.

'I don't know. It's disappointing not hearing from him, but in his line of work he could be dead... how would we know?'

'I say forget him,' said Jayne biting her bottom lip and to one side. 'But then I'm so desperate to get Libby back... I'll accept any help.'

'And me too.'

Both flinched as the window was knocked. A face appeared on Kramer's side and now his hand arrived on his chest to calm a racing heart. 'Relax, it's the park's owner,' he said dropping the window.

'Your ticket, Mr Kramer. Just leave it on the dashboard.'

'Of course. Thank you.'

'Another late shift I fear,' said Bomberger, listening once again to the bugged conversations captured recently at Sakamoto's rental.

He hit pause as Waxman spoke. 'If it yields something then great. If not, tough luck. The upside... working late saves my electric bill.'

'Yep.'

Waxman took a bite out of his take-away pizza and slipped his headphones on.

The boss sipped his diet coke with pleasure. 'Waxman, what are you doing?'

'I'm listening live, but no one's home. Sakamoto's obviously done a runner. That's very unfortunate for us because the Chief will want an update soon.'

Bomberger had been quiet for a few minutes. 'Hey Curtis?'

'Yeah,' with headphones lifting off one ear.

'I've been listening to the two we tangled with earlier.'

'Hold on,' said Waxman replacing his headphones properly. 'What is it?'

A hand went up, stalling the communication. Bomberger felt cut out and switched over to live streaming from Sakamoto's rental. Both looked at each other as they listened.

'Come on Sakamoto! Where are the keys to the pumphouse?'

'Can't you see, someone has turned my place over. Nothing is where it should be...'

'Salamander will not be happy. You're breaking the chain rules. What about your commitment?' came a shout.

'Hey! I've done my best. I caught Kramer and his wife and his daughter...'

'But you let them go. Kramer was the objective!'

'No. Correction. He escaped.'

'What about his wife? Where is she?'

'Something very strange happened here, like a weird force. I was floating then knocked out…'

'Floating!?'

'That's when she disappeared. I have memory loss…'

'Rubbish! Liar.'

'If you're so clever, why don't you go and find the Kramers. Then Salamander will be happy. Everyone will be happy.'

'That's not our job. We don't search and hunt… we look after the goods… in this case, we only have one out of three. Poor Miss Libby. She's so pissed off with us, but hey, when we get all three, Salamander can get the information she craves so much.'

'Help me look for the keys then…'

'That's not our job.'

'Ok, but it's not my fault if it takes all night.'

'Come on Waxman,' said Bomberger, jumping up and tapping a few keys. 'I'm transferring this live chat to my mobile,' now plugging in his Bose earphones.

Waxman pushed his chair backwards at speed, catching the Interceptor's keys flying through the air.

'You're driving,' said Bomberger, pulling a drawer out fast.

In he went and grabbed a box marked, CIA. After a few hectic minutes, the detectives were travelling at speed and making for Sakamoto's rental.

Bomberger was listening intently and waiting for any new snippets of information. 'What's in the box?' quizzed Waxman.

'The CIA box?'

'Yeah. What's that all about?' looking mystified.

'Car Information Access,' declared Bomberger looking smug.

'New kit?'

'Sort of…'

'What's happening at Sakamoto's place?'

'The gang's becoming more aggressive by the minute because there's still no sign of the pumphouse key.'

'What's the plan of action?'

'Park a few streets away, then cut across the field on foot and enter over the fence by the swimming pool.'

'Ok.'

'First job… put this CIA tracker on their vehicle.'

'Then with luck, we can find out where Libby's being held,' added Waxman knowingly, swinging their unmarked Interceptor around a sharp bend… the tyres screeching.

Parking in a side street, the two made their way across a small field until approaching a boundary fence. Bomberger stopped. 'There are three chain villains, plus Sakamoto. That's three on three, except only two guns on our side.'

'We've got to play it right,' said Waxman. 'We need at least one to run back to base with the tracker.'

'Correct. We can't have a full shootout… got to make them run,' added Bomberger struggling to climb over the high fence.

'Agreed,' replied Waxman following.

Both stopped by the bougainvillea wall, Bomberger out in front and breathing heavily. He put a hand up and a finger to his lips. Still listening to the conversation, the boss spoke. 'There are definitely two inside. We have to assume that a third dude maybe outside on guard duty.'

Waxman nodded. They remained stooped and aimed for the house before looping around. The gang's red Range Rover was parked and reversed into a space ready for a quick getaway. To complicate matters, the driver was seated and listening to the radio.

'Cover me,' whispered Bomberger as he crawled towards the rear of the vehicle.

In the darkness, the driver looked in his mirror and thought he saw a movement. He now switched to his near-side mirror. Nothing. The radio was turned off and a gun appeared. Further listening ensured he step out to satisfy his burning curiosity. Moving to the rear, he flicked his torch on before arriving on one knee. Bomberger was laid out between the front and rear, near-side tyres, when his tanned and dead-pan face was seen in the beam. Completely spooked, the driver dropped his torch. Then instantly a thud as Waxman barged from behind driving his victim's head into the vehicle's unforgiving steel panel.

'Good work,' whispered Bomberger as Waxman pulled the slumped villain away. Once secured and gagged, the tracker was placed securely. In the cover of darkness, the two detectives made their way to the rear of the house.

'One down, and two to go,' whispered Bomberger.

'Yeah,' said Waxman. 'And that vehicle has got to get back if we want any chance of finding Libby alive.'

Bomberger stood listening. 'Good news. They've got the keys. Now going down to the pump room... damn, the signal's fading.'

Both detectives crept around the side of the house and hid in the flickering shadows. Less than a minute had elapsed when the porch light illuminated. They flinched and froze on the spot – their safety catches off and ready for action. The lit door opened and Sakamoto suddenly appeared looking relaxed. He stretched and yawned casually. Bomberger then frowned and whispered. 'Hell... what's happened?'

'I don't know,' replied Waxman, his gun still ready.

In a daring move, the boss jumped out. Sakamoto went for his stolen weapon.

'Drop it,' said Bomberger moving forward, Waxman covering.

'Hey Chief, don't shoot! I'm on your side,' Sakamoto's hands rising. 'Remember... I'm your friend?'

'Where are the other two?' quizzed Waxman.

Sakamoto laughed. 'As one slipped on the stairs to the pump room and knocked himself out., I floored the other and put his brain in chill mode for a couple of hours.'

'Oh that's just great,' said Bomberger, not sounding pleased. 'We needed them to run.'

'It's good news,' said Sakamoto. 'Take those bastards in and lock them up.'

Five minutes later, and Waxman's plan was in its final stage. The two villains dealt with by Sakamoto were tied up and thrown in the back of the Range Rover. Once the driver was placed in his seat, the engine and lights were turned on. Lastly, a soda syphon now blasted into his face bringing him round fast. In shock and soon understanding the gravity of the situation, the spooked driver took off snaking madly as shots pinged off the bodywork.

Chapter 7

Escena Golf Club, Palm Springs, California: Wednesday

'Another sunny day,' said the President, strolling on to the first fairway. 'If I didn't have golf to take my mind off this crazy world, I'd go completely mad.'

Carrozza was amused. 'Hey Hal, I second that.'

'Myself as well,' said Penniman feeling jovial.

'Life is good at the top if you can take the shit,' added Hauk. 'My philosophy is, don't say anything you'll regret and be aware of people you don't know asking too many questions.'

'Yes,' replied Carrozza. 'You never know when an undercover journalist is snooping for the next big scoop.'

'The bloody press,' said the President. 'I hate fake news.'

He paused when selecting a club, then laughed. 'Unless it's my fake news.'

'Tell me,' said Hauk, with a ball and tee in his hand, 'who won yesterday's game at Swan Lake?'

Before an answer could be given, Hauk was back in. 'I can tell you,' now selecting his club.

Carrozza patted his shoulder. 'We would expect the Head of the CIA to know everything.'

All chuckled with amusement, Hauk included. He spoke. 'I thought I knew everything until my wife told me she'd been having an affair for six years.'

'Jesus!' said Penniman. 'How did you miss that one? You've got a billion or two microphones and cameras placed all around the world.'

'I'll tell you how I missed it... chocolate doesn't talk! She's in love with the stuff. It's an affair that's going to run and run... just like her waistline.'

Forty minutes later and the golf buggies were all parked as the four men lined up on the next lush fairway. Feeling relaxed, the Commander-in-Chief leant on his favourite carbon fiber driver while Penniman used a cloth to wipe his club. Carrozza smiled. 'Paul, it's too early to be sweating. I guess you think polishing your weapon will improve your game?'

'I'm already three over parr. I've got to try something new.'

'If it wasn't for carbon fiber,' said Carrozza, 'we would never have got the Stealth bomber.'

Penniman chipped in. 'True to say, that if I never found the money in the coffers, that project would never have got off the ground.'

'Smart materials,' said the President. 'That's a subject I like. I've been interested since they found samples at Roswell.'

Hauk looked more serious. 'That was a time when the truth nearly got out,' he said with a blue tee and ball in hand. 'I wasn't even born then, but I can tell you right now, if the truth had ever got out, we would be living in a much different world today.'

The Head of the Federal Reserve looked thoughtful. 'Do you believe that stuff? I mean, if that was really a real spacecraft, the mothership would have sent out a rescue mission, just like we always do... right?'

'Maybe they did,' said the President nodding.

'They didn't,' said Hauk. 'That's not what happened. We had been tracking them on radar for a few weeks.'

'What?' said Penniman, 'Aliens in their silver flying machines? Surely not. If that was the case, then seven decades on... we'd all have seen them by now.'

'Many have,' replied Hauk. 'Sure, there are a lot of hoaxes on the internet and some making the newspapers…'

'That's the fake news,' chipped in the President happily.

'But,' continued Hauk, 'while they knew one of their craft had gone down, they wrote it off to avoid further exposure.'

'Really?' half laughed Penniman.

'Yes,' said Hauk with his three colleagues facing. 'Imagine you are at war and spying on the enemy. If one of your men makes the wrong move and takes a hit… the rest don't step out and give their position away.'

'I agree with that,' said Carrozza nodding.

'Yes, me too,' added the President taking a full practice swing; blades of grass flying. 'You are second in command of all US Forces.'

'Nice action,' grinned Hauk, 'but the reason why the aliens didn't try and recover their spacecraft was because we got there first.'

'The CIA?' quizzed Penniman.

'And military,' added Carrozza quickly.

Hauk winked. 'You got it. Well, a couple of locals did snoop briefly, but our Men in Black called by to ensure they'd forgotten everything. All that was left to report was that a weather balloon had come down, not an alien craft. Over time, the majority of people got on with their lives and forgot about the event.'

The President smiled, placing his ball on to the awaiting tee. 'The moral of the story is… keep it quiet, play it down and spin spin spin!'

After the risky spying mission, Bomberger and Waxman had returned to their office to track the villains in their Range Rover. Once satisfied that it was back at base, both went home in the early hours of the morning. However, Lieutenant Bomberger was not a man to sleep-in, even at weekends, so made his way back to the office where he found Waxman already at his desk.

'Hey buddy, I didn't know you loved the job that much,' he jested, throwing a newspaper down.

Waxman had glanced up but then back to his screen. 'The jigsaw puzzle is starting to come together slowly...'

'Unfortunately, not fast enough for me,' admitted the boss. 'I want to have the Kramer's back in their house and all chain members behind bars.'

'Did you notice those three that we sent back with their tails between their legs had chains tattooed on their wrists?'

'Yes I did, and just like bracelets,' replied Bomberger booting up his computer. 'I'll tell you what does intrigue me...'

'What's that?'

'Does Sakamoto have the same tattoos?'

Waxman replied, still staring at his screen. 'If he didn't wear so many leather straps and bone-bead bracelets, then maybe we could see.'

A short pause.

'Curtis? Do you like flying?'

Waxman looked up. 'It's ok. Why do you ask?'

'We are going to San Diego at twelve thirty.'

'Tonight?'

'No, just after midday. We're bringing Libby back.'

'Ok,' said Waxman slowly and pausing for thought.

'The good news is that we're not flying. I would rather be shot at than sit in a cigar tube at thirty thousand feet. That's crazy,' he said before pausing. Now a smile. 'The bad news is that we will be driving. We'll share it... nothing like a little bonding time.'

132

'No problem. What about night vision glasses and a bag full of stun grenades?'

'Do you need that much stuff?' added Bomberger.

'What were you thinking... a fly swatter with a long handle?'

'Fair comment,' smiled the boss. 'No. It's ok, I've got it all covered. Don't worry. I wouldn't jump into a nest full of vipers without some protection. I'm a survivor and I want that pension.'

'Has the final destination changed?' said Waxman.

'No. The CIA tracker confirms the vehicle has not moved.'

'But probability suggests that Libby could be elsewhere.'

Bomberger shook his head. 'It's my gut feeling that she's there. I'm seldom wrong.'

'Ok. So, the plan is...'

'Firstly, we drive down to San Diego and then take the 805 south to Ocean View Hills, stopping just north of the Mexican border.'

'Essentially, Tijuana direction?' offered Waxman.

'Yes. Then we find the San Vista Ranch and hit them after dark, or in the early hours.'

'Sounds straightforward on paper. What about backup?'

Bomberger leant across to whisper. 'Unfortunately, we can't. And if they run south across the border, we'll go after them.'

Waxman blinked. 'That would be out of our jurisdiction...'

'Don't worry, Curtis, you won't get fired for taking orders. I'll plead diminished responsibilities due to UFO stress.'

Luis and Jayne sat eating in the back of their camper van, the sky slightly overcast and a light westerly picking up.

'Do you think it's worth contacting Bomberger or Waxman for an update since we are not home,' suggested Jayne, 'not that I'm meant to be there.'

'They have my mobile,' replied Luis, 'so I should try Fleming again.'

'He's a waste of time. Don't bother.'

'I have a different view. If he hadn't found me, I'd be dead right now.'

'Ok, phone him… but I bet he hasn't done anything.'

'To be honest, Jayne, you can't be lucky all the time.'

'I thought he had contacts in the LAPD?'

'Yes, that's what he said. Why wouldn't I believe him?'

Both finished.

'Jayne, tell me again what happened when both you and Libby were originally kidnapped.'

'As I said before, we had been shopping in Ventura when it started to rain…'

'I remember.'

'Then… when we got back to the car park, two men stepped out of a van. We thought nothing of it. Then they grabbed us. Something on a cloth was pushed up against my nose. And that's it. That's all I remember.'

'So, you ended up at Sakamoto's place and secured to a chair in the basement. Is that right?'

'I don't know if it was his house,' she confessed, 'but he was a big man and started to interrogate me. I was terrified. It was obvious from his line of questioning that this whole affair was about you… about your work.'

'There would have to be some motive,' stated Luis. 'No one does this for fun unless they're sick.'

'What do they want? You must have some idea?'

'If I put two and two together, someone with too much money wants inside information about Area 51, plus other related sites.'

'Then what? Publish a book... run to the papers...' she said looking frustrated.

'It wouldn't do them any good. Stories without proof carry no weight. Considered as fake news, the stories die quickly.'

'There is another angle,' she claimed.

His smile was small. 'I can tell... you've been thinking.'

'Yes, for days on end and hardly sleeping. Luis, I've been racking my brains to understand why.'

'If it's any consolation, me too.'

'I conclude that whoever is behind this wants you to step under the spotlight and tell all.'

Luis nodded. 'Yes, it had crossed my mind.'

'But why you, Luis? There are hundreds of people working in these sensitive areas. I don't get it. Why you?'

Waxman threw his hold-all into the rear of the Interceptor and closed the boot. He swung the passenger door open and stepped in. 'I've packed my toothbrush and a dummy's guide to making a will,' he said, placing his seatbelt.

Bomberger took off. 'I've got the military grade night glasses. Did you notice the other, kick-ass gear, in the boot?'

'Yes, but I didn't see a First Aid kit.'

'Real professionals like us don't need the stuff.'

'I like your confidence,' sighed Waxman, settling in his seat.

'The last time I wore a plaster, was on my trigger finger,' confessed Bomberger. 'I shot a lot of bad boys that week and had to cover a blister the size of a weather balloon.'

Waxman was amused as his boss continued. 'Here, take this and do two checks. Firstly, see if the tracker is still working and that the Range Rover hasn't moved from the ranch.'

'Ok,' said Waxman taking the kit.

'Then plug in the widget box and see if Sakamoto is back at his house. If he talks, we should pick up the signal. If it starts to fade, turn dial X1 and retune.'

'Did you borrow this from, Fred Flintstone?'

'Beggars can't be choosers with cutbacks forever eating into a shrinking budget.'

'Chad, I've just had a great idea,' sounding bright.

Bomberger laughed and turned. 'Ok Waxman, it's going to be a long journey, what is it?'

'I suggest we go and get, Sakamoto. I think he could be very useful.'

'I've never heard something so daft,' scoffed the boss.

'Don't forget, he's a tough guy who doesn't like the way the chain has treated him recently. Besides, he was driven there to see the one they call, Salamander.'

'You do have a point,' said Bomberger slowing to switch route.

Waxman laughed. 'We haven't asked him yet? He will never agree.'

'It was your great idea. Phone him now,' a quick glance in the mirror.

'What should I say?'

'You'll think of something.'

Just fifty minutes later, and Bomberger drove away from Sakamoto's rental.

'It's good of you to join us,' said Waxman, turning to view their new passenger.

'I've got to admit, I don't really like cops, but even worse... I hate trying to tidy up the whole house after those bastards ransacked the place.'

'What were they looking for?' said Waxman.

'I don't know, maybe information about Kramer. Who knows?'

'We haven't seen Kramer for a few days,' admitted Bomberger. 'He's done a vanishing act.'

'I know where he is...' confessed Sakamoto.

'Oh yeah,' said Waxman. 'We want you to sign up with us.'

'Obviously, he's in that camper van.'

'Really?' frowned Bomberger.

'Just a hunch,' admitted Sakamoto, cracking his knuckles.

'I like your hunch,' said Waxman, nodding.

'Me too,' agreed Bomberger. 'Why didn't we think of that, Curtis? We could have had our patrols out looking at camping sites.'

The San Vista Ranch sat just one mile south of Ocean View Hills. Salamander was extremely annoyed with the three men for returning without Sakamoto. They stood before her with hands tied behind their backs and under a tree with sturdy boughs, thick, gnarled and horizontal. Two other guards were close by, one with a gun, the other with rope and a noose.

'What am I going to do with you?' she said, standing close by. 'Look at you. Pathetic,' her mood angry and sounding frustrated. 'I could have you shot right now. In fact, I wish I had a ballista. You would be loaded up one by one and fired across the border into Mexico. All they would find is six feet sticking out of the ground. That would make me so happy,' she laughed before her face switched back to anger in an instant. 'But I haven't got a ballista so that leaves me even more pissed off with you three Brazilian clowns. Bolivians would have been better. Ok, what do you have to say for yourselves?'

Salamander stepped forward with her narrow bamboo cane. She struck the first man hard on his leg. 'Stand up straight!' she shouted. 'Have you no respect for those at the top of the chain?' her cane under his chin to push upwards. 'And if I was a man, would you respect me more?' she paused. 'Yes yes, of course you would!'

The wicked woman paced slowly looking at each one in turn. 'But as for me, you have no respect at all? You hate me. It's because I'm a woman, isn't it? You hate women having the upper hand... I know it. I'm not stupid. And your silence is wounding me more.'

All three men stood straight and taller than Salamander. Their silence was understandable; being tightly gagged was further humiliation.

'Ok,' she said, tapping the cane in her hand. 'I bet you are all thinking what an evil bitch I am, right?'

Salamander laughed. 'Don't be shy boys, speak up.'

Silence.

'Ok, so there's nothing to say in your defence? That's fine. It means the judge must sum up.'

Annoyingly, she paused to look at each in turn. Moving slowly in front, her menacing cane flicked collars, ears and hair.

'Listen. Two of you are going to go back and find Sakamoto and Kramer, then bring them back here. There can be no more failure. I will not tolerate it!' she said, stern-faced and switching direction every few seconds. 'However, that was the good news. The bad news is that one of you will be kind to the others and volunteer.'

Salamander laughed. 'Yes, a volunteer to set an example.'

She nodded to the guard with rope. He stepped forward and threw the noose over a sturdy bough where it swung to generate fear.

'Feel free to step forward and save your friends from dying.'

She waited no longer than two seconds.

'I don't have all day!' she shouted with anger, 'so I will decide who has the privilege.'

Salamander walked along, staring deeply into the eyes of her tormented men. 'I see your fear, but don't worry. I have made up my mind,' the cane lightly whipping her hand.

She stopped in the middle with an intimidating, fixed stare. The guard trembled. Not taking her eyes off him, she stepped back a pace. 'I have selected the one who reminds me of my first husband,' still staring without blinking. 'He was shit, so I dealt with him,' her face, thunder. 'What a pleasure that gave me,' a smile evident, now laughing happily.

Quick as a flash, she turned to her left and slammed the cane into the other prisoner. 'This one has volunteered, and the judge accepts with deep gratitude.'

The two overseeing guards moved forward, and very quickly set the noose in place.

Salamander smiled at her victim as the rope tightened until he was struggling on tip toes. 'Do me a favour,' her stick tapping his shoulder. 'If you see my husband in hell, tell him I'm having a great time on his ranch, spending his money and driving his sports cars. Oh, and finally, tell the stupid fool that I finished off two of his tarty girlfriends. What a pleasure.'

The show was paused. 'Listen to me you lucky pigs. After this memorable little lesson, get back in that Range Rover and bring me Kramer and Sakamoto... fast as lightning!' she glared.

In the silence of the yard, she nodded. 'Take it away, Sam.'

It was late afternoon and the Kramer's had just got back to the campsite after a long walk around the lake.

'I agree with what you say,' said Jayne. 'Go to Sakamoto's place and see what you can find. There has to be a link to Libby somewhere in that house.'

'I'll go after dark…'

'I'll come with you.'

'No, it's too dangerous. These people are ruthless.'

'I don't want to be left alone without you and Libby.'

They both stood and hugged in the back of the camper van.

Luis partially withdrew. 'If Bomberger and Waxman are out of the office, I'll have to risk going back for my gun.'

Jayne looked worried. 'If you have a gun, then a confrontation will be much more dangerous.'

'That's the risk I'll have to take.'

'Although I don't trust Fleming, why don't you try him?' said Jayne. 'Why not let him get in the front line. It's his job.'

'Let's call in on him. It's only a slight detour.'

'Why doesn't he pick up?'

'Your guess is as good as mine.'

'And where's the Mustang,' quizzed Jayne, flicking the kettle on.

'It's in Fleming's garage.'

'But why? He's a bit strange and you don't know him from Adam.'

Bomberger eventually pulled into the Ocean View Hills car park. 'There we are,' he said swinging around for the best view before parking.

Waxman opened his door. 'I need to stretch my legs after that laborious journey.'

'Me too,' added Sakamoto stepping out.

'Yep, I agree to that,' said Bomberger. 'Let's make the most of the calm before the storm.'

'This sure ain't going to be an easy ride,' admitted Sakamoto. 'Salamander's place is quite tight for security.'

'It's just a ranch isn't it?' quizzed Bomberger. 'A ranch that stretches right down to the Mexican border.'

'I've only been there once and that was as a prisoner. I woke up inside this whitewashed building, where I got interrogated, kicked and punched before being brought back. I guess I was lucky.'

Sakamoto laughed and continued while taking in the fresh air and scenery. 'There never was anything in the pumphouse. Just pumps, water and slippery steps.'

A few cars came and went as the small team sat inside the petrol blue Interceptor making plans for the night time raid.

The two Brazilian chain members were speeding northwards.

'Jesus, that woman is crazy as a witch!' claimed the passenger playing with his gun. 'When this is all over and we've got our money, I say we execute Salamander.'

'Yes, before we end up swinging from that same tree. That was unlucky for Rio.'

'Very unlucky for him… and only 24.'

The driver looked at his watch. 'It's going to take a few hours to reach Sakamoto's place. I'm getting bad vibes about this trip already. What if we come face to face with him? He'll kill us.'

'Don't forget, we have to take that ox alive.'

'Shit man. He's built like a brick house. How are we going to do that?'

'I don't know, I'm still in pain from the last visit.'

'What happened exactly?'

'You really want to hear it all over again? Oh God... what are you on?'

'I hope to learn from your mistakes.'

'Very funny.'

'No, I'm serious.'

'I was in the driver's seat and waiting for you and Rio to show up. Then I hear this noise...'

'What sort of noise... like a rat or something?'

'Yeah, somewhere at the back.'

'Ok.'

'And it's dark... remember?'

'Yeah... I was on my way with Sakamoto to the pump room.'

'Do you want me to continue?'

'Yes. Give me the story man.'

'Then I get out to investigate. I'm messing myself.'

'That's not good.'

'I get to the back and I bend down and flick on my torch...'

'And?'

'And I see two eyes looking back at me... just staring.'

'No shit?'

'No shit.'

'Was it the rat?'

'No. There was no bloody rat, ok?'

'What was it? Who was it?'

'I don't know... it all happened so quickly.'

'Then what?'

'I'm pointing my gun, finger on the trigger, when I hear this noise behind me... my brain goes into meltdown and I drop my torch. Next thing I'm rammed into the back door.'

'Yes, that was the dishing in the metal panel work. Salamander was not impressed.'

'She never is… the heartless dragon.'

'Then what?'

'I fell unconscious,' he said, pausing. 'Shit, that place is bad news. Sakamoto must have security guards. We need to be more careful this time.'

'For sure.'

'What about you?'

'I told you already…'

'Tell me again… I just repeated my story for you.'

'Ok. So, we were on the steps to the pumphouse. It was very dingy and with crap lighting. I'm at Sakamoto's side with my gun safely poking into his beefy ribs. Suddenly, I lose my footing and I'm going down fast like a snow-boarder. Next thing, I'm at the bottom on all fours like a dog and trying to grab my gun while it spun like a roulette wheel.'

'And?'

'And Rio slams in next to me.'

'That must have hurt… right?'

'Yeah, like shit. So, I'm nearly up and then Sakamoto lands a Mike Tyson shot straight on my chin.'

'Did you see it coming?'

'For about half a second.'

'Damn. This is going to be another hellfire trip.'

'Oh mother… I hate blood and pain… especially mine.'

'Me too, but when it comes to that crazy Salamander woman it will be an absolute pleasure to pay her back. I'm going to make sure she eats her hair extensions for Sunday lunch.'

Luis pulled on to their drive, the time; 6:33pm. Both looked around as cars came and went.

'And as Elvis once said, it's now or never,' claimed Kramer opening his door.

Inside the house, Luis checked the answerphone messages while Jayne thumbed through the mail. 'Thank God,' she said, 'there are no ransom notes. Having said that, at least it would indicate that Libby was still alive. I would gladly sell this place to raise the money and get her back with us.'

'Me too,' agreed Luis, checking his gun.

'You make me nervous with that thing.'

'Come and sit down. I'll show you how to use it.'

'That really isn't wise,' she confessed. 'I'm constantly having accidents in the kitchen.'

Once the short lesson was over, he left his wife and made his way to Fleming's home. On arrival, he was surprised to see a rent sign in the garden. *Oh no, that's not a good omen,* he thought, *Jayne would say, 'I told you so.'*

Never-the-less, he hadn't driven over to waste his time, so parked up and went to the front door. He was just about to knock when it opened.

'Hello Luis,' Fleming looking true and sincere.

'Hi Jack.'

Fleming stood aside and beckoned his guest in. 'It's been a few days since we met up.'

Kramer entered and was soon in the living room.

'Have a seat,' offered Fleming, pointing to several. 'I have no particular favourite.'

'Thanks. I see there's a rental sign up. Are you moving on?'

'Yes and no,' said Fleming seating himself. 'Let me explain. It's true to say that I'm moving on, but the good news is, it's not far away. Somewhere smaller and more convenient for access to Ventura. Besides, in this game it's better to be on the move.'

'Ok,' replied Kramer with relief. 'I've tried to get you a few times but without success.'

'That's because I'm sometimes out of the area or on a mission where it just isn't possible to answer. I'm sure you understand.'

'Of course. I've been in that situation myself.'

There was a short pause as Kramer looked around the room. It was sparse; no photographs, pictures, pot plants or lampshades to make the place look more homely. 'Have you had any luck with your contacts?'

'Unfortunately, nothing positive which is disappointing. But intelligence suggests something could be happening tonight. Typically, I may not get the information until the last minute, then I have to move very fast.'

'I understand,' said Kramer looking agreeable.

'What about you two? How are you coping?'

'It's difficult for me, but obviously harder for Jayne.'

'I can imagine... you have been through a lot just lately.'

'Jack, I'm going over to Sakamoto's place tonight. I want to snoop around if he's out.'

'Is that really wise, Luis? The people involved are potentially dangerous criminals and have no regard for human life.'

'I have a gun and I know how to use it...'

'You would be trespassing.'

'Only if caught and handed over to the police.'

'True. However, it's risky. You don't want to make Jayne a widow.'

'Does a burglar ever go out expecting to get caught?'

'No. And the majority don't. But it does happen. Things do go wrong.'

'Call it fool-hardy if you like, but we are desperate. Every day that passes is a day too long. As a father, I feel the responsibility to get involved. I can't just sit back. Imagine if something awful happened to Libby. I would spend the rest of my life thinking... if only.'

'I get it. I understand.'

'That would kill me, sure as day follows night.'

'Can you delay until tomorrow,' said Fleming.

'Tomorrow may never come.'

Bomberger and his small team stood at the back of the Interceptor, all lights out and only a half moon to help when intermittent clouds passed over. The three had been through their plan as best as they could regarding the layout of the ranch. Dressed in black, they took their weapons from the boot.

'Are you guys ready to kick ass?' asked Bomberger, placing his night vision glasses over blackened face.

'Yes,' replied Waxman doing the same.

'These night glasses are good,' claimed Sakamoto, looking around the car park and to the darkest corners.

'Ok,' said the boss, 'we've got a half mile walk from here, then we'll need absolute stealth and wisdom to succeed.'

'I'm ready,' said Waxman, holding his firearm.

'Are you ready, Sakamoto?' said Bomberger.

'I'm ready to kick butt. Let's go.'

The three men set off heading south and in the direction of the ranch. Waxman spoke. 'They say if the wind is blowing north, you can hear the Tijuana brass as it leaves Mexico.'

Bomberger led the way, his compass out. 'That background noise would be ideal tonight. We don't want any dogs barking as we approach.'

'That's right,' said Sakamoto. 'I understand they have at least two rottweilers.'

'How do you know?' said Waxman.

'Rio talked about them.'

'Rio? As in, Rio de Janeiro?'

'Yes, a nickname... he's Brazilian.'

Arriving in the extensive grounds of the ranch, the intruders stooped down and continued to cross a mixture of stony surfaces, where sporadic grass grew in clumps, and the odd cactus stood high and threatening. The boss had stopped. 'I estimate about two hundred yards to the house,' he whispered, and using his night vision glasses.

Stealth was the way forward; all silencers on. Approaching the veranda, Sakamoto took the lead, but stopped and stooped down behind a large water butt. A guard stood on the corner of this sleepy, white-washed ranch, chatting and laughing noisily on his mobile. Waxman was last in the line and turned to ensure the rear was covered. Sakamoto pointed at the guard. Bomberger craned for his own assessment. Then without warning, a door at the back of the timber-built building opened and a dog came out. Within a few quick strides, it arrived at Salamander's favourite tree. Seconds later, it seemed to look their way and started with a low guttural growl. Waxman lifted his gun and took aim. *Keep peeing dog, or you're dead*, he thought. But it stopped and then made a bee-line for their position and picking up pace. The gap was closing fast. In the seated position and leaning back on Bomberger, he took the shot. A thwack, and the dog fell forward and collapsed, tumbling almost at his feet. While it never moved, the guard had heard the pounding feet and inexplicable thud that followed. He ended the call. Grabbing his gun, he moved down the steps slowly to dutifully protect the ranch and, in particular, Salamander, the heartless boss. Creeping down and approaching the large water butt with his gun pointing forward, he suddenly saw half of the dead dog. His curiosity ensured he looked further. Waxman was seen. The very second that Sakamoto saw him raise his gun for the shot, he fired himself. As the guard fell, the rear door of the ranch opened and someone whistled. A few seconds later, a man shouted, his accent, South American. 'Hey Riu, stupid dog! Come on.'

Waxman and Sakamoto pulled the slumped guard in behind the water butt while Bomberger kept look out.

'Riu! Get back in here now, or I'll shoot you,' cursed the man, now standing on the corner and looking their way. Angered but also concerned, he brought out the second rottweiler on a short lead. The animal was pulling and straining, its front paws off the ground and choking. All three stood behind a tree in a line and five yards further away. In the semi-dark night, the dog handler followed his straining hound until it found the dead guard. From that position, it soon moved on to find the other dog at the base of the steps. Seconds later, the front door opened. 'Have you found, Riu?' said another guard arriving. 'Oh shit!' he exclaimed and turning back to run.

Immediately, the three stepped out from behind the tree to open fire, the detectives standing to the left and right, Sakamoto crouching in front of Waxman to take out the bounding dog. The pre-planned operation had worked well, but that was aided by the element of surprise.

'Come on,' said Sakamoto leading the way, Bomberger and Waxman close behind.

Into the building they went, covering each other while doors were kicked open and rooms, fast-scanned. A dog was barking further down the corridor. It had to be trapped in the kitchen.

'I'll go back and loop round,' said Sakamoto retracing his steps to the front door.

Bomberger turned out the lights and both detectives stood still and waited. Suddenly, a single shot was fired. The dog continued to bark, and aggressively.

'Bad news,' whispered Waxman. 'That wasn't silenced.'

'If we've lost Sakamoto, we could be surrounded.'

Both men experienced a light sweat breaking out, the dog up against the internal door and snarling.

'How long do we wait?' said Waxman with his night vision glasses back in place.

'Give him another minute.'

'Dead men don't walk.'

More barking, then a car was heard starting.

'Someone's leaving,' said Bomberger urgently. 'I'll try and stop them,' now up and moving towards the front door.

'But...'

'Waxman... the hound!' he shouted back. 'Shoot the bastard through the door.'

With the revving car and the sound of Bomberger running down the passage, so Waxman had not noticed that the dog had stopped barking. He was startled as the internal kitchen door swung open. 'Hey, don't shoot! It's me, Sakamoto.'

Both could now see each other in the darkness.

'And careful, don't trip over the dog.'

Waxman looked down. 'It's a bad day for the canines.'

'Where's Bomberger?'

'Chasing that car,' rotating to run. 'Let's give him back up.'

As they arrived at the front door, Bomberger pushed a man their way using the barrel of his gun.

'That's very efficient,' said Sakamoto. 'He'll talk once I start pulling his arms off.'

'Lock all doors and windows,' said Waxman with urgency. 'We don't know who's out there.'

'There's no one,' confessed the captured guard. 'They've gone in the car.'

Sakamoto scoffed. 'Why would we listen to you?'

'I'm only twenty-two and I want to live.'

'You should have stayed with your mother,' said Sakamoto without feeling.

'She's dead.'

'How come?' said Bomberger.

'My father was a drug dealer, but he messed up. The gang took revenge... killed my mother and traded me.'

'Where are you from?' quizzed Waxman.

'Tijuana.'

'You're Mexican,' said Bomberger. 'I thought I recognized the accent.'

'We should go. Salamander will be back very soon with her army,' stated the Mexican.

'Do you know where Libby is?' enquired Waxman.

'The girl?'

'A young lady about your age...' said Bomberger.

'She's in Mexico.'

'What?!' exclaimed Waxman. 'That's a game changer.'

'I can take you there, but it's risky.'

'You have a helicopter?' joked Sakamoto.

'No, but I know the way. There's a secret tunnel that we use for drugs and people smuggling.'

'Let's go,' suggested Bomberger. 'And no funny stuff.'

The three followed their captive down to the kitchen, the lights still all off and only a half moon to assist when clouds thinned out. Stopping at what looked like a pantry door, the three stared as a small torch flicked on.

'What now?' said Bomberger, aware of windows close by and dancing shadows outside.

The door opened to reveal a simple stairway going downward.

'Come,' said the young Mexican leading the way.

Bomberger felt a hand on his shoulder.

'Wait,' said Sakamoto. 'This could be a trap.'

'It's not a trap,' said their young leader. 'If you stay, you will be surrounded. Listen. This is a drugs trading route worth tens of millions of dollars. Anyone found here and threatening it will be toast.'

'Keep going,' said Bomberger following. 'I've never been to Mexico before.'

The tunnel was well made and about four-foot-wide by six high; dim lighting existed about every twenty feet attached to black conduit piping.

'How long does this take?' called out Sakamoto from the back.

'At a quick pace, about ten minutes.'

'Good. I can just about tolerate that.'

The Mexican laughed. 'Ten minutes to the border, and then another ten to the warehouse.'

'Who owns this warehouse?' said Bomberger breathing fast.

'Some drugs cartel, but it's never guarded that well because who would think a food warehouse is full of drugs. Clever, eh?'

'Yes,' admitted the boss, hating drug crime and itching to put people behind bars. 'So is Libby at the warehouse now?'

'There are a few girls at the warehouse. I don't know which one you want.'

'You don't know their names?' quizzed Waxman puffing.

'No. It's not my business. When we get to the other end, you are on your own. I cannot come with you.'

Sakamoto laughed. 'See, I told you. This is a trap.'

'But we can't return now,' admitted Bomberger. 'Also tricky, is how do we get back into the US? I don't have my passport. In fact, none of us have passports with us.'

'No problem,' replied the young Mexican. 'Do it the José way!'

'And what way is that?' asked Bomberger, also finding the pace tiring.

'The José way! I am José and welcome to my world.'

'Cut the crap,' interrupted Sakamoto. 'I've heard it all before.'

'Carry on,' said Bomberger with conviction in his voice.

'I can sell those night vision glasses for a good price so let's trade, yes?' said José keenly.

'What have you in mind?' asked Waxman.

'I can get you a flight back into the US.'

'Oh yeah,' said Bomberger. 'Unfortunately, I don't like jets.'

'This is a single propeller plane.'

'I'm not keen,' said the boss. 'It's a flying death trap.'

'Yeah,' said José, 'it does rattle a bit on take-off, but it's ok.'

'We'll be spotted on radar anyway,' concluded the boss. 'So we would be picked up quickly by the authorities... northside.'

'No, not so. You fly at twenty feet above the ground... jump up to fifty for five seconds to miss the border fence then down in to the car park at Ocean View Hills.'

'That will be very convenient,' added Waxman. 'Just where our taxi will be waiting.'

'Taxi?' said José. 'You also want a taxi? I can provide...'

'No thanks,' said Bomberger. 'We can order one. That's the easy bit.'

152

'So, we have a deal, yes?' said José keenly.

'Yes,' sighed the boss with the world upon his shoulders.

'Good. But the bad news is that I cannot go back to the ranch now. Plus, you will have to protect me at the warehouse. Ok? No protection, no flight...'

It was 11:16pm when the campervan slowed down to stop at the entrance of Sakamoto's rental. With the engine still running, Kramer spoke. 'Jayne. Pick me up at midnight. That should be plenty of time.'

They hugged briefly.

'Luis, please be careful.'

'Don't worry, I'll be waiting right here.'

'Ok,' she said looking and sounding pensive.

Kramer stepped out, winked and closed the door with care. There was no point waiting as her husband had disappeared into the darkness. Now moving quickly, with the distinctive sound of the campervan accelerating, he soon arrived at the front door. With an increased heartrate, Kramer stood listening. *What was the likelihood of Sakamoto being in?* he thought. *No lights on, no cars. And what would happen if he was in? How could he explain his actions? A father's desperation to find his only daughter?* So many questions and scenarios were running through his mind.

The steel crowbar rocked back and forth; the sounds of wood crunching and cracking during his aggressive assault. At last, the door sprung open and he was in.

The intruder was happier in the dark with his torch and so set about checking the house room by room, starting at the top. Most of the bedrooms were not in use, but he had come this far; it would be a pity to miss a vital clue.

Whenever he heard traffic passing slowly on the road, or a dog yap, he would go to the window and cautiously peep out. Ever conscious of the time, he crept along the hallway and now back down the stairs. The bureau was a nice piece of furniture that he'd seen briefly when entering, so made it top of his list. As he hunted for clues, a police car's siren could be heard in the distance. Kramer almost dropped his torch at the sound of a woman's voice. The central light came on to reveal a lady dressed in jeans, fancy Texan boots and a denim shirt, just sitting and rocking in a chair. 'Now who have we got here?' she said, looking amused. 'I was expecting the owner to be coming back from a Southerner's party. But what do I get instead? A common thief.'

Kramer was almost speechless as he scanned the two guards at the door, both showing handguns shoved down into their leather belts. He flicked his torch off.

'Come here,' she said beckoning with her finger, her voice almost hypnotic and controlling.

Kramer had little choice, so moved forward.

'Empty your pockets and show me what you've found,' her face and voice, firm.

'I'm sorry to disappoint you,' said Kramer. 'There's nothing upstairs,' he continued while turning his pockets inside out.

'But this is a mess in here,' she scowled, now standing to come closer.

One guard moved in support and arrived behind Kramer with his gun out.

'What have you found in here?' her tone slightly aggressive.

'It was like this when I arrived…'

'You're trying to tell me that it had already been ransacked?' she shouted. 'And how would you know?'

She slapped his face. 'Who are you? A friend of Sakamoto?' her eyes squinting. 'Maybe you are my enemy.'

'I don't know you,' said Kramer, still feeling the facial sting.

'Where is Sakamoto?' she glared. 'He should be here.'

'I don't know Sakamoto. I'm just a common thief who's down on his luck.'

She laughed. 'There's something about you I like, but a little voice inside my head tells me that you are trouble. Which is it?' she said, waiting for his answer. 'Are you good news or bad news?'

'To my friends I'm good news…'

'And to your enemies?' she replied coldly, 'bad news?'

Salamander paused. 'So, who am I then? Your friend or your enemy?'

'Neither, because I don't know you.'

'What's your name?'

'Luis.'

'Come on don't be shy, Luis. I'm not the bloody police!'

'Are we going to trade names,' he said, looking once again at the tattoo of a Salamander on the back of her hand.

She laughed insanely. 'If we were on a date, then yes that would be appropriate. But!' she said raising her voice, 'your only date is with death if you continue to play cat and mouse games with me. Have you got that, Luis? Now what's your surname?'

Kramer was just about to speak when he heard the campervan stop close by. Unfortunately, its distinctive and noisy engine was hardly providing a stealthy pick up.

Looking flustered, Salamander's pupils closed right down. 'Hey you,' she said pointing at the door guard. 'Go quickly and see who that is… and don't get caught unless you're tired of being on this planet. Go!' she pointed aggressively.

The house was suddenly plunged into darkness.

Bomberger and his gang had entered the warehouse where a frantic and wild scuffle followed a shootout. Searching through offices had revealed nothing, then Waxman thought he saw a draped cover over a large packing crate move. After further investigation, three girls were set free from wooden crates built like animal cages. With their tight gags removed, the escaping prisoners followed José out into the car park with Bomberger's crew covering. All entered a shabby beige Ford Fairmont.

'Before we go,' said José to Bomberger in the passenger seat, 'I must ring the pilot and negotiate.'

The rusty Ford took off with the driver holding the wheel and mobile to his ear.

'She will be in bed,' he said swerving to miss a dog.

'She?' said Bomberger, still trying to fasten his seatbelt in a slot filled with popcorn.

'I'm talking about the pilot's wife...'

'Oh,' frowned the boss with relief.

'She can fly as good as he can,' admitted José. 'The husband has a licence, but hers was declined. Poor eye sight.'

'That's comforting,' offered Waxman jammed in the back with Sakamotto and the three girls.

The call connected. 'Hey Maria... it's José.'

'I'm busy... what do you want?'

'Remember you said you owed me a favour?'

Driving with one hand, the other had to move the mobile back off his ear as she ranted. He now switched to his native tongue and spoke fast. Once the mobile had been thrown on to the dash board, he spoke. 'The good news is, she will do it.'

'The bad news?' said Bomberger.

'Just a small delay,' said José. 'Maria took sleeping pills.'

'That's great,' mumbled the boss.

'There's no other option,' said Sakamoto.

'How are you doing, Libby?' enquired Waxman.

'I'm so glad to be out of there. This horrible woman was giving me nightmares. She kept asking where my father was and trying to make deals.'

Sakamoto then spoke. 'Did she have grey blond hair with extensions, false eyebrows and tattooed sleeves...'

'Yes, and smelt like a cowgirl... breath like an ashtray.'

'That was Salamander, the psychopath,' offered Sakamoto. 'The crazy woman once shot her horse because she considered that its markings were bad luck.'

Jayne sat in the campervan and just inside the entrance to Sakamoto's property; her engine still running. Looking at her watch, she then viewed the house in total darkness. Biting her lip, her hand hovered over the car horn. *No*, she thought, it was gone midnight and didn't want any trigger-happy residents appearing. Feeling concerned, she moved through the gates and stopped as close to the front door as possible. Jayne cut the engine and stepped out. Instant shock as her wrist was grabbed. Her fear was made ten times worse by the fact no words were spoken. Shoved from behind, she arrived in the dark house with a racing heart. The lounge light flicked on. Relief and shock as she saw her husband kneeling on the floor and with a gun pointing at his head. Next, her attention was caught by the only other woman in the room.

'Hello,' she said slowly, walking over in a predatory manner, now circling. 'And who are you?'

Jayne looked at her husband... his ruffled hair and cut lip.

'Don't be shy and don't delay,' said Salamander. 'I always get there in the end... but it's late. What's your name?'

'Jayne.'

'Ok Jayne. Now you are about to get a gold star.'

She paused.

'Don't lie to me because I have gained knowledge from this man who calls himself, Luis. I know you know him, that's why you're here, isn't it?'

Jayne looked at the wall, the window and then at her husband.

'Isn't it!?' shouted Salamander, coming closer. 'Isn't it!?' now threatening a backhander.

Trembling, she nodded. 'Yes.'

'Good,' she said, pulling a closed smile that soon vanished. 'I like compliance.'

Still circling, now another question. 'I know you are husband and wife, so don't try and fool me again,' she said, grabbing her victim's hair from behind. 'You are due a haircut. I cut hair with a blunt penknife. Now do tell me,' coming around to face. 'What's your surname... and before you reply, he has already told me. Get it right and you have your freedom.'

She laughed. 'Then we can all go to bed, right? But hey girl, get it wrong and shit will fly like you've never seen shit fly before.'

Jayne was shocked and looked to her husband for comfort.

'What is your full name?' leaning in aggressively.

'It's ok,' said Luis.

He instantly got pistol-whipped and fell unconscious.

Jayne tried to move forward, but was blocked by her evil grinning tormentor.

'Your full name now!' she shouted at close range.

'Jayne Kramer.'

Salamander's face lit up.

'OMG! Well what do you know? I have hit the jackpot... and without Sakamoto's help... the useless idiot.'

She suddenly looked mad again. 'Tie them up, chuck them in the car and let's get back to the border.'

It was 1:50am as a light aircraft coughed and spluttered into life. All passengers were seated and packed like sardines in a tin. This was a low budget airfield – in fact, a farmer's field. Worse still, there were no runway lights, just some white-washed boulders that soon vanished up ahead.

'Ok everyone, ask no questions and I'll tell you no lies,' said their pilot, Maria, looking unkempt and yawning. 'I've got absolutely no idea why I gave up my bed, but I guess it's important for you. Obviously, you are criminals,' now laughing. 'You're in good company.'

'How long will this take?' said Bomberger, peering out and wiping dust off his side screen.

'Less than fifteen minutes,' she said, flicking switches. 'Into the US... out of the US... and into bed.'

A red plastic light cover dropped to the floor, 'Another job for me tomorrow,' she moaned, peering forward and wiping the inner screen. 'Come on, José. Hurry up!' yawning again.

Half a minute later and she could see his flashlight at the end of the runway.

'Ok, hold on tight,' she said, letting the brake off.

The plane juddered. 'Don't worry, it always does this.'

'When was it last serviced?' asked Bomberger at her side as the most privileged passenger.

'I said, ask no questions and I'll tell you no lies.'

'That's very comforting,' stated Waxman looking out sideways as white boulders seemed to accelerate by.

'Lastly,' she said. 'Under your seat you will find life jackets.'

'They won't be needed,' said Sakamoto. 'We're only travelling over land.'

'That's true,' answered the pilot, 'but on one occasion the tail rudder got stuck to the left sending us right over the ocean.'

'No way,' said Bomberger, wriggling in his seat.

She laughed. 'No, it didn't really happen. But a wheel once fell off. Now that was a tricky landing.'

As the plane bumped along, all could feel slight deviations from the center path. Bomberger gripped his lower seat with both hands to bring a greater feeling of security should they hit something. Turning halfway round, he spoke. 'Libby, have you ever flown before?'

'Yes, but only in a jet.'

'Jet's fly too high,' added their pilot. 'This is safe. Maximum height for this trip is about thirty feet. We need to stay under the radar.'

'But you can't see where you're going,' claimed Bomberger, feeling a light sweat.

I have memorized the route. Over to the left are the Tijuana lights and the glow on the horizon is Santiago. Once I leave the ground, please do not talk. I'm counting. It gives me the height and jump time when we reach the border fence. It's high and strong enough to stop a 747.'

Chapter 8

Area 51, Lincoln County, Nevada: Friday

A specially chartered jet had been organized through Janet Airlines to fly the US President and his friends directly into the highly secretive base at Groom Lake. The Commander-in-Chief and his Federal Reserve colleague had never had the privilege or time to visit, unlike Carrozza and Hauk. The President spoke as he looked out through his window. 'There's always a first time for everything,' he said, nodding and viewing hangers and other buildings. 'Before I got into politics, this place was always such a fascination for me,' he said with amusement. 'No wonder kids grow up in fantasyland; Batman, Ironman, Spiderman, the Hulk and all those other wacky characters.'

Carrozza smirked, 'You certainly won't be seeing any of those guys in here.'

Hauk spoke. 'Everyone remembers the film, ET. Children and families loved it. However, if that became reality, how would mankind see extraterrestrials then?'

'Certainly differently,' said Penniman. 'In fantasy, we see the innocence and fun in creatures that have been created in our image and, importantly, who act with feeling. Human feelings.'

Although keen and unbuckling, the plane was still taxiing. Carrozza spoke. 'Climate change will be hard to deal with when there isn't enough food to go around, but when knowledge of extraterrestrials is finally admitted in a Presidential crisis speech, that's when the world will change forever.'

Penniman sounded downbeat. 'I like being head of the Federal Reserve, but the consequential crash and problems that would be experienced around the world could be far more than I could handle… clever as I am.'

As usual, Bomberger arrived in the office first, yawning and slightly wobbly on his feet. Being the younger man, Waxman had dutifully volunteered to drive back to Ventura allowing everyone else to rest, especially Libby. The journey had been extended by stopping at the Kramer's home, but after finding no one there, it was decided that she stayed over at Waxman's house. Bomberger walked up to a row of vending machines and selected black coffee… no sugar.

Picking it up, he could feel his headache getting worse and walked to his desk. Placing it down, he spilt some. 'Boy, do I need a few days off,' he mumbled. 'This is total and utter madness,' now seating himself and booting up his computer.

Waxman showed up ten minutes later.

'What's your excuse,' said the boss, throwing his plastic cup in the bin.

'Flying by numbers shock, driving fatigue and lack of sleep.'

'Thanks for driving all the way back.'

'That will be easy one day with driverless cars.'

'How is Libby?'

'I didn't wake her. She's been through a lot.'

'Yeah, the poor kid,' said the boss.

'I left her a note to contact me if she needed anything.'

A pause. 'Sakamoto performed well,' said Bomberger tapping in on his keyboard.

'Agreed. I don't think that you and I could have pulled this off without him.'

'My sentiments too,' said Bomberger placing earphones.

Waxman now concentrated more on his own e-mails. The post lady arrived on her mail round.

'Thanks,' said Waxman and yawning. 'I must go to bed earlier... it's all these UFO reports playing havoc with my sleep.'

Bomberger was too engrossed. 'Waxman, I've got something from last night. Put your phones on...'

Minutes later, and the boss was scratching his head. 'This is stone-cold crazy. Kramer was at Sakamoto's place late last night when somehow Salamander turns up. Then quite miraculously, his wife Jayne arrives. Where the heck has she been hiding?'

Waxman looked thoughtful. 'An alien abduction?'

'Anything is possible in this crazy world.'

'The Kramer's sure have got some explaining to do. And who is paying that insane woman, Salamnder? She sounds like a nasty piece of work.'

'I've got a good idea,' said Bomberger. 'Let's get Sakamoto in here and see if he can help. And the last bit really bothers me... *tie them up, chuck them in the car and let's get back to the border.* Which border? Mexican.'

'Surely it's not the ranch we just raided?' frowned Waxman. 'What's going on?'

Bomberger rubbed his eyes. 'Kramer is central to all of this. We need to get him back here, screw him down on to a seat and get this thing sorted once and for all.'

There was silence for a minute as the two detectives played back the recorded event. Waxman released his headset. 'I just had a thought. Why don't we pay Fleming a visit?'

'Fleming?'

'The Private Investigator. The guy Kramer hired?'

'Ex-LAPD man?'

'Yes,' said Waxman. 'He may know something we don't.'

'Ok, so that's Sakamoto and Fleming to contact.'

Just as they turned back to their screens, the Department Chief stuck his head around the corner. 'Got a minute, Bomberger?' then vanished.

'Oh no,' he whispered, and rising slowly. 'Sounds like another damn job to investigate. I'm a bit too tired for this right now.'

Bomberger arrived in the Chief's office and closed the door. This was how the senior officer liked it. Total privacy.

'Take a seat, Bomberger.'

Sat behind his table, he paused. 'You're looking very tired and washed out this morning… is everything alright?'

'Yes. Waxman and I are working closely on the Kramer case. We were getting it under control, but a few complications and dead-ends have emerged.'

The middle-aged station commander didn't seem bothered as he spoke. 'That was always the story of my life when I was in your shoes.'

He paused. 'How is Waxman getting on? Is he going to make the grade?'

'I believe so. He's always thinking and doesn't seem to make any mistakes… plus, he has a good work ethic.'

'Good. And how's he getting on with the recent UFO activity in Ventura and surrounding areas?'

'To be honest, he's been giving me quite a bit of backup on the Kramer case.'

'That's what I want to talk to you about.'

'Ok.'

'Strictly between you and me, I had a visit yesterday.'

'A visit?'

'Yes, from the Men in Black, except they weren't in black.'

Bomberger obviously looked confused. 'Did they make an appointment, or just turn up?'

'The visit wasn't here as you may expect, it was at my home.'

'What did your wife say?'

'She was out. The one thing about the Men in Black, is that if you're on their radar, they'll know all of your movements... and in my case, family movements too.'

'What did they want?'

'Do you know what? By the time they left, I wasn't entirely sure why they came. But it has to be in connection with one of our investigations. I said I'd ask some questions.'

'Ok.'

'They're coming back next week.'

'Right.'

'They may even tap into the station's phone and computer network, so careful what you do... or say.'

Bomberger looked frustrated. 'Forgive me Chief, but I thought we were the good guys.'

'We are, but some subjects are very sensitive and connected to National security, etcetera.'

'I get that, but kidnapping, killing and drug running still need to be investigated, right?' said Bomberger, pushing his luck.

The Chief leant forward on his desk. 'Listen Bomberger, I want you to stop your current work on the Kramer case just for a few days and play catchup with Waxman on the UFO stuff. The state governor will be happy that all avenues are being covered and that his voters are getting their money's worth. That way, he gets re-elected and we still have our jobs and pension pots.'

'Just a few days then?'

'For starters,' stated the Chief.

'For starters?' questioned Bomberger and frowning.

'Yes. This whole episode will soon blow over and then we can all get back to relaxing and watching the LA Angels.'

'The Boston Red Sox, for me,' said Bomberger still confused.

'Ok, that's all,' then paused. 'Give me a UFO update report at the end of the week.'

Twenty minutes later, and Waxman drove back to his house after receiving a call from Libby. Bomberger decided to stay in the unmarked Interceptor and wait. Feeling more exposed to being spied upon, his eyes darted from the road ahead and then to the rearview mirror… back and forth as cars came and went. He even glanced sideways to look at houses and their windows. A curtain suddenly billowed from one, now anticipating a gun to appear. *God above! Calm down Bomberger, you fool. Men in Black don't want to kick your butt,* he thought, *well, not just yet anyway.*

At last, Waxman came out with Libby following. A short ride and they were at her parent's house. Bomberger walked to the front door. 'Actually, I do have a key,' he said, handing it over. 'I just thought it best you didn't stay here on your own.'

'Where did you get it from?' she asked, opening the door and going in.

'Your father gave it to me for safe keeping… just in case you came home.'

'Are you coming in?' she said, still looking tired.

'Thanks,' said Bomberger with one foot already crossing the threshold. 'We won't stay long. Just a couple of things to discuss if that's ok?'

Libby took a quick shower, and with some good advice from Bomberger, she packed a small case. The detectives had taken the opportunity to check the house and ensure the garage was secure. Once ready to move out, Bomberger had one final request. 'Libby, can we just have a quick chat?'

All sat down in the lounge. The boss started. 'I know we have asked many questions, but with your recent ordeal, do you want me to arrange counselling for you?'

'I don't know just yet,' she said, looking pensive.

'If you change your mind, let me know.'

Waxman looked sympathetic. 'We are going to drop you off at your aunts place where you can lie low till this whole affair blows over... and it will.'

'Do you still not know where my mum and dad are?'

Bomberger tried to be positive. 'We have some leads to chase up so hopefully they will be found soon.'

'What do I tell my aunt?'

'Whatever makes you feel comfortable,' replied Bomberger.

'Probably the truth,' added Waxman with a sympathetic tone.

'Can I ask you again about your kidnap ordeal?' said the lead detective.

'Yes. It happened in Ventura as we finished our shopping. Back at the car, two men arrived swiftly before we knew what was happening. I think they put us out with something like chloroform. The next thing I knew, I woke up with this weird woman's voice right in my ear. I thought I was dreaming. Then I felt a slap across my face and water hit me.'

'What did this woman look like?' said Bomberger.

'She had no accent, blondish, greyish hair with extensions and long green nails to match her eye shadow.'

'Anything else?' quizzed Waxman.

'She's about five-six, wears cowboy boots... and slim as a stick... even has tattooed sleeves.'

'Does she have a name?'

'I didn't hear one, but she has a bad temper. She kept asking where my father hung out and continually wanted to know what he did for a job. When I said I didn't know, she burnt me with her cigarette,' pulling up her top to show at least five red marks.

'She smokes?' said Bomberger.

'Yeah, like a trooper and never finishes them. Her breath is foul too and smells like an ashtray.'

Bomberger looked at Waxman. 'We need to bring her in as soon as possible.'

'Yes, she sounds like a fruit and nut cake.'

'Do you think mum and dad are also in Mexico?' she said.

'There is a chance of that,' admitted the lead detective.

'I just don't know what this is all about.'

'Ok, Libby, we need to take you over to your aunt's place.'

Sakamoto was up and still seething at the mess left in his lounge. He kicked a few things and continued out on to the rear patio where he found the swimming pool. 'At least they didn't trash this area,' he grizzled.

Sitting down, he contemplated his position and next move. His mobile rang.

'Hello.'

'Sakamoto?'

'Yes. Is that you, Bomberger?'

'How can you tell?'

'You sound like a policeman.'

'It is what it is,' said the lieutenant, riding as a passenger in the petrol blue Interceptor.

'Where are you? In Mexico and having a nice flight around the Teotihuacan Pyramids?'

'Fortunately not,' said Bomberger with relief, 'but Waxman and I are out in the car and thought we'd pay you a visit. A friendly visit of course.'

'Why? Surely you shouldn't be seen socializing with criminals too often.'

'An amnesty doesn't come cheap, remember?'

'I remember. But I think you already forgot how I helped you get Libby back. And to remind you that this involved travelling to Mexico. That was extra risk.'

'Come on,' laughed Bomberger. 'That was only a few yards across the border.'

'You broke the law,' said Sakamoto. 'Mexico was out of your jurisdiction and you know it.'

Ten minutes later, and Waxman turned off the road and pulled up at Sakamoto's house.

'At least I don't feel the threat of being shot at,' said the boss looking out at the five-bedroom building.'

Both stepped out and soon found their target sitting by the pool in his yellow palm-tree swimming shorts. While Sakamoto remained seated on his sunbed, the visiting detectives stood close by.

'Make yourselves at home. And take your sunglasses off... you look like the bloody Mafia,' said Sakamoto.

Bomberger pulled a small smile. 'We're way above the Mafia. We are the original Men in Black, except of course we dress down for our friends.'

'So, what can I do for you?'

'It's like this,' said the lieutenant looking more serious. 'We think that the Kramer's may have been grabbed and taken back down to the ranch or somewhere near there. Waxman and I are still on the case but have got something more urgent to look into for the next few days.'

'If that's the case, why are you wasting your time here?'

'We thought you may help us to identify someone by the sound of their voice,' said Waxman with his phone out.

The short playback started and was soon over.

'Yes, I know that bitch. She calls herself, Salamander, and is one ruthless mother. Mainly makes her money in drug dealing, but has a reputation in dark information.'

'Dark information?' added Bomberger, and frowning.

'Yes, information that should not be out in the domain. She's very good at it. The word is that she once worked for a national newspaper until over stepping her mark with fake news.'

'Interesting,' said the lead detective.

'That's why she set up the chain.'

'The chain of command?' said Waxman.

'Yes, an organization that in the first instance was involved in digging the dirt on people, mainly celebrities and politicians. Then moved quickly into drugs, gun running, people smuggling and, as I say, dark information. I was only a small cog in her machine.'

'That's all you were?'

'I did consider toppling her, but she's well organized and if I did manage it, then someone would soon be after me.'

'Very interesting,' nodded Bomberger slowly, and scratching his chin... now reminded that he'd forgotten to shave.

He had paused in deep thought.

'Listen Sakamoto,' he said, 'this could all be over very quickly, but we need your help...'

'My help?' he laughed sipping orange juice.

'Yes. If you can get Luis and Jayne Kramer back to us, I can close the case and you then just vanish and no more is said.'

'That's a big ask,' he replied. 'I don't have to remind you, but it's very dangerous. And now you say that you're too busy with something else. Does this mean that I'm on my own?'

'I would leave that up to you,' said Bomberger. 'Are there any disgruntled members in the chain that you could recruit?'

'I couldn't trust any of them. I'd be dead, quick as Jack shit. There is no allegiance in the criminal world. It's a dog-eat-dog world and where fathers kill their sons, kind of environment… you must know it… you're cops and not wet behind the ears.'

'I'll tell you what I can do,' said Bomberger. 'I'll get you all the equipment that you'll need, like, night vision stuff, guns without traceability, even stun grenades…'

Sakamoto laughed. 'You are more of a criminal than me!'

'No. I'm a collector. I buy a lot of this gear on the internet. Yeah, maybe some of it isn't exactly legal, but let's put it this way. I call it snooping to see what's out there and who's selling it. So, it's indirect police work. I have no guilt.'

'I don't know,' said Sakamoto. 'If I'm killed, you won't care. Just another criminal dude off the streets.'

'Ok, we'll leave it at that,' said Bomberger. 'But it's only a three-hour drive back down there. You know the place and have contacts…'

'Sure,' said Sakamoto, looking displeased. 'Go back to your cozy office, put your feet up on the highly polished desk that was paid for by the taxpayer and drink coffee till it pours out of your ears.'

The detectives were slightly surprised as he continued. 'Yeah, don't worry about Sakamoto, he'll have to take the heat and plan how to sort out your mess.'

Back at the ranch, the one who called herself Salamander had been strutting around the place; looking at all the damage and her dead guards and dogs.

'I want their heads,' she shouted, walking back to the house and throwing a cigarette down.

Two burly men followed. Salamander stopped and turned. 'And bring me the girl. I want her to see me execute her parents if I don't get what I want!' she ranted. 'No one messes with me.'

One of the guards spoke. 'I have just heard…'

'Heard what?' she shouted, and moving directly in front with her evil stare; her facial veins prominent, adding to her ugliness.

'The girl has escaped…'

'From where?!' she cried out. 'The cage? The warehouse? This shitty planet? Where where where?!'

'From the warehouse in the early hours.'

'Get me all those useless bloody people who should have been guarding her. I will teach them a lesson to remember!' her fists clenched and knuckles whitening.

'They are all dead.'

'What!' she screamed. 'Christ Almighty! They're so lucky… I'll get them in hell!'

Burning up, she went down the corridor and unlocked a door, her guards dutifully following. She faced them. 'Stand here and do what I'm paying you for. Guard!' came her shout.

Salamander entered and slammed the door.

'Ah, Mrs Kramer,' she said walking in fast to face her victim tied up in a chair. 'Bondage doesn't suit you, you do look tired,' stooping down. 'Is there anything you want? A taxi perhaps?'

'No,' sounding low.

'Oh,' said Salamander in a nonchalant tone. 'You're ok, are you?'

She paused before continuing. 'If there's one thing I hate,' she said with a bark to frighten her victim, 'and that is lying! Do you get me?'

Suddenly a quick slap. 'Liar! You're not ok. Why would you be ok when kidnapped and threatened by someone as horrible as me, eh? I bet you didn't know, but I now have your daughter,' she teased, 'but I can see in your face that you don't believe me.'

Salamander stood up straight and pulled out her iPhone before thumbing, sweeping and jabbing at keys. 'I'm going to show you that I'm not lying to you.'

The phone was turned and pushed in front of her victim's face. 'Look at this,' her own face one of delight as she enjoyed the resulting pain.

Libby was in full view and tied up much in the same way; it could have been the same room, the same chair and the same rope. Libby cried out as the cigarette burned her skin. Then quick as a flash, the mobile was shutdown.

'Now wasn't it kind of me to show you that. Every mother wants to see her child being treated reasonably. And why do I say reasonably,' she shouted, before switching to her sweetest tone, 'because we mothers care for our offspring, don't we, Jayne?'

The reply was too slow and secretly enjoyed.

'Don't we?' she shouted with her arm rising fast and ready to deliver a punishing backhander.

Jayne's head had moved back and her eyes closed at speed.

Salamander's laugh was quite crazy. 'For God's sake woman, anyone would think I was going to hit you?'

Jayne opened her eyes slowly, her tormentor moving behind.

'I don't like blood,' she said, pulling Jayne's shoulder length hair lightly. 'But hey, I do like cutting hair with blunt scissors. Now if you will kindly excuse me, I must pay your husband a visit.'

She paused. 'Can I give him a message from you?'

'Yes please. Tell him I'm ok. Thank you.'

'Sure I will. I'll tell him what you said, that you are not ok.'

Silence as she turned at the door. 'And what message for your lovely daughter, Libby?'

'Please tell her that I miss her.'

'I got that,' she winked. 'I'll tell her that you only asked after your husband. Hey, don't worry. We can all be forgetful. Libby's a sharp cookie and will understand.'

Sakamoto was still sat at his pool contemplating the raid, but not relishing such a dangerous mission on his own. Laid out peacefully on his sun lounger, he recalled the ranch layout; the crazy tunnel into Mexico and the risky flight back out. Amazingly it had touched down without crashing. Both eyes opened fast. A car had drawn up outside, so he automatically went for his gun. Stupidly, he had not brought it out this time. On full alert, the part-time gangster sat up and waited for evidence; evidence of an imminent attack or hopefully, something more innocent. A good sign; only one car door opened and closed. Then less than a minute passed before his front door was knocked several times. He could lay low or come out and face the visitor, the assassin, or perhaps his new found friend's, Bomberger and Waxman. But it was only one door, so he appeared from the side of the house.

'Yes, can I help you?'

The man turned. 'Sorry to bother you, but I'm looking for a man by the name of Kramer… Luis Kramer.'

'Why would he be here and who are you?' said Sakamoto approaching.

'I'm Jack Fleming and a friend of Mr Kramer.'

'But Mr Kramer does not live here.'

'Yes I know.'

'So?'

'So, he did leave me some details including addresses and this was one.'

'Are you the police?'

Fleming laughed lightly, almost with embarrassment. 'No, I'm not the police, just a friend. Just someone trying to help out.'

'With what?'

'It is sensitive and I have to be mindful of what I say and to whom?'

'You sure sound like a cop to me. Come on… come clean. Who knows, maybe I can help you.'

'Ok,' said Fleming, 'I guess it's only fair that you know, but I am a private investigator.'

Sakamoto nodded and laughed. 'I thought so. Have you got any ID?'

'Just a card,' he said going to his shirt pocket. 'For what it's worth, I'm new to the business.'

The card was taken. 'Who knows, Mr Fleming, I may need your services one day.'

'Just call me,' he said, turning to leave.

'Hey, wait a minute. So why are you here? Are you working for Kramer? Did he hire you?'

'Not exactly, but we met by chance. When I heard his daughter was missing, I said that I would help if I could… just a way of getting my name out there. It never was easy starting a new business. No one wants to give you a break.'

Area 51, Hanger 3

The base Commander was walking around and showing his guests their latest collection of military hardware. He looked at Carrozza. 'As you all know, this is Virgil's area of expertise.'

Carrozza acknowledged. 'Yes, I have always loved weaponry but this new Blue-ray laser stuff is the ultimate way to stay ahead of the game. Everyone knows it's not legal, but if there's a pre-emptive nuclear strike, then we'll shoot all the incoming missiles down and scorch our enemies wherever they hide.'

Carrozza then laughed. 'Who said the Star Wars programme had ended? Thanks Ronald. Good call.'

Moving on, they arrived at Room 12. Entry was only enabled by fingerprint recognition. The five-man group walked in.

'We call this our Gray area,' said the base Commander, 'and historically it has been evolving in different locations since the Roswell incident.'

The group's attention was drawn to several glass cases containing exhibits. Carrozza and Hauk had been to the base many times and seen this particular room, but the President had not; nor had Penniman ever had the privilege, or the misfortune. Both stood staring.

'Jesus!' said Penniman, 'I'd heard that these things existed but I didn't know we had hard evidence,' now walking forward to get a closer view. 'The damn thing is staring at me.'

Hauk was amused. 'It's just a model based on the Roswell crash victims.'

'That's right,' agreed the base Commander.

'Thank God for that,' replied Penniman with a hand on his heart. 'For a split second, the Federal Reserved just crashed.'

He paused when looking more closely. 'Did they really find bodies?'

'Yes,' replied the base Commander, 'but not intact. You have to remember it was a crash site.'

'Then, what you're saying is… that this really happened, not just a conspiracy story to debunk the church or all religions?'

'Correct,' added Hauk. 'We are not alone in the universe… in fact, very much a part of something bigger. Much bigger.'

'Hey Paul,' said the President patting his shoulder firmly, 'These beings… these things, they've always been here.'

'What?'

'It's a complicated story,' said the base Commander, 'but as the decades have passed, we now know this. Just as we have many different species here on Earth, so the same is mirrored out there. It's perhaps a bit scary until you get your head around it, but it's perfectly natural. Think of it this way. Here on planet Earth we have seven continents where many people live and in differing cultures. Just as Eskimos look different to Amazonian Indians, Europeans different to Chinese, Africans etcetera, so these beings also differ from each other.'

'Really?' said Penniman. 'Where's the proof?'

'We'll come to that soon,' said the station Commander. 'But just like nations here on Earth don't always get on, they don't either.'

Carrozza chipped in. 'We know that in times gone by, they were at war with each other. Scientists and explorers have found some ancient temples and unfinished structures… in a few cases, very heavy sections of granite strewn across the landscape.'

'And,' said the President, 'It reminds me how the Europeans fought over their colonies not so long ago.'

'We should never forget,' said Carrozza, 'it was our forefathers who did the same. They invaded this great land and claimed it from the native Indians as their own.'

'Yes,' agreed the President, thoughtfully. 'That's what our forefathers did. And if extraterrestrials decided to take over just as we once did... hey, that would be a bitter pill to swallow.'

'That it would,' agreed Hauk, looking closely at the gray.

Back in the office, Bomberger yawned and leant over. 'Looks like we have to spend the next day or so just tying up the loose ends on these UFO reports. Damn waste of time if you ask me.'

'And I have one here on a USO,' said Waxman.

'The Chief is balmy,' moaned Bomberger. 'Real people need our help and he's got us side-tracked with this garbage.'

'Some of it's quite interesting though,' said Waxman, flicking through an eyewitness's account. 'Look at this one from a trawler skipper just two nights back. He was fishing along the Ventura coastline when he saw a big bright light just under the waves.'

'How far from the shore?'

'He claims... approximately 400 yards out.'

Bomberger laughed. 'It was one of our subs practising with an illuminated decoy, a practice as old as the hills. While the enemy are distracted, the sub gets away.'

'Then this disc comes out of the sea and sits above the water for a minute. If that's not strange enough, three small bright orbs also come out of the water. They whiz around in all directions for about five seconds, then disappear rapidly into the mothership.'

'Mothership?' scoffed Bomberger. 'You sound so convinced. Are you sure you didn't write this stuff?'

'Then the thing zoomed up vertically at a phenomenal rate,' added Waxman looking bewildered.

'Huh! The captain was drinking rum. It's total nonsense.'

Silence followed as Waxman got engrossed in the same report.

Bomberger's mobile rang and noted the number was withheld. 'Hello.'

'Bomberger?'

'Yes, who is this?'

'Sakamoto.'

'What's new? And remember to only call me chief.'

'I'm going down to the ranch tonight. Are you coming? I need night goggles and your backup.'

'We could do this in a couple of days from now...'

'No, this can't wait. A quick counter attack is needed.'

'Yes, I know what's needed. Unfortunately, we're off the case to cover other urgent work.'

'Like what? What could be more urgent than this?'

'It's too sensitive. Sorry.'

If I say UFOs he'll laugh and my credibility will be gone. I'm not having that, thought Bomberger. *Anyway, it's not his business.*

'Listen Sakamoto, I know you understand.'

'No, I don't. I thought you wanted my help?'

'Yes, I do. And I'm sorry, but I don't have all the equipment that you requested.'

'If I go alone, there's a high probability that I will fail.'

'Just wait two days... there's strength in numbers.'

'I had a visitor today.'

'Oh yes. Who was that?'

'A private investigator by the name of Jack Fleming. Do you know him?'

'The name sounds familiar. What did he want?'

'He said he was looking for Kramer…'

'Kramer?' said Bomberger with surprise.

'Yes. Is Fleming legitimate?'

'I'll run a check on him.'

After Sakamoto had finished the call, he pondered the idea of going it alone, but the thought of getting caught by Salamander again was daunting. He went into the garage looking for things to take when he heard a familiar vehicle arrive. It was the velocity blue Ford F-150. In response, he moved out quickly where he saw Mondor stepping out.

'My God, look what the wind just blew in! Shit man, where the hell have you been hiding out?'

Mondor approached. 'I've been through some crazy shit that I just can't explain,' he said as they arrived together on the drive.

There was no handshake. To Sakamoto, it would be a sign of weakness, and friendly leaders rarely got respect.

'I never thought that I would be pleased to see you,' admitted Sakamoto. 'But I'll tell you something for nothing, Mondor… you look different.'

'In what way?'

'It's hard to say,' then Sakamoto laughed. 'You haven't had a spiritual experience… or near-death experience, have you?'

'When I remember, I'll tell you.'

A pause as both still looked at each other. Mondor continued. 'Now I'm looking at you and you've aged a couple of years. What have you been up to? Chasing women?'

'There's been no time for that. Listen, come inside. No, let's go and chill by the pool. We need to chat. Crazy things have been happening here too. I was kind of thinking that maybe you were somehow connected.'

Sakamoto sat on his favourite sunbed, Mondor on the next one. Mondor spoke. 'It's my observation that your character has definitely changed. You were always mad as shit, shouting and killing for virtually no reason.'

'I was, but now I realize that I was killing the wrong people.'

'Like César, the apprentice?'

'Yes, just like him,' said Sakamoto. 'When a mistake was made, someone always had to pay the ultimate price. That poor kid was in the wrong place at the wrong time.'

'Yes, just a young Brazilian like, Koga,' said Mondor.

Sakamoto frowned. 'And where the hell is, Koga?'

'If you remember, you said leave him in that coffin.'

'And that's what you did, right?'

'Yes,' agreed Mondor looking puzzled, 'but if you remember, when I returned, he had vanished. I was so spooked, I ran out of the pine woodland... my feet barely touching the ground.'

'We can't turn the clock back,' admitted Sakamoto, 'but listen, the chain is back on the Kramer trail. At last, we can get the job done. However, Salamander has flipped so much, that even you and I are in danger. She wants our guts for her savage dogs to enjoy. I've thought about it... we can't run... they'll track us to the ends of the Earth.'

'What do you suggest?' said Mondor looking concerned. 'I'm too young to die.'

'You drive us to the place where the Kramer's are being held and we get them back here.'

'But why? Salamander wanted them. That was the job.'

'I know, but just as the wind changes direction, so the world is constantly changing too. Come on. Let's get the gear ready. There isn't much time.'

'Where are we going?'

'To the San Vista Ranch near the Mexican border.'

'But the border is hours away?'

Salamander was no fool and had not returned to stay at the San Vista Ranch, but instead, at the much smaller ranch next door that her husband had acquired through money laundering. She stood on the veranda and alone as the sun was dropping down in the sky. 'Ok, it's time to go and be the worst bitch in the northern hemisphere,' now storming off and back into the ranch house. Once in, the guard locked the door and watched as she made her way along the corridor. Salamander stopped and withdrew a key. As the lock turned, she glanced back before shouting. 'Don't look at me, you fool, look out for the enemy,' she ranted. 'The vermin are everywhere. Do you want to end up like, Rio, swinging from a tree?!'

Once in the room, the door closed with a slam. Kramer was tied with hands behind his back and then to a steel wall-eyelet, the tethering too short to allow him to sit down. And just for further phycological torture was a chair so close by that he could touch it with his knee. Kramer had watched her walk over to a nearby table and pick up her cane. The woman with evil on her mind approached him slowly, all the time slapping the palm of her hand with the narrow weapon.

'So, Luis Kramer. I have you, I have your wife and I have your less-than pretty daughter.'

She then smiled after a stern face. 'That makes me the clever one, doesn't it?'

'What do you want?' asked her prisoner.

'What I want, Mr Area 51, is information. That's right. I want information that I know you have, because you have seen things that the rest of the world have not had the privilege to see.'

'What makes you think that?' he replied respectfully.

That remark brought a quick sharp whip to his left thigh. She enjoyed her power as she witnessed his face screw up with the pain. She shouted. 'Don't treat me like a fool! I'm giving you a chance. Further down the corridor is your wife. If you don't comply, I will arrange for her fingers to be cut off one by one until you tell me what I want to know.'

She paused to glare, her cane tapping on the floor at her own heart rate. 'One last chance to please your master, for it is I who decides whether you eat, sleep or die,' she said, starting to pace in a small circle and staring at the dusty floor. 'Ok, so now you work for me. Your pay… your reward, will be more than money can buy. It will be your freedom and to be reunited with your wife and daughter.'

Salamander stopped at the table and casually lit up half a cigarette. Remaining silent, she then picked up a photograph; something to provide further mental torture. *What was in the picture?* he thought.

'Hey Kramer, look at this,' she gloated, puffing out smoke. 'It's someone you know and someone that you like.'

She laughed at his facial expression once allowed to view for himself.

'You are cruel,' said Kramer struggling to release himself, 'Let her go,' still staring at Libby in a crate built from wooden timbers; much like a crude cage for a wild animal.

'I will, when you talk,' she said, throwing the picture on the floor like trash.

Still acting strangely, she stubbed her cigarette out.

'Ok,' said Kramer, 'ask your questions and I'll answer them to the best of my ability.'

'Oh good,' smiled his interrogator lighting up a new cigarette, 'Now you please me. That's rare for a man.'

Naturally, Kramer was steaming inside and just wanted this nightmare to end.

'Tell me where you used to work?'

'In Area 51.'

'How long were you there?'

'Nine years three months.'

'What was your title?'

'Manager…advanced weaponry.'

'It's a large base. Which section did you work in?'

'Hanger 3.'

'Now tell me. What happened in Hanger 3? You didn't play with weaponry all day. What else did you see?' she said, tapping the cane on her hip and moving closer to blow smoke in his face.

Kramer paused for a second and coughed. It was a moment too long. She whipped his left thigh again with a quick double stroke.

'I must tell you that I already know this.'

'How?'

'Remember someone called, Shahar?'

Kramer frowned; his response again was too slow. This time the evil woman brought the cane fast to his cheek, pushing it inwards to cause facial deformation.

'Again, you hesitate,' said Salamander with anger. 'Of course you knew him. Let me enlighten you… he is buried just a few hundred yards from here.'

She laughed. 'I can hear your pathetic cog wheels turning. Yes, clever boy, I interrogated him before carrying out his execution.'

Another pause to gauge his reaction. 'Kramer, you can carry on where he left off. If I get what I want, there will be no need for me to continue with this project.'

'Project?'

'Yes. Shahar gave me your name just a few seconds before he died. He claimed that you knew a lot more than he did... and why shouldn't I have believed him?'

'No reason. But I doubt that you ever met up with Shahar...'

'Why?'

'One day you might find out.'

'Stop stalling and trying to be clever,' shouted Salamander striking him with her cane. 'Tell me, Mr Kramer. What was in Room 12? A gray, a real gray that was captured after the Roswell crash?'

'No. I must add... that the word, captured, implies that live beings were taken from the site. The truth is that it was a recovery mission.'

'Therefore, a cover up,' she stated with probing and menacing eyes. 'The government didn't want the nation to know that we were being visited by beings from another planet?'

'I guess so.'

'This will please you immensely... I actually agree with you.'

Kramer was surprised by her sudden change of mood.

'Good,' she said, 'I almost feel like throwing my cane away.'

Salamander then laughed and started to walk as before; in a circle while looking at the floor. 'Tell me? What was in Room 13 that Shahar just couldn't bring himself to talk about?' her cane tapping her thigh as before. 'I think I know. I just want you to confirm it for me.'

She stopped, looked straight forward and then to the left at him, her eyes strangely evil. Her body caught up as she spun quickly to face him. Now the narrow cane was under his chin and lifting... worse, pushing into his throat. Kramer started coughing during the unpleasant ordeal.

'What was in Room 13?' her cane now removed.

'Just more of what was in Room 12. Put simply, the Roswell incident occurred in 1947 and was the first of its kind known to the US authorities. Everything was picked up and stored. Much of it was then examined.'

'And?'

'What I'm telling you is all well documented.'

'I know,' her eyes deeply penetrating, 'yes I know all about that... and reverse engineering to understand their technology. I must inform you that I was once a top reporter.'

'What happened?' said Kramer. 'You used these underhand tactics and got fired?'

Another swift whip to his left thigh. She laughed. 'Yes, it hurts in the same place doesn't it?'

'Perhaps if you could tell me exactly what you want to know, then maybe I can help?'

'Listen boy. We do everything my way,' she said, tapping the cane on his shoulder, sometimes his cheek. 'Back to Room 13. Be more specific about what was in there.'

'Room 13 was the autopsy room where anything unusual was taken for further examination.'

'Like extraterrestrials... and alive?' she said quickly.

'No,' frowned Kramer. 'Always dead. They always came in from the crash sites and dead.'

'What else was in there?'

'Just freezers to keep them stored.'

'What was next door in Room 14?' she said, looking down and starting her circling routine.

'Who said there was such a room?'

'Shahar. Your friend Shahar, said so.'

'When did you meet him? How did you meet him?'

'I ask the questions,' she said sternly, her cane pointing at his face with menace. 'What was in the room next door to Room 14?'

'It was my office.'

Chapter 9

The White House, Oval Office: Saturday

The President stood looking out of the tall window at the historical view of lawns, the elongated waterway and towering obelisk. 'I have enjoyed my mini break, playing great golf and reminiscing about times gone by. And I thought I knew all there was worth knowing about the universe. God bless America and God bless the Pilgrims who left Plymouth so long ago and found this wonderful land.'

'God bless America,' acknowledged his visitors as he turned to view them. 'And now I'm wondering if they actually found this great continent, or were they guided... just like the three wise men who followed that bright star to Bethlehem.'

'That's a deep question, Mr President.'

'Mr President!?' he laughed. 'Just call me, Hal,' now seating himself.

'Halleluia!' smiled Penniman.

'Amen,' said the President. 'Listen, Mr President is way too formal... even here in the Oval Office. And thanks for joining me on this old-boys trip. It sure gave you pleasure to see me in the bunker a couple of times. I thought I was in the Libyan dunes!'

Carrozza spoke. 'Hal, I speak on behalf of us all. We always enjoy your company whether it be work or clowning around on the fairway.'

'However,' said Penniman, 'I'm still haunted by what I saw in Room 15.'

'Room 16,' said Carrozza. 'Room 15 was an office occupied by a man by the name of Kramer.'

'Was?' added Penniman. 'That implies he's no longer there.'

'Yes, he left,' said Hauk. 'He was well respected, but when a work colleague by the name of Shahar disappeared in unusual circumstances, so questions were asked.'

'How do you know about this?' said the President.

'Because their internal police aren't super-hot. Anything odd happening on the Area 51 base is always flagged up for the CIA to investigate,' claimed Hauk smugly.

Carrozza nodded with amusement. 'The Men in Black with their own army of black vehicles, black choppers and dark arts...'

'That's us,' admitted Hauk. 'The very people that the general public view as suspicious, but if they only knew what we were dealing with, they'd respect us so much more.'

'Tell us more about, Shahar?' added Penniman.

Hauk obliged. 'Shahar was a very knowledgeable man who we recruited for Area 51. As a 42-year-old Israeli with secret-service background and no family, we borrowed him from Mossad.'

'Are you still investigating his disappearance?' said Penniman.

'Yes,' replied Hauk. 'We now know this. The Shahar we had working in Area 51, was not actually Shahar at all. The real Shahar never got here. There was a clever switch that we didn't detect.'

'Who was the Shahar you had?' asked the President. 'Surely not a Russian clone... therefore, the ultimate spy?'

'He was most likely an imposter working in one of the most sensitive Area 51 zones. So your guess is as good as mine. It's still a mystery and a National Security problem.'

'But I'm confused,' added Penniman with a deep frown. 'How did you know he was an imposter?'

'The real Shahar turned up in Israel,' said Hauk, 'and the day before Area 51 Shahar disappeared from the base. Furthermore, Israeli Shahar had complete memory loss. Mossad were afraid that they had been infiltrated, so questioned him under hypnosis.'

'Fascinating,' said the President.

'Yes,' replied Carrozza. 'Shahar's imposter was the spitting image of Shahar himself. Virtually a clone… maybe a clone.'

'My God!' said Penniman. 'Why was he in Area 51?'

Hauk nodded. 'They are everywhere.'

He paused before continuing. 'Paul, I hope the Federal Reserve is healthy…'

'Jesus, I feel it's about to crash.'

'Let me take you back to Room 16,' said Carrozza. 'That, *being*, that you saw in the glass case was not a replica for the New York museum or Madame Tussauds. No sir. It was real.'

'But it looked human,' said Penniman.

'Yes, it was,' answered Hauk. 'Everyone knows about grays but not this other species. And that's why Shahar was possibly there. An extraterrestrial in Area 51 to spy on our activities.'

'So where is Shahar, the extraterrestrial?' quizzed Penniman.

'Your guess is as good as mine,' nodded Hauk, looking tired, 'but now Kramer has become a suspect because he worked with Shahar.'

'The question that now begs,' said the President, 'is what did Kramer know?'

'I need to pull him in ASAP,' claimed Hauk, 'but he's done a vanishing act with his family, which is suspicious. However, we are acting on new intelligence right now. Things are moving.'

It was late afternoon, and Mondor was driving his velocity blue Ford-F150 with Sakamoto in the passenger seat.

'Hey Mondor, slow down. There's plenty of time. Don't get us stopped by the police with all this, bad-ass fire-power in the back.'

'If we get there early, we can have a rest. You know it makes sense... calm before the storm.'

'Slow down, man. Yesterday, we postponed because of the full moon.... but tonight, we have cloud cover and possible rain. So, it must happen without fail.'

'What are we up against?'

'The usual shit that we'd expect to find in the chain, except the one who calls herself, Salamander, needs to be dealt with swiftly, like cutting the head off a spitting cobra.'

'But I thought Salamander was some kind of mythical thing,' confessed Mondor, 'and if you think she's that bad, we may not make it back.'

'You can never tell,' said Sakamoto, cracking his knuckles.

'Tell me. What's in this for me if I escape with my life?'

'Would you prefer money or an amnesty from the cops?'

Mondor laughed. 'But you hate cops and cops sure hate you with your record.'

'Think outside of the box, Mondor. Some cops ain't too bad.'

'Shit!' exclaimed Mondor, swerving slightly. 'Have you had a near-death experience?'

Sakamoto nodded. 'Maybe I have Mondor, maybe I have.'

Bomberger cracked open a diet coke and leant back in his chair. 'All afternoon I've been looking at these two UFO files and it's driving me around the bend.'

'On the contrary, I find it interesting,' said Waxman, eating a biscuit with his coffee. 'I guess seeing is believing.'

A pause. Waxman continued. 'I was given a book on crop circles for a birthday present a few years back. Now that made me think. Sure, ninety-five percent could be explained away as hoaxes, but some of those circles were so sophisticated and large that no humans could have done them with such accuracy… and at night to avoid being seen.'

'I do admit, you do have a point, Curtis, but everyone knows that we are lightyears away from any similar planet to ours… so even if other worldly beings could jump in a rocket, they could never reach us.'

'What about wormholes, portals and the like? They may allow travel at the speed of light,' informed Waxman.

Bomberger laughed. 'Not if man passes out in a centrifuge pulling 5 or 6G. The speed of light would leave the astronauts eyeballs flat as pancakes at the back of their skulls…'

'Or,' laughed Waxman, 'bouncing back and forth on the brain like ping pong balls!'

'Now you're seeing sense,' said Bomberger taking a prolonged sip from his can. 'Talking of the speed of light, I'm going to give Sakamoto a ring and find out how he's doing.'

The call connected.

'Hello?'

'Sakamoto?'

'Chief?'

'Yes, it's the Chief. Where are you?'

'I'm on the devil's highway heading south.'

'Literally?'

'No, but heading to the San Vista Ranch. Somehow I don't think anyone will be there after we left a trail of destruction.'

'You never know,' said Bomberger with caution in his voice.

'Why, have you got some new information?'

'Unfortunately, not. Have you got support?'

'No. It's just me and my shadow.'

'Let me know how it goes.'

The call ended.

'Who the hell is Bomberger?' said Mondor, taking his eyes off the road.

'Just someone I met recently... someone that we could recruit.'

'He sounded like a cop to me.'

'Hey man, watch the road. This job is important.'

Salamander re-entered the bare room where Kramer still stood roped to the steel wall-eye.

'It's me again,' she said with her cane tapping her hand. 'I thought I'd give you a rest for a while. That's showing you how compassionate I am.'

'I would say thank you, but I don't like your hotel. No food, no water, no respect...'

Salamander laughed. 'But plenty of free entertainment... me!'

'That's rubbish too,' he said, testing her bad temper.

'I don't fall for your goading, Mr Kramer,' she said, standing back at arms-length and staring straight into his unblinking eyes. 'You are playing a silly game. You forget I have your wife and daughter. Would you recognize their fingers... if I brought them?'

'That's a cruel game... you're better than that.'

'I'm a cruel woman who always gets results.'

'Why not switch sides, I did?'

'What do you mean?'

'In the past, I worked with the CIA. With your knowledge, you could easily switch over and reveal who is behind all of this. I know what you want, but it wouldn't be wise to pursue this any longer. It's much bigger than you or I. You're way out of your depth, just as I am.'

Salamander's eyes had changed to a tight squint, her lips pursed. The cane tapping started. 'And why would I trust you?' she said in a blustery tone, the cane allowed to touch his shirt collar and drift slowly down to his belt. 'The CIA?! I don't believe it. Rubbish! You did not work for them.'

'How do you know what I did, what I saw and who I worked for in Area 51?'

'I can separate lies from the truth... it's in the body language.'

'Ok, so I tell you all that you want to know, then what?'

'Then the world will know the truth, Kramer,' she shouted, whipping his left thigh. 'It's time to reveal all...'

'What? On TV, in the newspapers? Who would believe me?'

'No one will believe you,' she said in a scoffing tone, 'but they will believe the President. Yes Kramer. When the President stands up there on his podium and tells the truth and apologizes for the thousands of cover-ups, then the world will tremble like never before.'

'Sorry, but I'm getting left behind here. I need you to enlighten me,' said Kramer still feeling the sting from the cane.

'The world is being visited by extraterrestrials!' she shouted. 'It's so well documented throughout the whole world and yet you people still cover it up,' her eyes mad. 'Why? Why? Why!?'

'If I were in your shoes, I would put two and two together and say, because the world we live in, the world that we've come to know... would literally fall apart. There would be mass panic and mayhem on such a grand scale, the predicted crash might be hell on earth spelling the end of civilization as we know it. That's the reality. Therefore, in summation, two plus two makes four... do you like the answer I just gave you?'

'I don't like your answer,' she glared. 'It's skimming over and trying to bury the truth. Come on! What's happening in hanger 3, Room 16? I've got the bone. You need to rapidly put some meat on it before I lose my temper for the last time.'

She paused and threatened a long stroke as the cane arced back for a sweeping strike. 'No luck with you then, you obstinate hell-bound mule.'

Salamander unleashed the cane at speed. Kramer's eyes shut fast and gasped as he felt the immense pain surging through his sparsely covered chest.

'You give me no choice,' she said, turning to leave. 'I'm just going to pay a visit to your wife and daughter now. Let's hope they aren't as stupid as you,' now reaching the door.

Without care, Salamander laughed. 'And don't worry, you won't hear their cries. They are a million miles from here.'

Mondor hit a large puddle as he drove into the Ocean View car park and found a corner spot. Despite the long journey, Sakamoto looked alert and ready for action.

'Where's Salamander's place,' said Mondor, switching off the vehicle's wipers before the engine shut down.

Sakamoto looked at his watch. 'Let's synchronize the time because we'll definitely have to split up. 7:32pm. Confirm.'

'It's too early to hit them,' synchronizing and confirming.

'We should've spent another hour at the firing range,' replied Sakamoto, looking out at the rain. 'It sharpens your mind.'

'Yes,' admitted Mondor, securing his waterproof camouflage jacket. 'And I love this Kevlar protection. It's a pity I can't wrap it around my head and face.'

A five second silence, both looking around. The driver spoke. 'What are you thinking?'

'I'm thinking… it's getting darker by the minute with more black clouds rolling in on the wind. We need to go out and do a scout job and see what's happening. Unfortunately, I can't even say that they're here for sure.'

'What did your cop friend say?'

'I didn't say he was a cop,' looking around the empty car park. 'You said he was a cop.'

Mondor laughed lightly while fitting a silencer to his gun. 'You would rather die in a stinking gutter than be a cop snitch, right Sakamoto?'

'Ok,' said the boss, his face blackened and looking pumped up. 'We're going now. Grab your things and be prepared for a tough mission. There will be dogs and bastards who want to rip your ears off. Let's go,' said Sakamoto, kicking his door open where light rain hit his body.

Mondor followed at pace as he tried hard to keep up. At the boundary fence, each climbed the slippery diamond-shaped wire mesh, pulling, grunting and heaving until tumbling over to drop nine feet on to a wet grassy embankment where both slid out of control in the semi dark. Jumping up, they ran, Sakamoto again in the lead and making for a wide tree trunk in the ranch's grounds. The rain had picked up, and as thunder rumbled overhead, water ran down their blackened faces. Sakamoto stood against the trunk and peered around to view the white-washed ranch house some twenty yards away.

'No lights on,' said Mondor, wiping water off his chin.

'Good observation,' replied Sakamoto. 'But don't be fooled. I was here recently on surveillance…'

'Surveillance?'

'Yes, killed a couple of crazy dogs and a few bogie men.'

'Bogie men?'

'Ok Mondor, this is where we split up. You take the front and work your way around. And listen! Find me... don't bloody shoot me.'

'I'll do my best... it is getting dark and the weather is crap.'

'I'm going to the rear. Check the windows. Don't be fooled by no lights on. You got it?' said Sakamoto peering out of his tight hoody.

Before Mondor could reply, Sakamoto was off.

Intermittent thunder continued, providing cover for heavy boots thundering onwards to the rear of the ranch where he knew the kitchen was. Anticipating dogs any second, his gun was ready and pointing in all directions at speed. Sakamoto found a window and peered in remembering the pantry door leading to the Mexican tunnel. Leaning against the glass, he stared intensely. As thunder rumbled over the coast, the sky lit up. In an instant, the kitchen illuminated, and like a ghost, Salamander appeared by candlelight. She was so frightened by the sight of the large dark hooded silhouette looking in, that she grabbed the pantry door at speed. Her hand with candle must have been holding something else. Its silvery surface flashed in a split second as it fell during another bolt of lightning.

'I remember that bitch!' he shouted, running to barge the rear door before firing a few rounds into the lock's mechanism.

Salamander was now on her hands and knees and searching frantically for something... but the pressure from the creaking and cracking door ensured she jump up and run for the pantry. The candle was thrown down in a last-ditch effort to delay the intruder's advances, followed by half a bottle of brandy that smashed on the stone floor. As Sakamoto burst in, flames flew upwards and across the tired wooden cabinets. His arm was up quickly to block the heat as he made his way swiftly to grab the pantry door... but it must have been locked or heavily bolted from the inside.

Mondor had worked his way around to the far side and, having met no resistance, shone his torch in every window.

Although the fire was taking hold and illuminating the room, Sakamoto didn't want the fire brigade turning up, so went for the light switch, but there must have been a storm power cut. Finding a fire extinguisher left his mind as the heat ensured he rush for the hallway door. During the act, he then part-skated on a small object that whizzed off at speed into the fire before hitting a kickboard and bouncing back out. Sakamoto spun and caught sight of the device as orangey flames danced and licked past it. Already halfway down in the splits, he rolled sideways and grabbed the slim device at speed; a burning sensation and smell of singed hair filled his nostrils. Seconds later, he was in the hallway and kicking doors open to search rapidly. Then sudden resistance as he was jumped from behind.

'Sakamoto?' a breathless and doubtful call in the dark.

'Yes, Mondor! Get off me.'

'I found her,' he replied letting go.

'Who?'

Mondor's light flicked on for three seconds to show a woman tied to a chair.

'Turn it off!' said Sakamoto with urgency. 'Don't worry, Mrs Kramer. We are on your side.'

'Please help me!' she cried out in the darkness and totally spooked.

'The place is burning,' claimed Mondor as the stench of acrid smoke moved down the corridor... his torch illuminating.

'The kitchen's going up,' replied Sakamoto cutting rope fast. 'We must go before a gas cylinder blows this place to hell!'

Suddenly, there was the sound of a large helicopter arriving over the adjacent ranch some two hundred yards away and with a searchlight powering down. Mondor rushed to the window to see rain sweeping through the beam. 'My God! There are men in dark kit whizzing down a rope like bloody ants on a string.'

'Come on,' urged Sakamoto, freeing Jayne of cut rope. 'This damn place maybe next.'

Running down the hallway with the orangey glow behind, the group leader slowed and pulled the front door open, his gun pointing. With pupils dilating and his heart thudding, he crept out with caution. Someone close by opened fire, the round slamming into Sakamoto's bulletproof vest. The sudden burst and thud in the chest ensured he dived forward on to muddy ground. In that split second, although Mondor was at the rear, he could see over Jayne's head and fired several rounds allowing Sakamoto time to recover and scramble behind a large shrub. In terror and with thunder rumbling overhead, Jayne slipped on the wooden steps as the military chopper hovered noisily in the background. Mondor took this opportunity to move out wide for a better view... and when lightning lit up the sky for just a few seconds, he released several rounds in a fast exchange until the villain pinning Sakamoto fell. Almost immediately, the desperate group made their way back, slipping, sliding and running through open ground until reaching the highwire fence surrounding the car park.

Hauk and Carrozza had arrived back at Groom Lake, Area 51 to spend some much-needed, catch-up time after their mini break with the President. The following day was to be their annual inspection and the opening of a new section. Certainly, the quarters afforded to these high-ranking men would have been seen as lavish and over indulgent to the outside world, especially by American taxpayers. But this was taken for granted as both men sat with their drinks and in deep conversation.

'Hey Carrozza, it's time you gave up smoking cigars. You look like Winston Churchill,' jested Hauk.

Carrozza scowled as he mimicked the once great leader. 'We shall defend our Blessed America, we shall fight on the beaches and fight in the sky, we shall never surrender,' a sip of whisky and a puff on his cigar.

Both laughed. Hauk spoke. 'Of course, Churchill knew that we were being visited. UFOs were seen all over mainland Britain in 1944. He then had secret meetings with MI5. Even met up with our old buddy, Eisenhower, to compare notes. I guess at first it was thought that Germany had some new technology. But they soon realised that this wasn't the case. The Roswell incident just a few years later confirmed what a select few were dreading...'

'That we weren't alone in the Universe,' added Carrozza. 'Do you think the President would be upset if he ever found out about our latest collaboration... with them?'

Hauk looked serious. 'The President has always been the nation's figurehead. He's the people's mouthpiece... the voice of America and the face of peace in the Free World. At the end of the day, he only needs to know enough to satisfy his curiosity. So, the less he knows, the more innocent are his answers when the muck raking press dig for dirt... and I mean, campaign dirt.'

Carrozza nodded agreeably. 'In the President's own words... keep it quiet, play it down and spin spin spin! Not that we need to spin.'

'It always surprised me that the night-time footage of eleven UFOs over Washington DC in 1952 never got taken seriously by the general public or the world. They were also spotted by air traffic control so there was no mistaking the event.'

'And,' said Carrozza lifting his finger, 'they all showed up in the sky one week later for the same reason.'

'Yes. Power. They didn't fear us or see the human race as a threat. Just out and about observing our lives... a bit like us studying gorillas in the jungle.'

A short pause, as Hauk continued. 'It makes you wonder where we would be today, if Kennedy had not wanted to know more about Roswell, the spacecraft and the grays. Personally, I don't agree that the President should be briefed in the first days of office about our extraterrestrial friends. Sure, tell him or her about any threats like North Korea etcetera, but draw a line in the sand when it comes to ET. I blame it on Eisenhower. He knew too much... he saw the grays in the glass cabinet and also the remains of the flying saucer. He was so troubled by it, he passed it on to Kennedy with warnings. No wonder JFK was so inquisitive. And if Russia had been a peaceful nation, then there would never have been a cold war or Cuban crisis. However, Kennedy wanted peace with Russia and no Third World War. Very gallant, but sharing our new alien technology with the Soviets was a step too far. But Kennedy pushed and pushed, then paid the ultimate price.'

Hauk's phone rang. 'MJ1'

'We have Kramer and he's alive.'

'Bring him to the base and let me know when you arrive.'

Hauk cut the call and spoke. 'Looks like we found our man.'

'Good work. Where was he?' said Carrozza.

'We knew he was down south on some ranch.'

'You must have spies everywhere,' added Carrozza sipping.

A smile from Hauk. 'Our agents have bugged his house and inserted micro homing devices in most of his clothing.'

Carrozza gave his fat cigar several quick puffs. 'I hope you haven't given me the same treatment.'

'Of course we have. If you get kidnapped, the Men in Black will kick ass and save your butt.'

Just before midnight, Mondor dropped Sakamoto off at his house and then drove Jayne back to her home. Feeling tired and barely able to keep her eyes open, she turned to Mondor. 'Thank you once again for all your help.'

'No problem.'

He paused. 'Do you want me to check out your place first?'

'I think I'll be ok… but thanks.'

'Sleep well.'

Once out, Mondor took off.

Approaching the front door, Jayne suddenly realized that she didn't have her key. In fact, she had nothing. At that moment, the returning wife could not recall when last having her purse or handbag. It was dark, she was cold and her thoughts started racing and spinning out of control. Feeling desperate, she rang the bell and looked in all directions, hoping and praying that the hallway light would come on and her husband, or daughter, appear soon. She shivered, then sat down on the step and slipped into a trance. And there she stayed until a car drew up several yards away. Its lights went out. Coming to, she looked up. The door opened and the curtesy light came on to reveal a man. It was hard to see who he was or to focus. As the door closed, so the light remained on. This person was approaching, his shape, large and imposing, somewhat threatening. Her heart started to pound; *should she make a run for it? Should she scream?* In that scary moment, Jayne had almost accepted the fact that her life was in danger once again. The mysterious figure spoke. 'You have nothing to fear. My name is Shahar.'

Chapter 10

Area 51, Zone 6, Conference Centre. 9am Sunday

Although Hauk was a very powerful man, he was short, so whenever the chance to stand on a podium presented itself, he grabbed the opportunity with gusto. In fact, he had ordered this particular piece of furniture especially for the occasion.

'Good morning gentlemen. It's great to see you all here for our annual MJ conference. Once, we were twelve in number, just like the twelve disciples, but we've grown as our responsibilities to create a safer world have grown too. Last year, I explained how and why the Men in Black were being strengthened and increased to cope with what is to come. You will be glad to know that we still lead the race to Mars which is very annoying for the Russians and Chinese, but hey, in this world there always have to been winners and losers. However, America is still top dog, and that's the way it's going to remain. To allow any other nation to take over would soon put the world in peril. World War Three would loom ever closer and we can't have that. Mankind already has new threats like the imminent return of Covid-19 in all its variants. But be warned... there will be worse things coming down the line. The brothers and sisters of coronavirus will be devasting. And as usual, the world has been fooled. This nasty pandemic virus was not engineered by man. It is the work of our extra special friends.'

Bomberger sat at his desk wearing headphones and listening for any signs of life or communication at Sakamoto's house. He sighed. 'Nothing doing. Damn, we need a break through.'

Waxman looked across. 'At least he phoned last night to say he had rescued Jayne.'

'We only have his word for that.'

'That is true.'

A brief pause. Waxman continued. 'We could pay him a visit and get all of the raid details. Perhaps even drop in and see how Jayne is. She will definitely be needing counselling.'

'As usual, I agree with you,' said Bomberger, standing up and throwing his headphones down. 'Come on, let's go out and do some real investigating. One more day on UFOs will kill me stone dead.'

Both drove to the Kramer's house, Waxman behind the wheel of their unmarked Interceptor. 'Jayne won't be in a good place having just had that ordeal. It's a pity we don't have Luis or Libby back to bring her a bit of sunshine.'

'Yes,' agreed Bomberger. 'I don't want the Chief breathing down my neck again.'

'Or mine,' said Waxman in sympathy.

Stopping outside the Kramer's house, Waxman cut the engine. 'All windows are closed. Why do I get the feeling no one's home?'

'Because you're a cop,' admitted Bomberger. 'You wait here, I'll go and knock.'

The boss rang the bell several times. He looked at the side gate and considered climbing over but thought better of it in broad daylight. *Too many nosey neighbours spying.*

He rang once more before rejoining Waxman. 'Ok, let's go and see Saka.'

As they sped along, Bomberger spoke. 'I suppose there is the smallest chance she stopped over at his place.'

'That's right. She was kidnapped and wouldn't have had a key.'

'Smart thinking, Waxman.'

Within fifteen minutes, the Interceptor turned into Sakamoto's property. There were no cars on the drive.

'That's not a good omen,' said Bomberger scratching his head and looking all around.

Once parked, both stepped out into the sunshine and strolled up to the front door.

'Your turn to knock, Waxman... I'm obviously jinxed.'

'Thanks for the privilege, boss. I hope I can please.'

On the third knock, the door opened.

'Hello Bomberger and Waxman,' said Sakamoto looking tired, a few evident raw scrapes on his face and arms. 'I hope you are here for a friendly chat and not to arrest me,' he said in mild humour.

'That depends,' replied Bomberger, 'on what you have to tell us.'

'I did the job, but fire away.'

'Is Mrs Kramer here?'

'No. She was dropped off in the early hours...'

'By you?' quizzed Waxman.

'No, by my driver. I had to have a driver on this job.'

'I thought you went alone,' said Bomberger. 'Who was he?'

'A guy named, Mondor. He's ok. Why?'

The boss nodded. 'We've just come from her place. She's not answering.'

'She's been through a lot and was under fed, under slept and probably took sleeping pills. I don't know.'

'Can we come in for a couple of minutes?' asked Bomberger looking around the garden.

'It's a nice morning, I'll come outside. We can sit by the pool.'

They ambled to the area.

'Do you want me to phone Mondor and check what time she was dropped off?'

'We will want to speak to him if she doesn't turn up,' informed Bomberger.

'What about my amnesty,' said Sakamoto. 'I kept to my side of the bargain. It was very dangerous.'

'Listen Sakamoto. It's not that we don't trust you, but we need to know that Mrs Kramer is alive and well.'

'What else do you guys know about the Vista ranch?' asked Sakamoto dipping his toes in the pool.

'What do you mean?' frowned Bomberger.

'There was some serious shit going on in the ranch house next door. In the lashing rain, a helicopter appeared with search beam then all these commando types dropped down a long rope, guns popping off, plus stun grenades. I thought maybe it was you, but on the wrong house.'

'No,' said Bomberger. 'It sounds like a smuggling gang being busted... maybe drugs or people.'

'Did you find out anything on Fleming?' asked Sakamoto.

'Fleming?' said Bomberger frowning.

'Jack Fleming,' said Waxman, 'the private eye.'

'Oh him,' said the boss. 'We've been too busy.'

Waxman laughed to himself. *Yeah, working on UFO reports.*

Jayne had slept well and woke up to hear a voice; a woman's voice. Opening her eyes slowly, she couldn't think where she was, but with a second call everything came flooding back. This curious man had stopped outside her house and, against all that she'd ever been taught, she had accepted his story and a lift to a safe house; a sanctuary, her sister's home. And now the door creaked open and a face appeared.

'Morning Jayne. Did you sleep ok?'

Bleary-eyed, Jayne half sat up as her sister came in. 'Someone's waiting to see you,' she said, looking pleased.

Libby appeared and ran in.

The Head of the CIA led his conference group out of Hanger 3 where they then boarded a coach for a short ride to Hanger 5. As the bus moved off, Hauk stood up. 'When you all return next year, the underground will be finished, but be warned. If you take a wrong train, you'll end up in Moscow chatting to the KGB.'

The nineteen strong group laughed and chuckled. Hauk loved the moment.

Two minutes later and they arrived.

'MJ19... Majestic brothers, I welcome you all to Hanger 5,' said Hauk stepping off.

All followed and entered through a door. This hanger had much larger sliding doors that were closed and for good reasons. As every man came through, they stopped and formed a semi-circle with Hauk in front. 'Gentlemen, when we pass through this next door, I want you to imagine that you are not here on Earth but, instead, stepping out on the far side of the moon. Yes, it will be dark when I shut the door behind us, but this is for realism.'

He paused and smiled. 'Anyone want the bathroom? We won't talk about you.'

There were no takers.

'Ok, follow your leader.'

All went through into the pitch-black hanger, Hauk in front. Everyone shuddered as the door shut behind with a hefty clonk. Hauk laughed. '*They* always shut us in,' he said.

'*They?*' someone whispered.

'Yes,' came Hauk's voice. 'And don't whisper, *they* have bionic hearing. Speak normally... to whisper is rude and suspicious.'

There was total silence as the group suddenly became aware of their own increased breathing. Now something was moving, the sound coming from overhead. The whole party looked up to see thousands of stars in a night sky.

'Jesus,' said someone in awe.

'Follow me,' said Hauk. 'If you can't see, just follow my voice.'

After twenty seconds, their leader suggested that they stop. Now an eerie sound came from behind them, a low frequency hum to ensure they turned.

'Jeeeze!' someone said, 'the hairs are standing up on the back of my neck.'

Now stars were being blanked out as something strange moved slowly towards them.

'Holy mother...' uttered someone craning upwards. 'Which way for the toilet?'

Amid the shuffles as all looked up, someone got touched and let out a short-spooked sound.

They all knew the object by the stars blanked out. A flying saucer. And as if this wasn't scary enough, two white orbs caught their attention and some way off. These objects were moving and progressing slowly but then took off at great speed turning at ninety-degrees, looping and spiraling; even joining to become one. Then two more appeared and pulsating; there for a second, and vanishing to reappear somewhere else. The group were gasping at the frightening display, some thinking what amazing technology, others now utterly convinced that extraterrestrials had landed on Earth. Without warning, all four orbs vanished into the flying saucer. Feeling some relief, many were heard to exhale and half laugh nervously, but then six lights burst on from the underside of the mysterious object. The group had ducked down in fright and brought their hands up to shield. Now a horizontal door opened on the underside before extending down to reveal a figure standing there and quite still. The group shuffled backwards but were stopped by an invisible barrier.

'Oh my God!' murmured someone. 'We're trapped.'

'Shit,' cried another, 'you're standing on my toes.'

Hauk, who stood bolt upright looked mysterious in the light emitting from the curious doorway. 'Excuse me gentlemen, I will be leaving you for a while. Jack Fleming will look after you.'

As Hauk stepped on to the platform, Fleming stepped off. The under door closed and the lights extinguished before the object disappeared leaving the group very shaken. In the darkness no one knew what to expect. One thing was for sure, the stars still twinkled way above. But even they now faded away. A door behind them opened, the very same door that they'd entered through. No one wanted to be left behind and almost tripped over each other as they made for the exit door. Once out in the sunshine, the previously jovial group looked pale and shocked.

'What the hell was all that about?' said one, dusting down.

'I don't know… where did Hauk go?'

'Back to the dark side of the moon, I think?'

'And who was, Jack Fleming. He's not in MJ19.'

'Shit,' someone exclaimed. 'Where did he disappear to?'

Another laughed nervously. 'I know we were all spooked, but that was one amazing Disney show. I can't believe I fell for that. We must congratulate, Hauk. Damn, that was clever.'

The two detectives were still talking to Sakamoto by the pool.

'You need to get your hands on, Salamander,' said Sakamoto, 'If you want to bring this crazy game to an end.'

'Who is she?' said Bomberger. 'Where does she fit in?'

'She's top of the chain. Get her, and you will get the one who is responsible for all of this. But you need to be ultra-careful. This woman is ruthless and involved in kidnap, people smuggling and drug running.'

'We need more to go on,' added Waxman. 'We aren't exactly filling up the cells.'

'I could help you a little bit more,' offered Sakamoto.

'That's wise,' said Bomberger, his eyebrows raised. 'You know withholding information is a felony.'

Sakamoto withdrew something from his pocket.

'What have you got there?' enquired the boss, perking up and looking at Waxman. 'Salamander's mug shot and new address?'

'I don't know,' he said dead pan and throwing the device in Waxman's direction.'

The small object was caught.

'What is it?' said Bomberger craning to view.

'A half-melted memory stick,' said Waxman with his hand opening fully.

'Where did you find it?' asked Bomberger still looking and now taking the evidence.

'At the ranch raid. Salamander dropped it when escaping.'

'Good work, Sakamoto,' said the boss. 'Carry on like this and you'll be promoted to station Commander very soon.'

All 19 visitors had left the hanger and boarded a coach that took them to lunch. Due to the unsettling event in Hanger 5, most enjoyed beer and wine at the table. One member leant over to speak quietly. 'This place is stir-fry crazy. I still don't know what that was all about. Was that a real flying saucer?'

'Don't worry, Hauk will explain this to us later on when we go to Hanger 7 and see the tank project.'

'The tank project? What is that? A new tank that can fire shells across to North Korea?'

'No. We already have Tomahawk cruise missiles.'

Forty minutes later and the same coach dropped the Majestic visitors off in the sunshine.

'Here we go again,' said one, mopping light sweat from his brow. 'I must see my doctor when I get back. My knees are knocking and my aging heart's fluttering like crazy.'

This elite group now walked in through another doorway; this time led by Fleming. Just as the door closed automatically, the lights dipped low... very low.

'Ok,' said Fleming with his back to a door. 'This will be a new experience for you. Some members may have heard of the tank project. All I can say is that it is unique in the world. I should know, because I've travelled extensively and seen every square inch that there is to see. We have given Google map technology to you and so much more.'

'Holy smoke!' came a whisper right at the back. 'What is this guy? An extraterrestrial?'

'Who would ever know?' said Fleming, creating uncertainty. 'Follow me.'

From one darkened room to another, although this time down a stairwell first and along a passageway. The group stopped.

'Why are the lights so low, I heard someone say? It's to allow your pupils to dilate further. Also, as you pass through into the next room, take a set of glasses and place them immediately. Otherwise, you may think that you have been blindfolded. You will not see anything and, consequently, the sounds may spook you. Is that clear, Majestic brothers?'

The group murmured in agreeance; others still whispering.

All nineteen men were ready and fitted with their special glasses as they walked single file into the next room. Now the penny dropped for all; this was no land tank with mega barrel but, instead, a giant water tank displaying the side of a ship, mostly submerged but with a waterline. This heavy fabricated section carried on for some distance each way that soon faded into blackness.

'What is this?' whispered someone in his lowest possible voice and expecting a colleague to answer.

'This is what *we* are doing here in your oceanic world,' said Fleming looking toward the man who posed the question almost in silence. 'Keep watching and don't blink.'

The 19 visitors stared through the thick-plate glass into the water where an artificial seabed had been created several yards below the keel line. Within seconds, something whizzed by from left to right... almost like a smokey apparition. Two frogmen soon appeared and following with air tanks streaming bubbles. They stopped and attached a magnetic mine. The dull clonk was heard by all. No sooner had they disappeared under the keel, eerie high-pitched sounds almost dolphin-like could be heard.

'It's the moment you've all been waiting for,' stated Fleming.

No one had removed their eyes, such was the tension created after the flying saucer show earlier. Swimming in at speed, came two elongated figures, but this time without air tanks or wet suits. Wearing no flippers or goggles, they stopped, removed the mine and took off vertically, bursting out of the water like racing dolphins, but not to return.

'Jeeze! What the hell was that?' gasped one.

Just as the group moved to within a couple of feet of the thick plate glass, the two burst back into the water and arrived at their position so fast, that the group all jumped backwards; some nearly falling over each other. MJ19 stood in awe as the beings remained there with their partially webbed fingers on the glass. These frightening divers were expressionless, scaly, had large fisheyes and stood at least seven foot tall.

'God Almighty!' said one visitor. 'I heard the stories... but...'

'Yes, Fleet Admiral Johnson, you did hear the stories,' said Fleming as the two divers disappeared, 'you heard the stories from other trusted naval men such as yourself, but never believed fully. Seeing... is the ultimate proof that mankind is not alone in this grand universe.'

Bomberger and Waxman had good reason to dash back to the office. A memory stick that had once been in the possession of Salamander could provide the breakthrough they'd been waiting for. The boss issued his orders the very second they entered the office. 'Hey Waxman. Grab me a diet coke from the vending machine and I'll get my computer booted up.'

'You must have shares in this stuff.'

'Bomberger?' called out the station's Chief seated in his office. 'Have you got a minute?'

Bomberger stretched over and hit the power button fast. He grimaced and muttered under his breath. 'Damn it! I've only got two hands. That's all God gave me.'

Arriving reluctantly in the office, he closed the door.

'Have a seat. How's the Kramer investigation progressing?'

'Hmm... sorry to disappoint, but it's a tough one.'

'Bomberger. You are my star detective. What's happening? Are the crooks getting too smart for you?'

'It's the old story, we just need a breakthrough.'

'How are the UFO cases progressing? Seems to me that every year there are more sightings. Either the nation is going ga ga, or we are being visited for sure. What do you think?'

Bomberger laughed respectfully. 'If I said we're being visited, I'm certain that you would give me a month off and a ticket to see a psychiatrist.'

Walking back into the office, Waxman looked up. Bomberger rolled his eyes. 'He's wasting my time again. Keeps asking me about the growing number of UFO reports in the vicinity.'

'He may have a point. I haven't been here that long and I've noticed an increase.'

'Oh no, not you as well,' complained Bomberger, placing the memory stick. 'I'm surrounded by believers in garden fairies.'

'Why don't you run me a copy from the memory stick,' asked Waxman keenly. 'I have a spare just here.'

'I thought you preferred UFO bull?' chuckled his coke swilling boss, now watching his screen with excitement.

Kramer had slept well and knew most of the buildings in Area 51. He had a few theories as to why he was there and spoke as his cell door opened. 'Now where to?' he said. 'The Supreme Court for my trial?'

'There's a car waiting outside for you,' said the guard.

'Could be worse, I guess,' now walking out in his kaki base kit. 'I'm surprised they still had my old stuff here,' he mumbled.

The car took Kramer past familiar buildings and to a place he knew well. As he stepped out alone, the driver spoke. 'You are expected. Room MJ1.'

'Thank you.'

Kramer walked up the ten steps to the top where he was saluted. Into the building he went and to an office that he had visited before and not so long ago. He knocked.

'Come in.'

Entering, he saw Hauk sat behind his desk and still writing. 'Have a seat, I'll be with you in a moment,' said the Head of the CIA barely looking up.

Kramer sat down with a straight back and chose to view the walls and their content, more so with his eyes than the obvious head movements. Hauk's pen went down.

'Welcome back, Kramer... and in your work clothing,' he said leaning forward. 'We were all sorry to see you leave.'

'My time here was rewarding. I learnt a lot, and I made some good friends.'

'Yes, some of them miss you for sure.'

'That implies some of them don't miss me.'

'I wouldn't worry about that, Kramer. It's the same the world over.'

'Since I left here recently, my life has gone crazy. My wife and daughter have been kidnapped... I too have been the victim of the same people, I know it.'

Hauk sat there staring and without expression.

216

Kramer continued. 'How did you know where to find me?'

'You know what they're like. They will find you when sensing danger. They are your protectors... the watchers.'

'I've worked here long enough to know what's going on, but this recent activity leaves me believing that not all is well at the base.'

Hauk smiled. 'And that's what I like about you, Kramer. You were always the sharpest pencil in my box. When you left, the programme seemed to falter.'

'Falter? How?'

'When you were the head of the Hanger 5&6 programmes, everything seemed to be running smoothly. You were the cement that held it all together.'

He paused. 'The big question is, would you come back? We want you, *they* want you.'

'To be honest, if I don't find my wife and daughter, I don't have a future anywhere. I may as well be dead.'

'Family is vitally important. There are many here who consider this to be their family. We all talk the same language. We all know what's going on here. It's wonderful, Kramer. Rejoin us and make history.'

Hauk was looking ecstatic. 'Luis, I know that you're a man who can keep a secret, right?'

'Yes, like all Area 51 staff.'

'Listen Luis,' and sitting forward to lean on his table. 'I would love to tell the world that I, Kevin Hauk, is the first human-being to ever land and walk on Mars,' looking expectant.

'Really?' said Kramer looking doubtful.

'Yes, no shit.'

'I know we have the technology...'

'As acting base Commander, they wanted me to be the first.'

'How long did it take?'

'Just two days,' Hauk's eyes glinting.

'Two days?!' uttered Kramer in disbelief.

'But how did your body tolerate the G-force?'

'Only they know how. It was something they did. All I did was show up?'

For the first time, Kramer smiled, although briefly. 'How can you be sure that this wasn't some sort of trickery? Sure, we work with them just like we work with the Russians, but do we really trust them? If crunch came to crunch, what would happen if their leaders suddenly turned up with a new agenda?'

Hauk nodded with a pulled smile. 'And that's where we part ways, Luis. They've been here since the Roswell incident all those years ago. We have given them friendship and access to our planet and they have returned our kindness with their weaponry and flying saucer technology. We are the winners, don't you see? They favour us over the Russians and Chinese. Their ancestors gave us the English language... that's why it's so wide spread. Can't you see?'

'You know I share your enthusiasm, and I like those who work with us in Hanger 5&6, but sometimes I just don't know if I'm doing the right thing for mankind.'

Hauk looked excited. 'Kramer, if I take you to Mars, will you come back and join us? Just stop and think, Luis. Mars... the red planet.'

'Of course, I'd love to, especially with Shahar... but,'

'Shahar has vanished. Listen, there are other extraterrestrials in Area 53 that you have not met yet. They are the caring type and ultra-intelligent.'

'Where are they from?' quizzed Kramer. 'Europa or Sirius?'

'Who cares,' said Hauk, still looking keen. 'They love us.'

'I'm sorry to disappoint you Kevin, but I don't have a burning ambition to visit Mars anymore. I just want to be a family man again... to go walking, surfing and enjoy the freedom that comes with less ambition.'

It was 5:10pm as Bomberger finished a short photocopy run.

'How's it going Waxman?'

'Working on a Sunday isn't fun, especially with the big boss floating around.'

'Yeah I know,' whispered Bomberger; now in a louder voice 'Found anything?'

'I'm still tracing these payments to Salamander's account. If we can find the person who paid her to carry out the kidnappings, then we have a chance to solve the mystery.'

'I like that,' said Bomberger, picking up his can to sip the last few droplets. 'Then we stop working such silly hours.'

'Yes,' said Waxman. 'The Red Sox are playing tonight.'

'And that reminds me, I must have a clean pair tomorrow,' admitted Bomberger.

'Have a look at this.'

The boss arrived. 'What is it?'

'Salamander's account shows money flowing in and out like water. It's very busy and is certainly busier than mine. However, there's quite a lot coming in with the ID MJ21. What is that? Mick Jones... and what does 21 refer to? A twenty-one year-old drug dealer?'

'Your guess is as good as mine?' said Bomberger.

Kramer had been allowed to return home after his nightmare ordeal. None of it made much sense.

A short flight back to Ventura and then a cab dropped him off. Entering the house, the first thing was to try Jayne's mobile, and then Libby's. With no response, he sighed heavily and went to the kitchen and flicked on the kettle. His phone rang.

'Hello…'

'Luis, it's Jack. I've been trying to get hold of you.'

'Sorry, I've been away…'

'How are you?'

'Depressed. I've just got home and the girls aren't here.'

'I have good news for you.'

'Really? I can't wait…' he said sounding brighter.

'Go to your front door.'

The doorbell rang. Kramer nearly dropped his phone and ran. True enough, his wife and daughter were stood on the doorstep and understandably looking a bit tired. He swung the door wide open. 'Jayne and Libby!' his arms out.

As they entered, all three were soon in a hug-trio.

'How did you get here?' said the father and husband, kissing them in turn. 'How did you escape?'

'Jack's been great,' said Jayne, 'I'm sorry that I ever doubted him.'

'I really owe him big time,' admitted Luis, now hugging his daughter. 'I've missed you so much, Libby.'

'I thought I was going to die,' she said, starting to sob.

Salamander wasn't happy and glaring at her guard.

'Why am I in Mexico and living in this makeshift hovel with a corrugated roof that leaks? I'll tell you why, you worthless piece of wet garbage!' she shouted at her restrained victim. 'Because you failed to look after me on the ranch. That was my safe-haven. And it grieves me to spend money on having you fixed up in hospital,' now tapping his chest wound with her cane. 'Since you're back in the land of the living, tell me once more what you saw?'

'There was some crazy shit going on at the ranch... wind was blowing, rain slicing down...'

'Rain doesn't slice,' she grizzled. 'Don't give me ideas because I have a love affair with sharp scissors. And so, why did you stop guarding Kramer?'

'When a black helicopter arrived like a demon in the dark sky, I ran away and across to the Vista ranch. I knew you would be there with Mrs Kramer. I came around the front of the house and saw Sakamoto coming out with two or three other people.'

'Who the hell were they?' her stick under his chin to lift aggressively.

'It all happened so quick. I shot Sakamoto. He went down.'

'Sakamoto!' she said, glaring. 'There were no bodies found. Now I'll have to pay him a visit before someone spills my blood. That is such an inconvenience.'

Bomberger was on the phone.

'Thanks for your call, Kramer. I think we should come straight over and see you all. There are many loose ends to tie up.'

'Please can we delay for just a few more hours... they are so tired and still sleeping.'

Bomberger frowned heavily during a pause. 'Ok. In that case, perhaps you would come and see us first.'

Twenty minutes later, and Kramer walked into Ventura police station before being directed to an interview room.

'That's great news about Jayne and Libby,' said Bomberger. 'I wish it was us who had found them. What's the story?'

'In a nutshell, it was Jack Fleming, the private Investigator who found them.'

'How?' said Waxman.

'Sorry to be vague, but when I got back home, they had just arrived and were very tired.'

'Ok,' said Bomberger, looking slightly doubtful.

'I'm sure Fleming will be in contact,' said Kramer. 'Then we'll have the full story.'

'If it's just a missing person's report, that will make my life a lot easier,' added Bomberger pausing.

He then cleared his throat. 'Luis, this is off the record and you don't have to answer, but we have some delicate questions.'

'I'll do my best.'

'We know that you worked in the Area 51 complex,' claimed Bomberger, now a small smile. 'Hey,' his hands up. 'I don't believe in grays or flying saucers, but I thought I'd get that out first.'

'It's a subject that interests many,' stated Kramer.

'I sit on the fence,' added Waxman. 'Who knows what's going on in this big wide world?'

'Ok,' said the boss. 'We have been scratching our heads about this whole affair, your kidnapping, your family's abduction, Sakamoto and other things.'

He winced with bridged fingers and looked up at Kramer sat opposite. 'We just sense that Area 51 has something to do with it. Your unfortunate experience may have a connection to what goes on there or perhaps there's some vindictive element. That's where we are.'

'I can't see any reason for it to be vindictive,' said Kramer shaking his head and looking mystified. 'I haven't upset anyone.'

'What do you know about MJ21?'

Kramer didn't look surprised. 'MJ21? Have you ever heard of MJ12?'

Bomberger looked over at Waxman, who shook his head. 'No, I've never heard of MJ12 in the sleepy City of Ventura.'

'MJ is the selected abbreviation for Majestic. Twelve relates to the number of its membership. This was set up a long time ago. I don't know much about why they exist, only that they did.'

'Did... or still do?' enquired Bomberger.

'We want to know who MJ21 is?' said Waxman. 'It is possibly the key to solving this dastardly riddle.'

'I can make a call for you, but I can never reveal the source.'

'Ok,' said Bomberger. 'How soon?'

'Give me twenty-four hours.'

'And when can we come and see your wife and daughter?' asked Waxman.

Kramer looked hesitant. 'Here's the deal. I will find out who MJ21 is, and for this, don't interview Jayne or Libby. Just let it be.'

'But...' started Bomberger.

'You will be opening a can of worms,' said Kramer looking serious. 'Your names will be flagged up on the CIA's data base. The Men in Black will appear and shut your voices down with all sorts of threats. Sometimes, things are just too big to deal with. Remember JFK? He thought as President that he could do as he pleased. Others had different opinions. The rest is history. My advice. Keep your heads down and look forward to your well-deserved retirement.'

Early evening, and Sakamoto was playing chess with Mondor by the pool. Out of nowhere, Salamander appeared with two bodyguards holding guns. Her smile was small, false and pulled for the occasion. 'Inside, you pigs. We have unfinished business.'

Urgent gun waving indicating they move quickly or suffer the consequences. Sakamoto didn't like being threatened, especially on his own property, albeit, rented. Once herded in, she made them sit down in independent chairs and with her armed stooges stood behind.

'Let's start with you, Sakamoto. As a key chain member, you have failed me dismally. And you know what?'

'Yes,' he butted in. 'You hate failure. But listen to me good. You failed. Maybe you should have spent less time on your green nails and crap make up... and it's about time you cleaned your stained teeth.'

She glared with fury and signaled. Instantly, Sakamoto was pistol-whipped from behind. Still reeling with pain, he spoke. 'As I was saying... and your grey hair looks crap too with those cheap blond extensions.'

'Shut up!' she shouted with rage.

'Ever had a date?' he laughed.

'Sakamoto, you have a big mouth. Pity you don't have the brains to know when to keep it shut. I know you have changed sides and betrayed me, but even I, the shrewd Salamander can forgive... if I want to.'

'As I'm going nowhere,' and looking at blood after touching his head, 'I guess there's no harm in listening to what you have to say. Who knows, maybe you can tempt me back.'

'Listen to me carefully,' she said, walking slowly around in a circle before him. 'When you foolishly raided the Vista Ranch, you took something of mine and I want it back,' her hand out and fingers beckoning fast.

'What was it?'

She stopped, stooped forward and glared. 'Don't play cat and mouse with me!'

'Ok. So, you want me to deliver the Kramer's back to you?'

'Too late for that now!' she shouted.

'What then?'

'You broke into the kitchen and found my memory stick on the floor... I know it.'

'You are mistaken... the place was on fire.'

'I saw you through a gap in the pantry door. You picked it up.'

'Do you want the good news or the bad news?'

Salamander cussed and cursed. 'Sakamoto! Stop this shit. Where the hell is it?' her teeth clenching.

'The good news is that I don't have a computer. The bad news is that my friend does, so I gave it to him.'

'You damn fool!' cursed Salamander. 'Phone him now!'

'If you insist,' he said with a hand sliding into a side pocket.

'Careful,' said the guard from behind and shoving his gun's barrel against Sakamoto's bleeding gash.

Sakamoto tapped in a number. The call connected.

'Hello. Is that you, Chief?'

'Sakamoto?'

'Yes. Listen. You know I found that stick and gave it to you? Can I have it back. I located the owner and they are here with me and offering a reward. A very big reward.'

'Really?'

'Can you bring it over to my place now? It's urgent and you must come alone. Do not contact the police.'

Bomberger did as instructed. He left his dinner on the plate, drove to the station where he picked up the stick from his drawer. There was no way that he could have swapped it for another, the manufacturer and wear marks were too distinctive and probably well known to its owner despite the partial melt zone.

Fifteen minutes later, he turned off the road and drove up to the house.

Strange, he thought, *no other vehicles. Perhaps the visitors took a cab.*

The detective stepped out and walked to the door, casually dressed in old jeans and a faded blue denim shirt. After knocking, he was ushered in by a gun-waving guard.

'Have you got a licence for that thing?' said Bomberger.

Once inside, he could see that it was a situation of control. Sakamoto remained seated as the second gunman came forward to frisk him.

'Who do you think I am?' he said, looking at Salamander. 'A damn cop or something? Get real. I'm not a loser.'

'You better not be a cop,' she said, squinting her eyes and trying to read his body language. 'What's your name and where is my stick?'

The daring detective smiled and engaged with those fiery eyes. 'Call me Bomberger. And listen. My parents taught me manners.'

'I don't care, Bomberger... and what sort of name is that?' she scoffed.

'There's no need to get personal. I thought you wanted my help?'

'Just give me that stick,' she said with pursed lips and a hand out at speed.

'So, who are you?' demanded Bomberger.

'That's none of your business.'

'You sure are an angry person. Can I help? I'm a paramedic, my mother and father were both phycologists.'

'I don't take no shit from a man like you,' she said angrily and hating the loss of power in front of all. She nodded at one of her guards. Instantly, he fired a shot over Bomberger's shoulder that then took out a wall light; glass flying. Bomberger had hardly moved, just shut his eyes and waited for the thud and thrust of penetration. Opening his eyes, he stared at his aggressor. 'He missed. Personally, I would sack him on the spot.'

'Hey, stupid!' she shouted with a deep scowl. 'Where is it?'

'That's an interesting question,' he goaded calmly.

'I must inform you,' said Salamander pointing rudely. 'It's very easy to search a dead man's pockets... and let me tell you something else. It wouldn't be my first time...'

'But,' interrupted Bomberger, with a finger up to match. 'It's not so easy to ask a dead man why he never brought the stick in the first place, is it?'

'Puh! You think you're smart.'

'I am. Look,' he said, pulling out both pocket liners to flap like dog ears. 'There's nothing but yesterday's fluff, a sign of poverty.'

Fully out, Bomberger looked down and flicked each in turn. He then laughed. 'I suppose you want me to pull a white rabbit out next?'

Salamander caught a few smirks. She exploded with rage and walked fast to her closest guard. 'Give me your gun.'

Halfway through presenting it, the weapon was snatched. She moved quickly towards Mondor who remained quiet and seated. 'Hey, do you like walking?'

Before he could answer, she shot him in the thigh. Mondor gasped in pain but this never deterred Salamander as she turned on Sakamoto. The gun flew up and aligned with his face. 'Do you like talking?'

Bomberger shouted. 'Wait! I have it. It's in the car. It's in my paramedic bag on the back seat,' he said, throwing her the keys.

'I love it! I love controlling you men,' she gloated. 'Huh! You think we women are stupid and don't know what's going on. I have news for you, Bomberger. When I get that stick back, you are dead!'

A window smashed and startled the group. Half a second later, a shot was fired making everyone stoop before diving for cover... except Mondor, who sat in his chair with eyes squeezed shut and praying. A gun battle followed.

Chapter 11

Two men sat in deep conversation about their futures, each having differing views in relation to how the world should, or shouldn't be.

'You know what, Virgil?' said Hauk standing and walking over to his window. 'When things get a little heated, it's time to step back and look and see what a wonderful world this is. Just think, we are sitting here in comfort on a spinning globe that is hurtling through space and on a massive journey around the sun. It's incredible. And to consider that we are a minute speck in our own galaxy, I think it's incredible that we've been found.'

Carrozza nodded. 'It is incredible how everything works like clockwork. Certainly, we need all that nature can give us but, in reality, nature sure doesn't need us. If the human race died out tomorrow, the planet would carry on regardless. The only thing to stop it functioning is when the sun burns out in six billion years from now.'

Hauk returned to his chair. 'Virgil, I just got to say that of all the men on this earth, I respect you the most. You're a man with compassion and yet you are highly respected as second in command of all US Forces. It goes without saying that I need your support even more now.'

'Kevin, as you're the Head of the CIA, I will do my best to support you. And yes, sure we do have a few things we disagree on... but that's life.'

'Virgil,' said Hauk looking down at the table, then back up. 'I know this will come as a shock, but I want to stand for President. Will you give me your unconditional support?'

Carrozza was surprised by this revelation. 'My God, Kevin. I never thought I'd hear those words come from your lips. Are you serious?'

'I certainly am, Virgil. It's been a dream of mine for decades,' he confessed.

'I thought you would stay in your position until retirement.'

'No. I want to become President. I know I can do that job. I'm the man who can see both sides of a coin at once. Where Kennedy failed, I want to be the one who brought mankind together with his long-lost brothers.'

'You don't mean to expose the truth, that we are not alone in the Universe? Surely not.'

Hauk nodded. 'Yes Virgil. It is the only way, for if I don't do it now, when *they* decide on arriving in bigger numbers, we will have no control. We will become subservient... the underdogs.'

'But...'

'But, if it comes from the President, the world will listen, just as they did when we dropped those atomic bombs.'

Carrozza looked out of the window, his thoughts swirling like never before. 'This will be opening Pandora's box. Once the lid opens, it will never shut again. If you leave things as they are, we have a chance to announce things in a different way. For you to stand up on a podium and tell the world that extraterrestrials have been living on earth alongside us for years, decades or centuries will spook the world's population. Life as you know it, including the markets, the power and the control, will all crumble.'

'Virgil, I see your concerns, but listen. This is a journey. Man has always come up against brick walls. Look at our history. Don't you think that intelligent beings could show us a new and better way forward?'

'We could debate this for weeks, months or even years. I can't imagine changing my mind.'

'When I'm the President, I'll be the convener, the ultimate peacemaker. I'll make it work for all mankind.'

'If you take up that position, there will be a gaping hole in the CIA at the top. Who's going to fill your shoes and take the reins of a million wild horses?'

'I'm working on a replacement team right now,' said Hauk.

'No one from my vast network I hope?'

Hauk laughed. 'Kramer would be number one. The head of ET advancement into society.'

'Kramer?' said Carrozza. 'Is he up to it? You're making a big mistake.'

'Yes. I've put him and his family through the standard CIA test for those at my level.'

'You don't mean your unorthodox tests? No one in this world would put family members through such torture,' said Carrozza in dismay.

'Sure they would,' smiled Hauk.

'Come on Kevin, you're losing the Presidency before you've even got a single vote.'

Hauk laughed. 'It's ok, Virgil. The family passed with flying colours. We are all winners. The kidnappers couldn't get them to talk and then my boys flew in and got Kramer out. A great raid and good practice for my crew. All I've got to do now is float the idea to Kramer. He'll come back. Every man has his price.'

Bomberger sat at his computer typing out a report.

'The pain of my life,' he sighed and turning to Waxman. 'That was good timing on your behalf last night.'

'I could see things getting out of control and fast.'

'Yes. Salamander definitely hated men,' stated Bomberger. 'I thought I was going to be dead in seconds.'

'Funny thing,' said Waxman. 'I still don't like killing women, but I saw no choice. She was going wild.'

'Every day the chain gets shorter. We'll never find out who's pulling the strings now. Mondor and Salamander have gone. That just leaves Sakamoto,' said Bomberger.

His mobile rang. 'Hello.'

'Chad, it's Kramer.'

'Luis, did you get the information?'

'Yes. I was shocked. Best we meet up. Let me know when.'

The call was short and ended.

'Interesting,' said Bomberger, looking over at Waxman. 'It looks like MJ21 has a very high profile. It could be a person or even an organization.'

'Interviewing the remaining bodyguard isn't going to reveal him,' stated Waxman. 'Besides, he's possibly still in a coma.'

Bomberger rolled his eyes and picked up his diet coke. 'Wait until our Chief gets this updated report. He'll go ballistic. More dead bodies at Sakamoto's place.'

Hauk was still at the Area 51 base and talking on the phone. 'Shit! Listen. You need to cover our tracks fast before someone puts two and two together and knocks on my door. That just ain't gonna happen, do you hear me? All evidence no matter how small and insignificant needs to vanish.'

'What about the chain?'

'Break it up into the smallest pieces. Melt it down until there is nothing left. No houses, no cars, no fingerprints or DNA that could lead back. Got it?'

'Yes sir!'

Carrozza had been over to Hanger 3 where his interests were in the latest weaponry development. As second in command of all US Forces, it was imperative that he remained completely up to date.

'How was it?' said Hauk, leaning back in his chair.

'I'm always impressed,' he said sitting down, 'but equally, always thinking where is this undeclared experiment leading us to? What if…'

Hauk laughed, placing his hands behind his head. 'A wise commander with so much power at his fingertips, still asks the question, what if? Take my advice, Virg. Don't even go there.'

'But you know me, I'm a deep-thinking man.'

'Listen Virgil. We have nearly a hundred of them working with us every day on new technology.'

'New technology for them, maybe. But we haven't caught up with their old technology yet. Please just allow me to finish before you butt in again. Consider this. Who has the greatest wisdom and know-how? You or them? It's ok, I'll answer it for you. Them. How do you know what their ultimate intention is? Why do you think it's good? You and I know how a double agent deceives. It's rife in our own culture. Tell me why these beings wouldn't be here gathering data to report back on us. Yes, you think that you have all their new gadgetry to help us rule our fellow human beings, but the extraterrestrials are the Trojan Horse,' he said leaning back. 'Sorry, but that's where my thinking takes me. A cautious commander survives to fight another day.'

Hauk nodded without smiling. 'I'm sorry that you feel this way, Virgil. There always has to be trust. When the First and Second World Wars ended, all sides signed the peace treaties. When you got married, both sides accepted each other. That's the way it is.'

'But we are dealing with beings from who knows where?'

'I told you before,' said Hauk sounding frustrated. 'They are not visiting us from outer space. Many of them have always been here. They never left.'

'How do you know?' said Carrozza. 'Where's the proof?'

'Intelligence as always. Their bases are under the sea.'

'I don't have to remind you, but the oceans of our world are vast. We know more about what's on the moon and Mars than down there.'

'Virgil. At least I can agree with you on this point,' admitted Hauk. 'And listen. I have something else that you ought to know.'

'Oh yeah? I'm not sure I want to hear this.'

'When I become President…'

'If you become President.'

'When I become President, I will announce to the world that it is true, there have always been cover-ups regarding flying saucers and visits from extraterrestrials. The way in which it's announced is critical, and so I propose a fly-over Washington DC at night just as it happened way back in 1952. Just as Truman covered it up, I will go down in history as the first President to settle this once and for all… that we are not alone in the universe and that these beings are, in actual fact, our distant cousins.'

'Cousins?' half-laughed Carrozza. 'There will be mass panic across the world. How will you deal with that?'

'We've started that part of the programme already.'

'How?'

'It's true, Covid-19 isn't man-made or engineered. 'It's the product of our friends. They have done it.'

'What?' said Carrozza looking annoyed. 'You mean this is a deliberate act?!'

'Yes, I'm afraid so. Just like in war... and you should know this well. Remember that saying... cannon-fodder? Those that have died, have gallantly paved the way for the biggest ever lockdown ever known. Sars, Covid-2 and Mers have been the forerunners as we ramp up to this next level. Numerous lockdowns have been practiced and accepted. We may have to have much more virulent strains in the future to ensure total control when announcing the truth. That's how I will be accepted so well. Just like the messiah sent to save the world. The vaccines will appear quickly and confirmed as developed by our new friends.'

Carrozza closed his eyes for just a second as he shook his head. 'I don't know, Kevin. It sounds like a disaster for the human race.'

'It will be a bigger disaster if everyone wakes up one morning to see hundreds of flying saucers and their motherships have arrived. That would be an outright confrontation. Us against them. Don't you see that my way is peaceful and ensures that we join and accept these beings?'

'The resistance will be huge,' admitted Carrozza. 'If Nations on Earth can't get on, how do you expect the human race to accept an alien race living along side? Whose rules would we abide by? What would you do if they said they suddenly wanted the USA for themselves and we got kicked out?'

'But they wouldn't.'

'Huh! I love your confidence, but you forgot how the people of Diego Garcia got pushed off their island so that we could have it as prime territory. Yes, the Brits helped too, but as you know, it's our military base now. What if these beings have enemies on other planets? Kepler 186F, for example. Could the US become the new Diego Garcia?'

'No. Never.'

'Have you forgotten our forefathers arriving in America and pushing all the native Indians on to reservations? Look how they have lost their culture and way... wearing baseball caps, eating burgers and drinking coke. These beings could mirror our actions or just kill us off like the dinosaurs.'

'Virgil, you're overthinking this massively. Listen to me. Just like Truman announced, project Bluebook... so I'm going to announce, project Greenbook. It will be our green light for, Go. How would you like to help me construct it? I would greatly appreciate your input.'

Bomberger replaced his phone. 'I have just heard that Salamander's bodyguard has passed away. The circumstances are suspicious and it looks like we have to investigate.'

Leaning over to Waxman, he continued softly. 'He was a chain member, so I say we just do the bare minimum, take a few notes and then call in on Sakamoto.'

At the hospital, it was a done and dusted event. A forensics team were about to start and there was nothing else to see apart from a deceased body and tubes pulled out and hanging. 'Hopefully, there's a corridor video,' said Bomberger. 'Come on, let's go and pay Sakamoto a visit.'

Just as they arrived, another car followed them in and parked alongside. Out of curiosity, both turned sideways.

'A black car, and with blacked out windows,' said Waxman, looking back at the house, then to Bomberger. 'Friends of yours?'

'I don't think so,' looking at the garden and subtly checking his gun placement. 'Come on, Waxy.'

They both stepped out.

Bomberger said nothing and walked towards the front door, Waxman following. As they did so, they heard several doors behind opening and closing. Glancing back, they noticed four men walking their way. The boss spoke. 'CIA... Men in Black.'

'Who do they want?' said Waxman like a ventriloquist. 'Not us, surely?'

Bomberger knocked the door and rang the bell. 'First come first serve. And get ready to draw in case they're hit men.'

The boss knocked again as the group of four arrived close by.

'No answer,' said the first with a stern face, black framed sunglasses; the others like peas in a pod.

'That's right,' said Bomberger, 'No answer. Do you want to try?'

'Ok, that's it,' said the first. 'Guess you'll be leaving now,' looking back at their Interceptor.

'Not quite,' said Bomberger in a slow and deliberate manner. 'We are visiting by invite. The owner's possibly in the swimming pool,' moving away.

'No. That's really not advisable.'

'Oh, why is that?' continued Bomberger, looking mystified.

'Because I said so and that's good enough.'

'Not in my neck of the woods, it isn't.'

'So you run things around here, do you?'

'Yes, you could say that. Why, who are you?'

'That's not your business right now.'

Bomberger smiled. 'Ok, I guess you are small-time private investigators trying to earn a crust.'

'You're too cocky and ask too many questions. I suggest you move on. And remember this. You did not see us and you are banned from here. Got it?' said the leader, leaning in.

'That's classic CIA bullying tactics,' said Bomberger looking at Waxman. 'They tried it on the people of Roswell in 1947 after the incident. Yeah, told folk who saw the dead bodies and crashed saucer that they didn't see anything and were never to speak about it.'

'You sure are a mouthy individual. If you're a cop, show me your badge.'

'Yes, on the condition that if you are CIA, show us your ID's.'

Both Bomberger and Waxman produced their badges and held them up.

'I thought so,' said the leader. 'Small-time Ventura cops doing nothing all day but getting fat on biscuits and coke,' now viewing Bomberger's protruding waistline.

CIA badges appeared.

'It's like a game of poker,' said their spokesman confidently. 'You've got all the aces, but we've got a Royal flush,' now leaning in. 'So, detectives, Waxman and Bomberger, it's time you left the party. Take some good advice, Lieutenant. Change that stupid surname of yours and, who knows, maybe you will get some credibility. Oh, and one last thing. There's a good gym down on the High Street… but don't jog too fast, you just may miss it. Now run along.'

'Don't worry, we're going,' said Bomberger, 'smells like a pig farm here.'

Both arrived at the Interceptor, stepped in and closed their doors. As the four stood at the door ringing the bell, Waxman spoke. 'Wow Chad, I've got to say you have balls of steel.'

'That's why I never run anywhere. I just shoot the enemy with bullets or punchy words.'

'I loved the way you turned the game around without taking the shit. It was pure magic.'

Still in view, the leader looked down at the Interceptor and, in particular, to Bomberger who then spoke. 'Sitting here is winding that knob up like crazy. I know what will happen. Word will get back and I'll be called into the Chief's office to explain.'

Sakamoto appeared at the door and within ten seconds, all had vanished inside.

'What now, Chad?'

'I say we sit and wait. We are within our rights to be here on investigative work. When they go, we pay a visit.'

Waxman startled Bomberger. 'Quick, Chad! If you've got that receiving device, we can listen-in right now.'

Bomberger grimaced. 'Damn, it's in the office.'

'Oh, that's bad luck,' sighed Waxman, as he viewed the vehicle with its blacked-out windows.

The disappointment didn't last long. A gun battle broke out in the house. Both went for their guns and crouched down fast in their leather seats. Bomberger spoke. 'Four against one. I guess we won't be speaking to Sakamoto again.'

'Yeah, and we don't have to arrange his amnesty now,' offered Waxman, deep in thought but still peeping over the dashboard.

The gunfire had lasted about ten seconds.

'We could circle the place,' said Waxman.

'We could go home and watch the Red Sox on your TV.'

'Now you're talking, boss. We did work the weekend.'

'But,' said Bomberger, 'I don't trust these guys. I don't know their agenda... they could frame us and pin Sakamoto's death on us.'

'That's not good for my pension,' added Waxman.

'And no good for my marriage prospects,' offered Bomberger.

Both circled the house before finding Sakamoto sitting with a guest by the pool.

As Waxman and Bomberger appeared, Sakamoto went for his gun.

'Whoa there!' said the boss with his hands flying skyward. 'That's enough shooting for one day.'

'We saw you both arrive,' claimed Sakamoto, 'but then those bastards turned up.'

His companion nodded in silence.

Sakamoto spoke. 'This is Lieutenant Bomberger of Ventura police and his colleague, detective Waxman.'

The visitor spoke. 'Jack Fleming. Private investigator.'

'Glad to make your acquaintance,' said Bomberger, now with his thumb pointing back over his shoulder. 'What happened in there? I get the impression an ambulance isn't required?'

'Correct,' said Sakamoto. 'They're all dead.'

'Four against two,' stated Waxman, 'That's impressive.'

'If I hadn't called Jack earlier, I guess I'd be dead right now.'

'You know each other?' quizzed Bomberger.

'Yes,' said Fleming. 'I came here recently looking for Kramer.'

'Ok,' acknowledged the boss. 'Just a case of the bodies and their vehicle then,' said Bomberger deep in thought. 'My boss is going to hate this... wiping out the CIA's Men in Black will stir up a hornet's nest.'

'If it makes your life less complicated,' said Fleming. 'I can arrange it. Their car as well.'

Bomberger frowned as Fleming continued. 'You three were never here, you never saw me, and you never witnessed this event.'

Sakamoto and the two detectives felt a strange calmness, almost as if under some hypnotic spell. Both detectives were now back on the highway, Bomberger in the passenger seat. 'Waxman, I thought we were going to see Sakamoto…'

'No. If you remember, we left the office to call in on Kramer.'

'Why are we near Sakamoto's place?'

'I think I took a wrong turn,' now pausing. 'Yes, we've come out to see, Kramer.'

The boss looked confused. 'For what reason?'

'You took the call, but Kramer couldn't speak over the phone. You said it was something about the identity of MJ21.'

Bomberger blinked and frowned. 'Yeah, that rings a bell. MJ21. Who is… I mean, what is, MJ21?'

'That's what we want to know,' added Waxman.

'Let's go and see him. In fact, no. Let's arrange to pick him up a hundred yards down his road. We need to be more discreet.'

In less than twenty minutes, Kramer was in the Interceptor and cruising towards a recreational park. Once there, Waxman cut the engine.

'How are you all coping after that ordeal?' said Bomberger turning to view Kramer on the back seat.

'It's going to be a long hard road. I've just got both Jayne and Libby booked in to see the same therapist next week.'

'Good,' said Waxman. 'What about you? Are you ok?'

'Yes. But I worry about the girls and our future. Could this all happen again? Or maybe something even worse, next time.'

'Who can tell?' said Bomberger. 'It's a crazy mixed-up world?'

A pause before the boss continued. 'Luis? You said that you knew the identity of MJ21.'

'Yes I do, but what are the implications of giving you this information? Will it be my downfall? I couldn't put my wife and daughter through this again. That would be irresponsible of me.'

'I get that,' said Bomberger. 'What about we do a deal?'

'What sort of deal?'

'We close this now as resolved. It was just a missing persons' case. Mother and daughter went to visit Grandma. The car broke down. No signal in the area.'

Silence.

Bomberger pulled a smile. 'It wouldn't be the first time I've done a deal. Off the record, we have to do this more often than we like to admit. But if we didn't, we'd be snowed under with unresolved cases.'

Silence.

'Have we got a deal?'

'I guess we have.'

'Good. So… who is, MJ21?' said Bomberger, hopefully.

As Fleming's visit to Sakamoto's rental had mysteriously become a non-existent event, so Sakamoto remained alone at the pool and in the shade to consider his future. His mobile rang. 'Hello…'

'Sakamoto?' said the mysterious male caller.

'Who is this?'

'You don't know me, but I know you.'

'If you know me, where do I live?'

'In a rental costing $4000 per month.'

'Why the mystery?'

'That's how it works.'

'What do you want?'

'Where is Salamander? I have not heard from her and so I'm going down the chain until I get some answers.'

'Salamander is dead. She was killed in a shootout.'

'When?'

'Yesterday.'

'How do you know?'

'I heard it on the grapevine. It was a police sting. The bastards.'

'Here's the deal. The chain is breaking up and there's much that needs doing. If Salamander has gone, I need a new leader. Sakamoto, that person is you.'

'Me?'

'Yes. Any problem with stepping into Salamander's shoes?'

'No.'

'Are you in?'

'How will you pay me?'

'Used cash. It's not traceable.'

'When should we meet?'

'Tonight... 11pm at your place.'

'Will you be alone?'

'I'm always alone. I am, Fire Salamander.'

Hauk and Carrozza were still at the Area 51 base, both having differing duties throughout the tedious day. It was 5:25pm and by previous arrangement, they both met once again... this time, in Carrozza's office.

'Kevin, how's it going in Hanger 6?'

'You should come over more often and see where we have got to. All the reverse engineering that we once did to learn about their technology has now been scrapped. Our gain is having access to their things, things that are so much more advanced than found after the Roswell incident.'

'That was a long time ago…'

'Yes. And talking to them over the years, I found out that the crash was planned.'

'Planned?'

'Yes, the Kings of Kepler saw the two atomic bombs fall on Nagasaki and Hiroshima. They didn't want mankind to wipe themselves out, so they sent us a distraction.'

He paused before continuing. 'The grays were their scouts and a sub species. The craft was crashed by their superiors remotely and on American soil. Why? Because they saw that we were the most powerful nation on the planet and trying our best to keep peace in the world.'

'Really?'

'Think about it. The time and place had been carefully selected. This was done two years after the Second World War had ended and also in a zone that no one would be interested in… a desert.'

'A coincidence to some…' said Carrozza.

'No. The perfect timing to initially introduce themselves to us,' nodded Hauk knowingly.

'That's right,' replied Carrozza with conviction. 'They saw us as the leaders of the Free World. That was our destiny.'

'Mighty rivers always find the best way forward. We must go with the flow.'

'But must we?' questioned Carrozza. 'I'd rather be in control of my own destiny. I don't want to be told by someone else what I can, and can't do. That's why we have our own boarders and awesome Forces to protect those hard-fought frontiers.'

'Virgil, it's called progress. Without progress, people of the world would still be fighting with bows and arrows.'

Bomberger grabbed a diet coke from the vending machine and arrived at his desk, Waxman already booting up his computer. The Chief stuck his head around the corner. 'Everything alright, Bomberger? You seem to be dashing around quite a bit. Urgency generates interest.'

'Everything's under control. Waxman and I have just been out investigating some UFO sightings.'

'And?'

'And, we are waiting to get some footage. People can report anything, but without proof… well, it's wasting our time.'

With the boss gone, the two detectives started searching all avenues to confirm the identity of MJ21.

Hauk looked excited. 'Come on Virgil. We must take the plunge. Why not be the second man on Mars?'

Carrozza laughed lightly. 'I'd rather go whitewater rafting down the Colorado strapped to an alligator's back than risk that journey. What makes you think you'd get back?'

Hauk smiled. 'I've already done the journey with them.'

'You mean, you've been to the Red Planet?' said Carrozza with a mixture of surprise and disbelief.

'Sure. They took me there and back within a week.'

Carrozza looked deadly serious. 'Kevin, you're getting in too deep with these extraterrestrials. They will be your downfall and ultimately result in mankind's demise. We need to fight them with wisdom,' he said sternly, banging his fist on the table, 'not get into bed with them. Hell no... this is a big mistake.'

Hauk frowned and now looked angry. 'Look here, Carrozza. You either come on the journey or get left behind. I have offered you a fantastic opportunity to be my righthand man. When I take over the Presidency, Kramer and a few key men will run the CIA, and *you will* support me to the bitter end!'

Bomberger was staring at his screen, Waxman on his shoulder. 'He's our man,' said the boss. 'The accounts match with all the regular payments made into Salamander's account.'

'So, King, is the missing link?' said Waxman. 'Very weird. He's moved out of his house and, through an agent, paid for Sakamoto to stay there. That's nuts.'

'Suggesting that he is, stone cold crazy,' stated Bomberger.

'Unless King is an ex-CIA member. Remember, Kramer said he was seen at Area 51 and, in restricted zones. King's ID is MJ21.'

Bomberger grimaced and whispered. 'Listen Curtis. We are digging ourselves a very big hole messing with the CIA.'

'I have to agree with you. Maybe it's time we just walked away from this one. Yeah, why not take a break and think about that retirement... then get a season ticket to watch the Red Sox.'

Sakamoto drove off towards Ventura, where he parked up and went for a meal. It was boring eating on his own but his head was buzzing with the crazy idea of meeting, Fire Salamander. *Who the hell was he?* he thought. *And was he who he said he was or an assassin?* Afterall, the chain that he'd relied on had collapsed.

Back on the road at 10:35pm, he drove in a trance until within half a mile of his rented house. Almost like telepathic messages, something told him he should pull over, and urgently. Parking up, Sakamoto sat forward and close to his screen as he witnessed three white orbs in the sky coming down to disappear over the area behind his house. A quick eye rub before peering back out into the darkness. Two taps on his window made him flinch. Angered, and with near heart failure, Sakamoto had got a quick glimpse of a weather-beaten face staring in. The mysterious man shouted. 'Jesus is coming!'

'Get lost, vagabond.'

Spinning his wheels, Sakamoto took off at speed and soon reached the house. He had left the lights on, but the place was now in darkness. A hand reached down swiftly and pulled out his loaded firearm, all the time scanning the surrounding area with difficulty. Sakamoto jumped out into the darkness, running for the front door. A sudden flashback of the strewn and bloodied CIA bodies appeared. Without fear, he threw the front door open and edged his way in before flicking all lights on. Instant shock. The place was immaculate and all four bodies had gone... even the blood.

'Shit! Who the...?'

Suddenly, he heard the CIA's vehicle start up, but the keys were in his pocket. *How could this be?* Sakamoto flicked all lights off and crept over to the window where he pulled the curtain back to peek. The vehicle's headlights illuminated causing him to dive down; now flashing. *Morse code?* he thought. *No it can't be*, not that he could decipher it anyway. The 4x4 reversed at speed, spun round and took off. Sakamoto felt relief until someone flicked the lights back on. He turned quickly in shock to see his visitor.

'Who are you?' he demanded and pointing his gun.

The mystery man was of medium build, mid to late fifties.

'You will only know me as, Fire Salamander,' his back to the front door.

'How did you get in?'

'Through the front door. You left it open.'

I don't think so, said Sakamoto to himself.

'Put the gun down. You are going to work for me and make up for where all others have failed.'

'Have you brought the money?'

'As I told you previously,' walking forward, 'you'll be paid in used, US dollars.'

'What's the business?'

'The business my friend is the biggest opportunity of your life.'

'I'll be the judge of that,' said Sakamoto.

'You are to assassinate the President. That's all. Job done.'

'You're crazy. That's way out of my scope.'

'Take it or leave it.'

'And if I say, no?'

'Then you get executed.'

'Why don't you use your own executioner to assassinate the President?'

'They don't do that type of work.'

'And I don't assassinate Presidents, especially those that I voted for.'

'You will… because you have to. Look behind you.'

Sakamoto turned to see two people standing with their arms by their sides. He felt faint and bewildered all at once.

'Koga and you…. you César … but you drowned.'

'Yes,' said César, stepping forward. 'I was your apprentice but you tied my hands behind my back and pushed me into the pool where you left me to drown. It's true, humans do drown. But that's not me…'

'What do you mean?'

'I'm from Kepler 186F.'

'What?' said Sakamoto feeling dizzy.

Koga spoke. 'We are from another planet. Our civilization is a thousand years in front of yours.'

Sakamoto was speechless.

'Yes,' said, Fire Salamander. 'You humans are messing up your planet. It's a beautiful place. We've been here years just watching and trying to guide you forward. But you're still trashing it. Our leaders have decided that if you don't want it, we'll have it for ourselves in the near future.'

'This is trickery,' said Sakamoto, suddenly raising his gun and shifting his back to the wall… all were in view. 'Get out of here before I fill you with lead.'

Koga laughed. 'You can't kill us. We have a skin that's ten times more protective than Kevlar. Shoot if you wish.'

'Leave now, I don't want to kill you. You go and assassinate the President.'

'No,' answered Fire Salamander abruptly. 'It has to be done by a human being. That's what our masters have requested. So put the gun down,' he said firmly. 'Now, Sakamoto. Now!'

Sakamoto fired at the center light and with the second shot, he hit the bulb, not that he heard the glass falling, his ears were still ringing. Remembering their positions, he fired many rounds with the hope of taking them out. Then when pulling the trigger again, he just got a click, and another. *Damn,* he cursed to himself, *this could be the end of the line.* The large room was in silence. No one seemed to be moving. Perhaps they were getting ready to pounce in the dark. The door to the room was heard to creak. *Departing or reinforcements arriving?* he thought *hopefully just a breeze*. His heart was beating harder and he was certain that they could hear him breathing. Suddenly, he was totally surprised as twin wall lights flicked on. In the brightness, Sakamoto saw a figure that soon became identifiable. 'Fleming! What the hell are you doing here?' he said standing up and looking bewildered. 'And where are…?'

'Koga and César? They've been picked up by Kepler scouts.'

'Kepler scouts?' he frowned deeply.

'Sakamoto, the world has a lot to learn.'

'And Fire Salamander?'

'I let him go. We can deal with him later.'

Sakamoto was still in shock. 'Tell me about Koga and César?'

'Your chain was infiltrated by an undesirable group from Kepler 186F.'

'Sorry… I'm not with you. Please bring me up to speed.'

'The planet Earth has always been home, or a destination for other beings… in some cases, it's a halfway stopover.'

'Am I dreaming? What just happened here?'

'To put it plain and simple, you were visited by a species who want to take over your planet.'

Sitting down on the arm of a chair, Sakamoto half laughed. 'You want me to believe that I just had extraterrestrials in here?'

'Yes, just two. Koga and César. Try and remember this. When humans die, that's it… but you drowned César.'

'I remember. He was face down in the pool and I left him for dead.'

'Kepler beings can breathe under water.'

'No shit. Jesus, this is an absolute nightmare. What about Fire Salamander?'

'He's ex-Area 51, and has links to Keplar 186F. He's one of yours...'

'One of mine?'

'One of your species... an Earthling.'

'When you say, your species, you imply that you're not of the human race yourself.'

'Correct. I'm from Sirius...'

'Sirius in the Orion belt?' frowned Sakamoto. 'God Almighty.'

He then laughed. 'Come on, this is a game. Stop bluffing.'

'It's true. Listen. We also have an interest in the planet Earth. Ours is more one of helping you and guiding humanity forward. We are trying to inspire mankind not to kill his brothers, but to be more like us... peaceful and kind. Unfortunately, so many men have nothing but greed in their futile minds. It's so pointless, for you can only leave this world with what you brought with you. Essentially, nothing.'

'You are right about that.'

'Listen to me, Sakamoto. I was never here; you never saw me and you never witnessed this event.'

Sakamoto felt totally at peace with the world as Fleming spoke slowly. 'I was never here; you never saw me, and you never witnessed this event.'

Chapter 12

Area 51, Hauk's office midmorning: Tuesday

Hauk's red phone was ringing. 'Hello Mr President,' he said with a smile in his voice.

'Kevin. We need to talk…'

'Sure Hal, go ahead?' now more serious.

'There are rumours going around that don't make me feel too happy.'

'What type of rumours?'

'There are two that I would like you to investigate.'

'Ok… what's your source?'

'The FBI.'

'We know how the FBI works,' said Hauk. 'They're not so smart. But I am going to take this seriously.'

'First and most important… someone wants me assassinated which isn't a great feeling. I'm doing my best for the country and in the face of world-wide adversity. I need you to find out what's going on and report back to me, ASAP. Take the bastards out if you have to. No evidence, no questions.'

'Yes, I've got that, Hal.'

There was a pause. Hauk continued. 'In my opinion, I think because you are near the end of your Presidency, the risk is low. Very low.'

'Yes, but I'm going to stand again and that obviously increases the risk considerably.'

'In that case, Hal, you do have a point. I'll get to the bottom of this right away.'

Once the call ended, Hauk laughed to himself. 'Yeah right, Mr President. What will be, will be.'

Bomberger was seated at his desk with headphones on and listening-in on Sakamoto's phone conversation.

'Listen to me, Fire Salamander. You'll have to find someone else to assassinate the President, I'm not your man.'

'Do the job or die... I'm not asking again. You remember how the chain works?'

The senior detective was transfixed; a mild sweat broke out under his arms, *oh shit!* he thought, *this is mega serious.*

'Reject the chain's work and your family members go first. And you know how we do it? You will be present... so, which is it to be? Your family, or the President?'

'My family,' said Sakamoto, playing a risky game. 'All I have left is my mother and father.'

Naturally, Bomberger was shocked. Waxman arrived and placed a diet coke can down.

'Are you prepared to sacrifice your mother and father?' asked Fire Salamander, his voice high-pitched. 'You are crazy, but if that's the way you want to play it, that's the way you'll get it.'

'I'll be waiting for you. That's the way I want it?'

The cruel caller laughed. 'The shame is, you'll never know the moment. It may be tonight... it may be in a year from now. Sleep well... Sakamoto.'

As the phone went down, the senior detective dropped his headphones on the table and grabbed the ring-pull with urgency.

Waxman's brows shot up. 'What's happening?'

'Things are getting out of control.'

The station's Chief appeared. 'Hey Bomberger, have you got a moment?'

'Sure.'

His phone started ringing.

'I'll take it for you,' said Waxman.

As Bomberger disappeared, the call was taken. 'Waxman here.'

'Call coming through,' said the station's operator.

'Hello, I want to report a strange event last night north of Ventura.'

'Ok, I'm detective, Waxman. Go ahead and then I'll take your details.'

'We saw strange lights in the sky… like, like balls of light…'

'You mean orbs?'

'Yeah, dashing around by this house. Then they disappeared before returning five minutes later. Damn things shot up into the sky ten times faster than a rocket.'

'Anything else?'

'No.'

'Ok, I'll take some details from you.'

Five minutes later and Bomberger returned looking pissed-off.

'What's up?'

Bomberger seated himself and grabbed his can. 'The Chief is severely hacked off. Said he's had a call from the Men in Black…'

'Not the CIA again?'

'Yeah, about our inappropriate intervention into one of their undercover operations.'

'Meaning?'

'In relation to Sakamoto.'

'He's like a red-hot potato straight out of the oven.'

'Correct. They also know that four of their men went to his house and then vanished. Even their vehicle with tracer has gone missing.'

'We don't know anything about CIA men disappearing,' said Waxman looking puzzled. 'Probably whisked away in a flying saucer.'

'I wish,' stated Bomberger, looking more troubled than usual. 'But we couldn't be so lucky,'

'Imagine writing that in a report and putting it on the Chief's table. CIA men whisked away in a flying saucer. He would go bananas.'

'He certainly would,' said Bomberger.

'Hey Chad, while you were out, I took a call…'

'Oh yeah? About what?'

'Flying orbs.'

Bomberger rolled his eyes. 'Waxman?'

'Yeah?'

'I need a day off. My head feels like it's been hit a thousand times with a baseball bat.'

Once Sakamoto had put the phone down on Fire Salamander, he walked out to the pool.

'Hey, ma and pa, I see you're still chilling in the shade?'

'It's a nice place you got here son,' said his father, seated under a parasol. 'I'm envious of you, but also mighty pleased for you.'

'Me too,' said his mother proudly. 'Your car sales business must be doing really well.'

'You know me, ma,' a twinkle in his eye, 'I'm always wheeling and dealing.'

He paused.

'Ok, two small piña coladas before we leave?'

'That sounds really nice,' said his mother. 'And I'm sure looking forward to going to see the Niagara Falls,' squeezing his hand.

'Anything for you, ma,' he winked.

Two men walked towards each other on an isolated beach just north of Ventura.

'Albert King, alias Fire Salamander,' said Hauk as he arrived. 'It's good to see you, MJ21.'

Both men stopped and shook hands before King changed direction.

'It's always good to see you too, Kevin,' he said, then looking out to sea. 'I love coming here when I want to be away from it all. The fresh Pacific air, the sound of big rollers crashing, and the swirling foam sweeping in.'

'Have you got that hitman lined up?' said Hauk. 'The day is rapidly approaching and my campaign is about to start. I will become President and it will be unfortunate for Hal to be in the line of fire, but that's how the cookie crumbles. One moves out, one moves in, and the world moves on.'

'Yes, I have the ideal assassin. One by the name of Sakamoto and an ex-marine. Sure, he was chucked out quite a few years back for dealing in drugs, but he's a survivor and highly capable.'

'Good. Once the job's done, he'll go down the same route as Oswald.'

King laughed as white foam whizzed up to kiss his exquisitely fashioned cowboy boots. 'So, when you get into office, how long before you announce to the world that ET is here?'

'Within the first month.'

'And will you have all your witnesses lined up, like Kramer and others from Area 51, 52 and all the rest?'

'Yes, there will be a well-rehearsed timetable of events to support the revelation. In this way, the people of the world will hear it from me first and, therefore, accept the inevitable, that we are not alone in the Universe and never were.'

'And when do I step into your shoes as Head of the CIA?'

'As soon as I become Commander-in-Chief, you'll be my top man, overseeing the FBI and other law enforcement agencies. We've got to keep all those boys in line too.'

'I can't wait for the day,' confessed King. 'And Kramer?'

'Kramer? Oh yes, Luis Kramer. He knows too much, and if he doesn't join the CIA's top-table party, it's the end of the road for him and his family. A car crash will soon be forgotten.'

'Agreed. We don't need the opposition to trip us up.'

'I've got a little treat arranged for us, Albert.'

'What's that?'

'Are you doing anything tonight?'

'That depends…'

Hauk smiled. 'MJ21, you will not want to miss this historical event.'

'Really?' replied King with great interest. 'What is it? I hate not knowing.'

'Don't worry, but we're flying back to Area 51 by helicopter in about five minutes.'

'Where from?' frowned King.

'This beach, Albert. My men will drop in shortly and whisk us away.'

'What about my car?'

'Don't worry, I've got it covered.'

King smiled. 'There's no doubt about you, Hauk. You'll make a great President.'

Waxman was driving; Bomberger not happy and crushing a coke can in his right hand. 'Ok,' he said. 'I know we have to investigate this orb extravaganza, but it's sure going to be a waste of time. While we're out here and passing by, let's go and see Sakamoto. I picked up a snippet of conversation about him going to see Niagara Falls.'

'Sounds like he's taking a vacation,' suggested Waxman.

'I also heard other people in the house. It's a good time to snoop.'

'Just one problem,' said Waxman looking cautious. 'You said the boss is pissed off with you...'

'With us.'

'Let me guess. Far too many bodies in our jurisdiction.'

'The Chief is not happy,' claimed Bomberger, frowning. 'What would Arnie do?'

'The Schwarzenegger would do exactly the opposite and go in all guns blazing.'

'That's right, Waxman. Arnie would say; to hell with UFOs, I'm coming to rip the heads off real villains!'

'I guess we're going to Sakamoto's place?'

'Yes. First stop... to hell with the boss and the Men in Black. We are going to sort this mess out ourselves.'

Ten minutes later, they pulled into Sakamoto's rental.

'As usual, there's no car on the drive,' said Waxman pulling up and cutting the engine.

'Damn,' cursed Bomberger. 'I wanted to ask him a few more questions before he vanished into thin air. Plan B. Let's go and do a bit of snooping.'

Having knocked and looked around the pool and gardens, so Bomberger used his tumbler keys to gain access.

'It looks quite tidy for a bachelor's pad,' said Waxman walking in and peering at anything unusual, sometimes lifting things.

'Maybe he's got a girlfriend,' offered Bomberger, looking out of a window. But the two people I heard sounded like older folk. Unfortunately, there wasn't enough conversation to get details.'

'I've got it,' said Waxman. 'They were cleaners.'

Hauk and King had been picked up by a black helicopter with no identification markings, the pilot wearing green tinted Ray Bans. Once out of Ventura County, the land became desolate, not that the two passengers cared. They were too busy talking.

'Tell me about this surprise,' said King, seated next to Hauk.

'Have you ever wanted to be an astronaut and leave the planet to explore space… even if just for a day?'

King laughed lightly. 'Yeah, when a kid.'

'Wouldn't you like to be on the International Space Station and two hundred and fifty miles above the globe? What a privilege. Just imagine us, the cream of society looking down upon the plebs of the Earth.'

'I have dreams when I actually fly… my arms out like wings, but right now, I prefer my feet on the ground.'

Suddenly, the helicopter started bleeping.

'What's happening?' shouted Hauk, looking at the pilot's back.

'I don't know, but I'm losing power,' he replied while flicking switches and trying to assess the situation.

Both Hauk and King peered out of their window. Hauk spoke. 'Looks like we'll land in the sweltering desert.'

King was now over at the opposite window. 'I think I just saw something.'

'All I can see is the back of your head,' replied Hauk, craning to see past. 'What was it? A condor?'

'No, a flash.'

Hauk laughed. 'Not a UFO?'

The pilot called back. 'Look out of your left window and upward.'

True enough, outside Hauk's window was a UFO, no lights, but the sun glinting off its saucer-shaped body as it tracked them.

In just less than a minute, the helicopter was controlled and brought down to the ground. Hauk then stepped out knowing that this fifty-foot circular saucer was from Area 51. 'Come on King, it's a surprise. We're being transferred.'

King looked apprehensive as he stepped down on to the sandy desert floor. Without warning, the helicopter's rotor picked up speed creating a bigger dust cloud. Both Hauk and King ran in a stooped fashion towards the saucer's opening door.

'This is scary,' shouted King, his mouth dry. 'Are you sure that it's one of ours?'

'Yes, I know the geometry and markings,' returned Hauk as he arrived confidently.

'Welcome aboard, MJ1,' said a crew member appearing.

'Fleming?' said Hauk, 'I didn't know you cared so much.'

'Welcome aboard. I thought you might like a faster trip back to Area 51.'

Hauk stepped aside. 'Come on, King. Enjoy your first flying saucer experience.'

'Welcome MJ21,' said Fleming watching the helicopter lift off.

Detectives, Bomberger and Waxman, were snooping around in the bedrooms of Sakamoto's house when a 4x4 raced up the drive.

'That sounds urgent,' said Waxman, arriving at a window to spy.

As doors slammed, he had witnessed men jumping out and now running to surround the house.

'We've got trouble,' informed Waxman going for his gun.

'How many?'

'Four.'

Both dashed downstairs and just got to the living room as one came in... gun pointing. He fired straight away at Bomberger, who had anticipated the threat with a dive down behind the sofa. Waxman was close behind and fired, as he too had to seek refuge... but not so lucky with a smaller sofa chair. And in all the mayhem, the intruder had stooped low and not been accurate with the dual distraction. While Waxman became the focal point in the shootout, Bomberger very quickly slithered to the end and hit the gunman with a single shot. He screamed out in pain, his arm dropping but still holding his gun.

Bomberger shouted. 'Police! Stop firing and put all weapons down. Now!'

Two more men appeared quickly at the doorway, opening fire aggressively, both Bomberger and Waxman hearing bullets whizzing by, sometimes bits of shredded sofa flying, other times, the walls and skirting collecting rounds. Waxman felt a twinge as a bullet ripped through his trousers to tear the flesh on his right thigh. Now the stinging and blood seepage began. Suddenly, there were shots being exchanged outside. *That's impossible,* thought Bomberger feeling pinned in. *We have no back up... no one knows we're here.* As quickly as the shootout had started outside, so it stopped. Now the two at the doorway had turned to fight a rear-guard attack. Waxman was mystified and, with the two pinned front and back, he started shooting. Another crumpled to the floor like a stone. All three were firing from a surrounding position when the remaining villain ran out of ammunition. Unaware of the mystery gunman's identification, Bomberger shouted. 'Police! Put all guns down and show yourself.'

The last villain stood in the doorway with his hands up and half facing Bomberger who was standing up slowly. Waxman, with a hand on his thigh, followed suit. Suddenly a shot from nowhere. The fourth villain collapsed. *Shit*, thought Bomberger, *who the hell…!* Right at that second, a man appeared in the doorway.

'Chief?! What are you doing here?' looking totally surprised.

The detectives watched as their boss walked in. 'I was never here; you never saw me and you never witnessed this event.'

Both Waxman and Bomberger stood mesmerized and as their boss turned to go, he continued. 'I was never here; you never saw me and you never witnessed this event.'

The flying saucer was moving at Mach 1 and at a height of two thousand feet. King sat next to Hauk and both were viewing a monitor of their flight's progress. King spoke in a soft whisper when leaning in. 'Without windows, how do we know that this screen shot is our true view of what's going on outside? I mean, it could be fake.'

Hauk laughed. 'Would I trick you? No, of course not.'

'I trust you, but what about Fleming?'

'He's one of our top men. Have faith.'

At that moment, Fleming entered the passenger zone.

'How are you enjoying your flight, Mr King?'

'It's wonderful, thank you… very smooth.'

'We just made a quick detour…'

'Oh,' said Hauk. 'Any problems?'

'Not for us,' stated Fleming. 'But it was very lucky that you switched places. The helicopter went down just after take-off.'

'Really?' said Hauk with surprise. 'That was one of our best pilots.'

'Type in HC1,' stated Fleming, 'and it should come up on your screen.'

As Hauk did so, the last thirty seconds of the helicopter's flight appeared. 'It's a rearview shot. Who took it?' he quizzed. 'Us?'

'Yes. Unfortunately, a mechanical fault flashed up in the ill-fated chopper. As our systems are linked, I switched direction to see if we could help out in anyway.'

The three watched the final moments before the crash and fireball.

'Damn,' said Hauk.

'Jesus, we were so lucky,' claimed King.

'Yes, you were incredibly lucky,' added Fleming.

King coughed and cleared his throat. 'Who's flying this thing?' he said looking at Hauk and then to Fleming.

'I am,' admitted Fleming with a small closed smile. 'I'm doing it remotely using MCP.'

'MCP?' said King for clarity.

'Mind Control Pulsing. It's a standard way of communicating with machines when back home?'

'Back home?' said King. 'Where's that? Silicon Valley?' his eyes stuck on Fleming and half smiling.

'Sirius.'

'Sirius?' replied King, looking shocked and surprised. 'You're joking, right?' he half laughed, and looking across at Hauk for reassurance. 'Surely not.'

'Now I suggest you both fasten your seat belts as we pick up speed and disappear from radar.'

Bomberger and Waxman left A&E, Waxman having enjoyed the attention of several young nurses who, in turn, appeared and disappeared while patching up his thigh wound. Back in the Interceptor, it was Waxman's turn to relax as Bomberger sat behind the wheel. The boss spoke. 'You should take a day or two off and make sure your stitches are ok,' he claimed.

'Yes, I should. What are you going to tell the Chief about our lack of progress and that Sakamoto is now missing?'

Lieutenant Bomberger pulled a face. 'That place is jinxed. I can't remember why we were there or when we went there. If the Interceptor hadn't been parked on the drive, I'd suggest we must have arrived by cab.'

'But we never go anywhere by cab?' said Waxman frowning.

'I know. It's all a complete mystery and I hate being vague.'

Only back in the office five minutes and Bomberger had just started his second diet coke. The Chief appeared. 'Got a minute, Bomberger?'

'Sure,' he replied, standing up and rolling his eyes the second the Chief's back was turned.

Bomberger strolled in.

'Close the door and have a seat.'

The Chief leant back in his black leather chair. 'Now tell me Bomberger, why do you roll your eyes when my back is turned?'

'I...'

'Forget the excuse... I know that it will be pathetic. How are the UFO cases coming on? Have you solved anything yet?'

'Waxman's on to it and carrying out a few investigations.'

'Good,' he paused. 'And what about your progress? What's happening about the Kramer kidnappings and all the dead bodies appearing at Sakamoto's house?'

'Well…' said Bomberger, ready to explain.

'Your clear up rate is poor just lately which is disappointing. Be careful. I may have to put Waxman in charge of the case and place you back on UFO sightings.'

Both Hauk and King sat tightly braced in their seats as the spacecraft seemed to be accelerating after a very sharp turn. The passengers felt lightheaded and woozy; they were without doubt, climbing at great speed.

'Man oh man, I feel odd!' exclaimed King, his voice wobbling and sensing his stomach down on his shoes like a cement bag. 'It's like being in a rocket shooting off to the moon.'

'I'm glad you like it,' said Fleming, suddenly appearing on their large monitor. 'You must be psychic, Fire Salamander. That's exactly where we're going. I thought you both may like a little treat. The unexpected is always much more fun.'

'Fleming,' said Hauk with authority. 'I have a few things I need to do at the base. This unnecessary trip can wait.'

'Sorry, but I'm in control of this mission.'

'No Fleming,' replied Hauk, sounding stern. 'I order you to take us back to Area 51.'

'This must be disappointing for you, but we can see that your plans for the future of this planet are disastrous and will not proceed.'

King felt real fear as he witnessed the power slipping away from Hauk. 'How long will the moon trip take?' looking even more shaken.

Fleming reappeared through the connecting door. 'I guess it's only polite to speak to you in person. Your position is grave. However, please feel comforted that you men will not be alone.'

'What do you mean?' asked Hauk, looking mystified.

'It's for your own good, but you are being dropped off...'

'Dropped off!' fired Hauk, trying to rise up.

'Your belt is locked. There's no point trying to escape.'

'Shit!' cursed Hauk angrily while struggling desperately for his freedom. 'Fleming, you'll pay for this.'

'I don't pay for anything in your world. As I was saying, you will be dropped off on the dark side of the moon.'

King's mouth opened to speak. His jaw trembled but no words came out, such was his shock.

'The dark side of the moon?' quizzed Hauk. 'What do you mean... there's nothing there?'

'You consider yourself to be so powerful and all knowing, yet your knowledge is so weak. We have several bases in place... and when I say, we, I mean the people of Sirius.'

'This is outrageous!' shouted Hauk.

'So were your plans for the planet Earth. But your big mistake was to jump into bed with those from Kepler186F. They are attacking your planet with Mers, Sars and Covid-19. Let me warn you, there is far worse to come. Now you will have to excuse me. However, I do have a colleague who will look after you.'

As Fleming left, a new crew member arrived. Hauk's mouth dropped open. 'What the...'

A tranquil voice filled the air. 'Hauk, we have met before. However, it is only polite that I should introduce myself to Mr King,' he paused. 'I am, Shahar, but listen, it's irrelevant where you are both going.'

'Shahar,' said Hauk looking pale and starting to tremble. 'You are dead. Salamander killed you and I saw the photographic evidence.'

'I fooled her. She was so stupid,' he said, displaying a small though gratifying smile.

'This is a betrayal. I'm the Head of the CIA and the future President of the United States of America. I order you to take us back to Area 51.'

Shahar's voice was totally calming. 'You were never there on planet Earth; you never saw us, and you never witnessed this event.'

Both Hauk and King felt drowsy as the words became faint. 'You were never there on planet Earth; you never saw us, and you never witnessed this event.'

Printed in Great Britain
by Amazon

63940299R00159